BARRACUDA

PENS

BARRACUDA PENS

A MACDUFF BROOKS FLY FISHING MYSTERY

by

award winning author

M. W. GORDON

Published in the United States by Swift Creeks Press
swiftcreekspress@gmail.com
www.swiftcreekspress.com

SWIFT CREEKS PRESS EDITION, NOVEMBER 30, 2014

There are some churches named after St. Peter the fisherman, but not in the places used here. Playa Larga, the Zapata Reserve, and Las Salinas exist, as do the Hemingway locations. St. Augustine, Gainesville, Mill Creek, Paradise Valley, and Bozeman are real places but are used fictionally in this novel. This is a work of fiction, and the characters are either the product of the author's imagination or are used fictionally. Any resemblance to actual persons, living or dead, or to actual events or locales is unintentional and coincidental.

Library of Congress Cataloging-in-Publication Data
Gordon, M.W.
Barracuda Pens/M.W. Gordon

ISBN-13 978-0-9848723-5-0
Printed in the United States of America

To the people of Cuba, from Piñar del Rio to Guantánamo, who in 1957 and 1958 inspired me to spend my career with a focus on Latin America.

ACKNOWLEDGMENTS

Special thanks to Iris Rose Hart, my editor, friend, and patient instructor in English grammar, who has assured me that I am improving. I believe she omitted to mention how many years it may take at my pace of learning.

Particular thanks go to Elsbeth Waskom, Josh Dickinson, Marilyn Henderson, Roy Hunt, and Johnnie Irby.

Several people have provided quiet places for me to write in Montana, especially Joan Watts and Johnnie Hale of Livingston and Julie and Jason Fleury of Bozeman.

Always thanks to my wife Buff who reads chapters and at times of self-doubt urges me to go on.

To Christine Holmes for designing advertising and developing my website.

To the graphic design staff of Renaissance Printing of Gainesville, Florida, for assistance with the cover as well as bookmarks, posters, etc.

I benefitted from trips to Cuba in 1957, 1958, 1993, 1997, and 2000, covering much of the island, and one attempt by the Department of State to get me to Havana in the mid-1970s, which was rejected by the Cuban government as I awaited a plane for Havana in Mexico City.

PROLOGUE

Elsbeth's Diary

The wedding of Lucinda and Dad was a quiet affair. Not a word appeared in the newspapers. They were joined as husband and wife in a small church on the crest of a hill in Oyster Bay, Florida, which received a large anonymous donation allowing the church to be beautifully restored for the wedding and years thereafter. Not one of the women of the six families of Oyster Bay allegedly involved in the gill net murders was invited, which they understood was for the best. But the church was filled with flowers they donated.

Dad and Lucinda loved their friends too much to make distinctions among the many roles to be played at the wedding. Gathered around them at the altar were Grace Justice and Jen Jennings (along with husband Jimmy and son Tom) from St. Augustine; Dean Hobart Perry from Gainesville; Dan Wilson from D.C.; Erin Giffin, Ken Rangley, Amy Becker, Wanda Groves, and Mavis Benton from Montana; and Huntly Byng, John Kirby, Juan Santander, and my friend and college roommate, Sue Thomas, from Jackson Hole. Only two others played a role. Lucinda asked me to give her away, a moment that continues to bring moisture to my eyes. Carrying the ring hanging from her collar was Wuff, who trotted down the aisle with Lucinda and me.

Lucinda and Dad honeymooned on Captiva Island for a week, staying at the house they had rented the previous year but never used because of their separation. After a week they returned to the Montana cabin to relax and close up for the winter and drive back to Florida.

Perhaps the most significant announcement Lucinda made at the reception was that she had withdrawn permanently from her investment firm, although she planned to keep the Manhattan apartment for periodic trips with Dad to a city they both loved.

They soon expanded the garage in Montana and the cottage in St. Augustine, adding a room for me and space for Lucinda's photography. To further her interest, Dad arranged admission to a photo workshop at the Murie Ranch at Moose, Montana. That week began what would be her rise to prominence principally as a photographer of nature and especially of both the mountains of Wyoming and Montana and the salt flats of Florida.

I felt like I was the luckiest girl in the world. Maybe I should have held that off, considering the trouble Lucinda and Dad were about to face in Cuba.

Dad put in writing the memories that follow, filling in some details he never told me. But I remember most of the Cuban experience because I was involved. I still have vivid nightmares about what I saw in the hotel manager's office in Playa Larga, Cuba.

1

A SUMMER DAY ON THE SOUTH COAST OF CUBA AT THE BAY OF PIGS

NACHO GOMEZ ARRIVED at the Hotel Playa Larga at the head of the Bahía de Cochinos on the south coast of Cuba at 6:45 a.m., driving his personal variation of what once was a 1950's red and white two-tone Chevy that didn't appear able to travel another mile. He took the small crucifix dangling from the rear view mirror and kissed it, thanking Jesus that without breaking down his car again made it across the waist of the island. His client, Juan Mendoza, was waiting on the hotel's veranda and was ready to fish.

"Nacho," Juan asked, as they departed, "how long have you been a fishing guide here?"

"Long time, señor. I fled Cienfuegos in early 1960's to avoid being gotten by Castro's army and taken to his 'Second Revolution' in Angola. I lived quietly in battered wooden shack on the edge of town. Cuban officials look for me and I hide in Zapata Reserve swamp. I live on fish, mostly snook and Cubera snapper.

"Russians came to Cuba so I keep hiding. I not like Russians; they look and act like common street criminals.

"When Czechs begin to arrive, I learn some of them like to fly fish. I take them out, and they pay me; it was a little capitalism working between two communist countries. I live better than most Cubans. When communism in Russia and Eastern Europe end in the late 1980's, most Russians and Czechs left Cuba, but others came—bringing *real* money. I especially liked to see Canadians arrive.

"I work hard learning English; I guide Americans since the late 90's, most coming to Cuba and ignore U.S. boycott and no got U.S. license. Now lots more come, most from Miami through Bahamas or Jamaica. So, maybe I guide for almost fifty years. I live same good as hotel employees in Varadero and where workers get tips in real foreign money, not no good Cuban pesos. My earnings more than Cuban doctor or lawyer gets. Most who work for state earn about twenty Cuban pesos every month.

"And you, Señor Mendoza, you been to Cuba before? You are from the United States. Both your names are Spanish, but you no got accent."

"My grandfather came to the U.S. in 1960 with his wife and son, who became my father," Juan explained. "I was born in Miami, as was my sister Elena, who is four years older. This is my first visit to Cuba. I'm with a group from Washington. We would like to see better relations with Cuba, and we've been meeting with Cuban government officials, including your president."

"I think you happy come to Cuba, señor," he said, flashing a broad smile that highlighted crooked teeth. "We hardworking people and welcome everybody. Fishing we gonna do not like what you got in U.S., where too many Americans look for only few fish left. Americans and Canadians give me old

4

fishing magazines with stories how fishing was more better thirty or forty years before.

"*We* got plenty fish, Señor Mendoza. Me and you spend three days in *Parque Nacional Ciénaga de Zapata.* I not know what it means, but park is called a world preserve that got best unused wetlands in whole Caribbean. I just call it 'our swamp.'"

An hour's drive over dirt roads took the two to the Hatiguanico River. They stopped at a military post by the river, where the government operated a fishing concession. One of a half-dozen fourteen-foot jon boats with a 25 hp Honda outboard was reserved for them. Nacho ran downriver for fifteen minutes to where they could see tarpon rolling.

Juan joined the three sections of his rod while Nacho scanned the river. Nacho fumbled through a small bag with several lines and plastic boxes with a few dozen flies.

"Floating or sinking line?" Juan asked.

"In between. Cuba tarpon like feed below surface. But after they hooked spend time leaping above water."

"What do you recommend for a fly?"

"Hand me rod," Nacho said. "I like Black Death fly made by guide you can know, Stu Apte, from Florida Keys. Fly has long head and behind head got red and black fur and hackle. Long head helps stop wind trouble casting and red and black to tarpon is like red to bulls. . . . You ever tarpon fish, Señor Mendoza?"

"Maybe a half-dozen times," Juan responded. "One was near a place called Seven Mile Bridge in the Keys. I hooked two, watched one tail-walk and the other leap clear of the surface. Both dove and I never saw them again.

"A few years ago I was invited to the annual tarpon tournament at Boca Grande in Southwest Florida. Called the Professional Tarpon Tournament Series, it was about as professional as a pit bull fight. PTTS was more entangled in haphazard litigation it initiated against an 18,000-member non-profit group called Save the Tarpon, than the fishermen were entangled with tarpon. Tarpon *snagging* would be a better word. PTTS calls it using a Boca Grande Pass jig, or a jig rig, but it's snagging whatever it's called. It's a circle hook attached to a lead head with a scented plastic minnow imitation. It's made to snag the tarpon when the jig is pulled up from the bottom through a close-packed group of fish. The Florida Fish and Wildlife Commission finally decided the Boca Grande Pass jig is a snagging device."

"That's not good, Señor Mendoza. Cuba never allow that."

"It wasn't fly fishing, and it wasn't sportsmanship, Nacho. During the tarpon season, Boca Grande Pass is overcrowded with boats run by people who've never heard of right-of-way rules and use unethical methods that threaten the tarpon fishery. It's like too many people at a carnival. If tarpon could vote, only mouth hooking would be allowed. I never picked up my rod that day. I'll never go back."

"You don't find nothing like that here. We probably be only boat we see all day. We fish ethically. Some days many fish. Some days no fish. We like the many fish days and we accept the no fish days."

Nacho's words proved true. They didn't see another boat, but they did see tarpon. Hundreds of tarpon. The Hatiguanico was truly a tarpon nursery. Juan hooked a dozen tarpon and landed three, ranging from eleven to forty-seven pounds. He also caught a few fish that Nacho said were pests. Juan recognized them as snook. On the way home, he asked, "Nacho, it can't get any better than what we saw today . . . or can it?"

"Señor Mendoza, choices got to be made when fishing Zapata peninsula. You want to fish for the Silver King—tarpon—you go to the Hatiguanico River as we done today. But Zapata has flats off Salinas where a bone fisherman can fish his whole life and never see another person. We go there tomorrow. The inner flats are protected by outer barrier islands called Bocas; that's where we go third day. Bocas are roaming grounds for large snook and Cubera snapper, barracuda, and some monster tarpon."

The second day Juan fished the Zapata flats in a tiny two-man skiff that used only the power of Nacho pushing a pole. They returned an hour before dusk with Juan exhausted from the best bone fishing he could have imagined existed. He hoped that within the next decade he would be allowed to purchase or build a small vacation house outside Playa Larga. He dreaded the thought, however, that after Cuba emerged from its economic funk the bay's coastline soon would be lined with condominiums.

After dinner Juan sat on the porch with a Cohiba cigar and glass of Havana Club *Máximo Extra Añejo* rum from a bottle given to him in Havana by the trade group's Cuban government hosts. He thought he would take the bottle home and the next time he visited his cousin Rodolfo in Miami—Rodolfo was chief legal counsel for Bacardi—he would offer him a glass of *real* Cuban rum. Bacardi had claimed rights to the Havana Club name, to little avail outside the U.S.

Juan welcomed the coming night's sleep, but as he lay on his bed pleasantly imagining his final day of fishing along the Bocas, he heard sounds coming from outside and rose to investigate. When he stepped out the door, two men grabbed him, each taking an arm and bending back a hand, forcing him to follow them. When Juan struggled, one of the men pulled a knife from his belt and made a long shallow cut on the side of Juan's face that began to bleed and drip on the porch cement. He knew the men were serious and bent his head down on his shoulder to stop bleeding.

One of the two spoke to him quietly. "Señor Mendoza, hope you enjoyed fishing the past two days. We taking you for little *night* fishing."

They dragged Juan to a rusty old Ford truck with its bed piled with junk, shoved him into the middle seat of the cab, and drove what seemed to Juan to be a very short distance, perhaps exaggerated because of his fear of what might be next. The truck slowed half-a-block beyond a church with a sign that identified it as St. Peter the Fisherman and pulled off onto an unmarked dirt road that wound past dense sea grape shrubbery. A few dozen yards down the dirt road, a worn and faded sign said *Centro de Investigaciones de Aquacultura* (Center for Aquaculture Research).

The truck pulled up alongside a narrow wooden dock at a tiny harbor. Several pens were submerged off the end of the dock. Suspended a few feet above the pens was a makeshift maze of walkways. Pulled from the truck, Juan was guided through the dark along one of the walkways until they stopped over the center of the largest pen. He knew from talking to Nacho that the area was the habitat for the Caribbean *maniti*, a relation of the Florida manatee, and he thought that might be what was below in the shadows. But he soon learned otherwise.

One of the two men quietly called to someone on the land, "Luces!"

When the lights on the poles came on, Juan could see clearly into the water. Several long, thin fish hung suspended, their fins moving only enough to hold their positions. They might have been mistaken as pike were this cool fresh water of Michigan or Wisconsin. They were mostly silver, with upper bodies a mixture of gray, dark-green, or dark-blue. Black spots were scattered randomly along their sides. When one turned, Juan noticed the caudal fin was forked with a double curve on the back edge. No doubt the fish in the pen were barracudas.

Juan looked more carefully and saw a barracuda, perhaps as long as five feet, begin to move slowly to a position immediately below the men. Then they did something Juan at first did not understand: after pulling off his pajamas, they took from their pockets and placed on his bare body several pieces of bright reflective silver—metal bracelets, a necklace, anklets, and a belt.

One man reached up on a pen support pole and turned a switch that ignited underwater lights. The barracudas began to stir. Finally, from a bucket the two men took four mangrove snappers, cut them open, let the blood drip into the pen, and tied them to Juan's wrists and ankles. Six more fish from the bucket were made into a necklace that was hung below the one of silver.

One man stood on each side of Juan. The older of the two whispered, "Buena pesca, submarina," and, quietly laughing, pushed him in.

The feeding frenzy that ensued scared the two men, and they left the walkways as fast and carefully as possible. One stopped and threw up into one of the pens. When they reached the shore and looked back at the pen into which they had pushed Juan, they saw only a frothing mass of scarlet water where barracudas were slashing at the snapper and at the flashing silver jewelry and at other barracudas. And soon they were fighting for the final morsels of what was left of Juan.

One man turned off the lights while the other handed some cash to the man who had waited on shore, and said, "Remember what you saw happen to this man. If you say a word about this, we will be back, and you will be the next meal for the barracudas."

The man took the cash and stuffed it into his pocket, dropping half the wad of nearly worthless Cuban pesos. He was trembling and wanted to see the men leave. He wondered why he had agreed to this, but his willingness had saved his life. He would never say a word, or he would lose what little he had.

The two men drove off in their truck, facing a two-and-a-half-hour drive back to Havana to receive payment of the second half of what they were promised for "feeding the fish" in Playa Larga.

In the morning the local man—still terrified by what he had witnessed—completed his instructions. He went to the fish pens where the barracudas were calm and again hung suspended in the water. With a net on a long pole, he removed Juan Mendoza's skull, a few pieces of bone, and pieces of silver he would sell, including a man's watch that had engraved intials: J.M. Wrapping the skull and bones in an old towel, he carried them into a building. He scrubbed the skull and took it to the roof where he hid it in a place where the sun would bleach it white. He next took the bones and buried them in the dense woods in the nearby Zapata Reserve.

2

A FEW DAYS EARLIER

THE TOWN WHERE Juan Mendoza's life abruptly ended had seen little excitement since the invasion of Cuba at the *Bahía de Cochinos* or—as better known and best forgotten in the U.S.—the Bay of Pigs. On April 18th, 1961, Playa Larga was code-named Red Beach and became the landing point for a few hundred Cuban exile troops of Brigade 2506. They occupied the town for little more than a day before Castro's artillery, tanks, and infantry retook the area on their way to driving the brigade into early graves, the sea, or a Cuban prison.

Twelve hundred invaders were captured, convicted of treason, and later—if not summarily executed—traded to the U.S. in exchange for millions of dollars of food and medicines. The episode remains an embarrassment to the U.S., as well as one of the darkest times in the history of the CIA, members of which admittedly lied to U.S. Ambassador to the U.N. Adlai Stevenson and Secretary of State Dean Rusk. The town of Playa Larga had changed little in the ensuing years.

Mendoza was scheduled to stay at the modest Hotel Playa Larga. Not far from the hotel sat an infrequently visited church—St. Peter the Fisherman. The church's name was fitting since Playa Larga was on the edge of the fishing paradise Zapata Reserve, which consumed nearly a third of Matanzas province. The province straddled the island from the Florida Straits to the Caribbean, similar to many of the fifteen provinces, like rings around the island, from Pinar del Rio province in the West to Guantánamo province in the East. The Zapata Reserve area remained undeveloped, a positive irony of the failed economy that was the outcome of the Revolution.

Where there were undeveloped wetlands there were bound to be fish and wildlife. A road wound from Playa Larga for miles through the reserve to a small launch site—Las Salinas—that opened to a fisherman's paradise. Just what St. Peter must have spent hours praying for and where Juan Mendoza fished his last day.

Not far down the road from the church, set behind lush vegetation, was the small marine research center. Its focus was not on the gamefish of Zapata, unless one considered barracuda to be gamefish. A half-dozen pens held barracuda up to five feet long. Wobbly rotting wooden walkways were suspended over the pens, making feeding time a challenge for the one research center resident employee, a seventy-five-year-old weathered veteran who helped repel the Bay of Pigs invaders a half-century ago. Some of Brigade 2506's members who were seized had soon learned that capture did not mean incarceration but being thrown into a pen with a dozen huge barracudas whose usual food had been withheld until they would eat anything. They did, and like grizzlies in Montana that have tasted human flesh, the barracudas came to favor it.

3

YEARS PAST

Juan Mendoza had been excited to be finally in the land of his father, grandfather, and great grandfather. Now, he would be the last of his branch of the Mendozas. He had not married and would bear no sons to preserve the Mendoza name. But if the family history was repeated, carrying on the name was a challenge that could not go on forever.

Alfonso Mendoza and his wife, carrying their infant son, Miguel, fled Franco's Spain in 1937 destined for Cuba, leaving behind three small hotels they owned in Madrid as well as their classic Spanish Renaissance house in the Salamanca area. Penniless, Alfonso started over as a baggage handler at the Havana airport.

A generation later Miguel Mendoza and his wife, with their twelve-year-old son, Ricardo, fled Castro's Cuba in 1960 destined for Miami, leaving behind three modest hotels they owned in Old Havana as well as their classic Art Deco house in the Vedado part of Havana. Penniless, Miguel started over as a baggage handler at the Miami airport.

As Ricardo reached his teens, he first thought he would someday own three large hotels in Miami, but then remembered the old adage "once bitten, twice shy." He assumed it even more appropriate that, if one were "twice bitten," one might be "thrice shy." But he owed his father and grandfather more than a life worrying that he would someday have to flee Miami and start over as a baggage handler at some distant airport.

By the time the new century arrived, Ricardo owned three of the most luxurious Arquitectonica designed hotels in Miami. He was a generous man and much liked except by one segment of the Miami community—persons mostly of his father's generation who, when they arrived in Miami, assumed they would soon return to a Cuba ridden of the revolutionary Castro. But the years passed, and Castro did not. Surviving early exiles in Miami increasingly were bitter. They used their considerable power to elect representatives and senators to both the state and federal legislatures who would fight any attempt to restore relations with a Castro led Cuba. Their fight succeeded, but time was not on their side. New generations thought differently.

Ricardo's son Juan rejected attending college in Miami and enrolled at Duke. Eventually, he settled in New Mexico where he served a single term in the state senate before being elected to the U.S. House of Representatives. He was considered the favorite to replace a retiring senator in the fall elections.

Ricardo's daughter Elena also rejected attending college in Miami and enrolled at Dartmouth. Eventually, she settled in Connecticut where she served a single term in the state house before being elected to and joining her younger brother in the U.S. House of Representatives. She also aspired to be a senator.

Neither Elena nor Juan accepted the politics of the early exiles. Neither wanted to live in Cuba; they were both born in Miami and were both U.S. citizens. They did not want their ancestors' properties returned to them. They did hope that someday they might own a small vacation home in the Cuban countryside. Those were their personal decisions; what caused them conflict with the early exile members of the House and Senate was their introduction of legislation repealing the U.S. Helms-Burton law and renewing full diplomatic relations, trade, and tourism with Cuba.

In Washington, Elena and Juan frequently were subjected to various forms of persuasion to curtail their outspoken rejection of the early exiles' demands. But their Connecticut and New Mexico constituents applauded their positions and urged them to vote in favor of renewed ties with Cuba and to convince the current President to use the powers of his office to bypass Helms-Burton, the law that so divided U.S. citizens' views on Cuba, because of its fierce focus on retribution and the restoration of expropriated property.

Neither Elena nor Juan had ever visited Cuba, aware that their father Ricardo and his very aged and ill father Miguel might be upset with such decision. But several months ago Miguel died. At his funeral in Miami, Ricardo took his two children aside and urged them to follow their hearts as elected legislators who had succeeded so well in the new land of their birth.

Ricardo asked to be cremated when he died and to have his ashes evenly scattered on the waters off Key Biscayne and the Malecón in Havana. If they wanted to visit Cuba now, their father said they should do so.

Juan had called Elena in Connecticut the week after their father's funeral.

"Elena, no sooner did our father tell us he wasn't opposed to our visiting Cuba than I received an invitation to join a delegation of twenty from the House, the Senate, and the Departments of State and Commerce to visit Havana and meet with a high level trade group of Cubans, including the aged remnants of the Castro brothers. . . . I'd like to go. What do you think, Hermana?"

"Go, but be careful if you have to fly from Miami."

"We fly from D.C. on a government plane."

"I know why you really want to go to Cuba, Hermano. You want to go bone fishing and tarpon fishing. Am I right?"

"Yes. I called a friend in Key West who put me in touch with the owner of a Canadian-based fly fishing tour business. He can arrange a couple of days for me to fish in a place called the Zapata Reserve. Maybe the best fly fishing in Cuba."

"I knew it," Elena answered. "You should have been a guide like our friend Macduff Brooks, not a politician. But *I* don't want to be a guide. I want to be the President of Cuba," said Elena.

"I've been thinking the same," said Juan.

"Not if I get elected first," Elena responded with an edge to her voice.

"I'll bring you some rum and cigars. You can hand them out to the early exiles who have overstayed their welcome in Congress."

"Forget that. Call me when you're back safe."

Juan immediately emailed some Florida fishing contacts who frequently arranged for Americans to break away from rigidly scheduled People-to-People trips and fly fish. While Juan had no difficulty leaving his group, he needed a contact to arrange the three days of fishing.

One essential item Juan carried with him to Cuba was a long tubular case containing two fly rods, one a 9' 7-weight for bonefish, the other a 9' 10-weight for tarpon. They were the sizes he used fishing the flats north of his parents' Duck Key weekend house in the Florida Keys and along the eastern shore of Abaco in the Bahamas, a short boat ride from his sister Elena's vacation cottage overlooking the harbor at Hopetown.

CNN televised the meeting of the trade group in Cuba throughout the U.S., but coverage was blocked in Miami and seen only by those who owned a satellite dish that avoided local censure. Apparently, the pendulum of opinion had reached its half-a-century apogee and had begun swinging back to adopt policies toward Cuba mirroring those applicable to other socialist or communist nations including Vietnam, China, and Tanzania, and perhaps soon also Bolivia, Ecuador, and Venezuela.

The early exiles were furious at the U.S. delegation because it was traveling to Cuba. Some took to the streets in Miami, mostly to shout and hold rain-stained and faded placards derogating Castro, placards that once again had been dragged from storage for a futile use. Some exiles adopted more violent means of protest, and the three hotels owned by Juan's father were damaged.

Most of the delegation to Cuba returned to the U.S. immediately after the meetings, but Juan remained. He spent the night at the elegant Hotel Nacional and in the morning hired a car and driver to take him to Playa Larga, where he had booked one of the small cement-walled bungalows at the hotel that bore the name of the town. The bungalows had long ago been painted bright colors, but—along with the Revolution—had faded over the years.

That evening a poorly dressed but elegant in stature local met Juan on the hotel's veranda and said, "I'm Juan Mendoza. You must be Señor Gomez."

"My name is Ignacio Gomez. Please call me Nacho. I guide you for three days."

Juan was amazed that Nacho would have the stamina to guide for three days in a row. He was rail thin, missing several teeth, and had hairless skin darkened more by sun than genetics.

"When do we go?" asked Juan.

"Tomorrow. I will come exactly at 7:00 a.m. The hotel will feed you breakfast one hour earlier. Buenas noches, Señor Mendoza."

"Buenas noches, Nacho."

Juan slept soundly that night. Partly exhaustion from the days of meetings put behind. And partly the prospect of three days of fly fishing that lay ahead.

But little did Juan know *what* lay ahead. It was not all *catching* fish.

4

PARADISE VALLY MONTANA—MID-OCTOBER

L UCINDA LANG BROOKS AND I were standing shoulder against shoulder by the large window of my cabin, looking out at leaves fluttering down along Mill Creek in Paradise Valley, Montana. I was celebrating my survival of the first month of marriage to Lucinda. She was celebrating the absence of any murders on my wooden drift boat, *Osprey*, since we were married.

At least I *assumed* I was still married. From the September day we said our vows, not a word had been uttered by either of us about any fly fishing related deaths on land or water, in or out of a drift or flats boat, at my cabin in Montana or my cottage in St. Augustine, or anywhere else in the world with some link to one or both of us. But such bliss could not last.

"Am I safer from my adversaries now that we're married?" I asked, turning to admire her profile.

"Of course, you're safer. Our marriage is a warning to all others that any attempt on your life will be viewed by me and my attack hound as an act we would respond to immediately and with savage vengeance." The "attack hound" is a twenty-five pound Sheltie named Wuff. I rescued her eight years ago from a combative couple in Bozeman.

"Do recall, dear husband, that I am a better shot than you with a pistol. You'll learn to understand that marriage does have its benefits!"

"I feel safer when we're under the covers at night. Time will tell if I am safe with you during a day floating in *Osprey*. . . . Another matter, since we now share all things equally, do I get to choose half of what I eat?"

"Not a chance. I remain the family nutritionist with full authority for all meals. Except you clear the table and do the dishes."

All day we moved some of Lucinda's odds and ends from her nearby extensive, elegant Arrogate Ranch to my modest cabin, and then went to dinner at the Chico Hot Springs restaurant to celebrate our first month.

"Lucinda, since we'll soon have additional space here at my cabin, you have lots of room for your things."

"No," she answered, which surprised me.

"No? What do you mean? Didn't I plan enough room in expanding both my cabin and my cottage?"

"There's plenty of room."

"I've said something wrong?"

"You did. The cabin and cottage are now *ours*, not *yours*. Henceforth, please refer to them in the collective rather than personal form. May I remind you that we are now tenants-in-common on the deed for each property? If something happens to you—or more prophetically expressed, *when* something happens to you—I get both houses free and clear. When we're both gone, Elsbeth inherits them. And that applies to my ranch and Manhattan apartment."

"Are you saying I can't cast you out if you misbehave?"

"Try it! Remember that if it comes down to a vote, Elsbeth will vote with me, and I'll win."

"That's called alienation of affections. It's unlawful."

"Any such action was prohibited by very fine print on our marriage license."

"I don't read fine print."

"That's good. You wouldn't have agreed to some of the other provisions."

"I don't want to hear another word about my, I mean *our*, cabin and cottage. I suppose you also share ownership of the drift and flats boats?"

"Of course, especially *our* drift boat. Remember, Macduff, that Wuff and I shed some blood from a shooting on *Osprey*."

"But *I* was also shot on *Osprey*—by Park Salisbury."

"You wouldn't have been if you had known how to use your Glock and not kept it in an inaccessible pocket. I had to do the shooting to save the three of us. All because you embarrassed Salisbury in front of his wife, Kath, when you guided them on the Snake River."

"He deserved it; he was clubbing to death a native cutthroat trout in Grand Teton Park. My not letting him back in the boat and making him walk out four miles while I took his wife with me in the drift boat didn't justify his later attempts to kill me. First trying to shoot me from the shore while I was guiding a float and then again when you, Wuff, and I were together with him on that later float where he wore a disguise."

"That's when *I* shot and killed him," she commented.

"But I shot him, too," I pleaded.

"True, but *after* he was dead."

"I did execute a perfect *coup de grâce* by running *Osprey* into the tree limb in the river that impaled Salisbury and left him hanging while we floated past."

"Also *after* he was dead."

"And then you faked amnesia for nearly a year, trying to get my sympathy so I'd marry you."

"I think you have early dementia. That's worse than amnesia."

"Did you give me dementia?"

"Of course, it was all part of a plan Wuff and I devised. We intended to strip you of all you have."

"Just what have *you* stripped from me?"

"All of your clothing every night since and taken a share of everything you own now or will ever own, down to your old, worn toothbrush. They are called appurtenances."

"What have I gotten in return?"

"Other than *my* clothing on those same occasions, you share ownership with me of a beautiful apartment in Manhattan and the Arrogate Ranch here on Mill Creek."

"The apartment where you suggested that the concierge search me for jewelry and silverware after I stayed once at the place in your absence?"

"The very same."

"We'd best leave for dinner. I'm losing my appetite."

There may be benefits to marriage after all, I thought. As our waitress brought drinks and an appetizer to the table, I was returning from sprucing-up in the gentlemen's quarters. But any amount of sprucing was insufficient to shift others' eyes already directed to Lucinda, who sat across from me looking spectacular in a salt and tweed split skirt, a white turtle-neck top, and a black, gray and white cardigan. She wore small silver hoop earrings and a slender silver necklace from which hung an eight *reales* coin retrieved from the 1715 wreck of a Spanish galleon heading from Havana to Spain and sent by a hurricane to the bottom off Florida. I gave the coin to her years ago while she was recovering from amnesia.

"You look ravishing," I said.

"You're saying that only because it will make you feel you're entitled to criticize the appetizer we're sharing."

We were sharing *Escargot Mountainere.* I didn't dare complain. As I took a bite, she nudged me under the table, smiled, and said, "You've come a long way in your food fetishes, Macduff. I never thought I'd see you eating mushroom caps with snails."

"But they live in shells and are cooked in wine. I eat anything that lives in a shell—oysters, mussels, stone crabs. Anyway, the wine neutralizes any disagreeable flavors."

"I wondered why you told the waitress 'heavy on the wine.' To you it should be listed on the menu as *White Wine with Bits of Mushrooms and Snails.*"

"That's right. The mushrooms and snails are really garnishes, like parsley. It's the wine that is the essence of the dish."

Lucinda lifted her hands with palms up and rolled her mesmerizing green eyes in a display of futility. I watched her and remarked, "Love me, live with my quirks."

Rather than staying at Chico's dining room for a nightcap, we drove back to the cabin, made drinks, and went outside and leaned against the porch rail. It was chilly, but windless and lighted by a near full moon that appeared to slide across scattered clouds. Lucinda sipped a Montana Roughstock Whiskey; I had my usual Gentleman Jack.

5

NIGHTCAP ON THE PORCH

LUCINDA TOOK A SIP OF HER DRINK, set her glass down, turned and looked at me, and abruptly asked, "Can we go to Cuba?"

"Cuba! That came out of the blue," I said. . . . "The answer is we *can* but probably *may not*. There's a federal trade and tourism boycott and likely we don't fit into any class of persons permitted to go to Cuba. At least I don't."

"Because you're a threat to America?" she asked. "Who *is* permitted to go?"

"It depends on who you are and what your purpose is."

"I want to photograph the Hemingway locations for an article in a Canadian travel magazine. We signed a contract. I would include his house—Finca la Vigía—outside Havana; his boat—the *Pilar;* his favorite Havana hotel—Ambos Mundo; the bars he frequented—El Floridita for daiquiris and La Bodeguita for mojitos; and the harbor and La Terraza bar at Cojímar, which partly was the setting for his *Old Man and the Sea*. Are journalists allowed to go?"

"Maybe."

"Maybe? Who's in charge, and why would I not be permitted to go? I'm not trading U.S. or Cuban goods."

"The Treasury Department's in charge and you're considered to be a threat to the Cuban early exiles in Miami and some in New Jersey."

"New Jersey? I didn't know the New Jersey mafia was Cuban."

"It isn't. It's separate from the Italian mafia, whose people don't care where you go as long as you gamble, drink, and hire prostitutes while you're there. But there's another group in New Jersey. Cuban Americans. It's where many of the cold-tolerant early exiles settled. But the biggest group lives in South Florida, mainly Miami—which is really a suburb of Havana."

"What did you mean by the *Treasury* Department controls travel to Cuba?"

"For the most part you *may* go to Cuba. The act of going and returning is not the catch. It's that you aren't allowed to spend any money in Cuba. Treasury controls money."

"What if the Canadian travel magazine pays for the trip?"

"You can't spend *anyone's* money, even if the trip's paid for in Canadian dollars. Or Mexican pesos. Or whatever."

"What if I flew to the Bahamas and went from there to Cuba?"

"When you re-enter the U.S., you have to list the countries you've visited. If you list Cuba, you're in trouble?"

"What if I *forget* to list Cuba? You often complain that I'm forgetful."

"The Treasury Department doesn't equate 'forget' with 'forgive.'"

"But U.S. customs won't know where I've been."

"Aha! You'll have a passport with an *entry* stamp to the Bahamas when you first go there and a second entry stamp from the Bahamas when you stop there on the way home from Cuba. How can you enter the Bahamas twice without leaving it sometime in between the two entries?"

"What if I admit to customs that I've been to Cuba?"

"They may take you away in chains and turn you over to the early exiles in Miami. That would relieve me of supporting you. But more than likely they will tell you you're a very bad American, let you in, and send information about your travel to the Treasury Department in Washington. Treasury might fine you. Or not."

"How do you know so much about travel to Cuba?"

"Because I've been there."

"But you just told me you can't go there."

"I had a permit from the U.S."

"How come you could go then and I can't now?"

"You're not supposed to ask questions, just do as the Miami early exiles say. They don't want anyone to go, except for Cubans in the U.S. visiting and taking money to their relatives. The U.S. rules keep changing."

"Do many Americans go to Cuba?"

"Thousands of Americans go each year with or without Treasury's permission. We are one of the nations sending the most tourists—legal or not—to visit Cuba each year."

"That's strange."

"Stranger still is the fact that we have no embassy in Cuba, but we have the largest number of diplomats in Cuba from any country. They're based at what once was our embassy but now is supposed to be called the Interests Section. And don't call the ambassador Mr. Ambassador. He's the Chief of Mission."

"How does the chief of mission differ from an ambassador?"

"If there is someone called the ambassador, then there is no chief of mission. If there is someone called the chief of mission, there is no ambassador. The key is whether we recognize the other nation sufficiently to establish relations. If so, we have an ambassador. If not, a chief of mission. I'd wager that the chief of mission in Cuba has a more challenging role than the U.S. ambassador in dozens of nations."

"That's silly," she exclaimed.

"No. That's called diplomacy, Mrs. Brooks."

"I like that—the *Mrs. Brooks* part."

"One last comment," I said, before she equated "Mrs. Brooks" with being chief of mission at our cabin. "The U.S. is one of Cuba's principal trading partners even though we have a trade and tourism boycott in place."

"It gets stranger all the time. . . . I still want to go."

"Maybe we can arrange it. I'll look into it. I'd like to go with you and fish."

"Is fishing a reason the U.S. might give you permission to travel?"

"Not officially."

"Are we getting ourselves into another dispute with our State Department?"

"No, but likely with Treasury and some frustrated early exiles from Cuba who live in Miami and think they control our foreign relations with Cuba. . . . They do!"

"Are any of them dangerous?"

"Yes, mainly Al Pacino. Also known as Tony Montana or Scarface."

Not wanting to go further with the conversation, Lucinda suggested we go inside—the temperature had dropped, and the ice in our drinks was no longer melting. Once inside, she took a sip of her drink and opened *The New York Times*, while I went on my iPad searching for current restrictions on travel to Cuba.

Five minutes later she looked ashen and said, "I don't want to go to Cuba."

"An epiphany?" I asked.

She shook her head. "No, one of our House of Representatives members was in Cuba last week and is missing. An unsigned and unidentified note was received at the U.S. Interests Section that said 'Representative Juan Mendoza will never be found. He has paid for his sins in promoting a termination of the boycott.' The *Times* article goes on to say that a large poster had been unlawfully plastered on billboards and electric poles throughout Havana, saying 'Cuba is free only if it remains separate from any U.S. domination. No more U.S. diplomats, no more U.S. trade, no more U.S. tourists. Independence forever! The FF.' What suggests that more than one person is involved and that persons in both Cuba and the U.S. are jointly seeking something is that similar posters were placed in public places in Miami and D.C."

"What is the FF?" she asked.

"I'm not sure. It may be a group of militant early exile Cubans who call themselves the Freedom Fighters. Others call them the First to Flee. They want the U.S. to invade Cuba, again. . . . But it's more likely a group *in* Cuba that doesn't want any renewed relations with the U.S. They aren't adamant that the U.S. stay out altogether, but that the early exiles don't take over—like before."

"Who is Juan Mendoza?" she inquired. "And please don't tell me you know him?"

Nodding, I added, "I do know him, but not well. He's an avid salt water fly fisherman. I met him more than fifteen years ago in D.C. at an international law meeting where I spoke on trade with Cuba. He was in the audience and after I finished came up and we shook hands. We talked for no more than two or three minutes. A couple of years ago, I guided Juan and his sister Elena on the Snake River in Wyoming. I wore very different clothes, a hat, and sunglasses. He never even hinted that he had met me before."

"It was probably because you've aged so much," she added.

"It's the company I keep."

"At the international law meeting, did you speak in favor of ending the trade boycott?"

"Yes, and I wrote some articles that supported ending the boycott. This happened when I was Professor Maxwell Hunt. It was a few years before I met you. Meaning literally that as Macduff Brooks I have never been to Cuba. . . . Does the article say when Mendoza was last seen?"

"Mendoza was in Cuba with a U.S. government trade group," she answered. "He remained when the rest of the group left for home."

"I think he was on the important Committee on Foreign Affairs of the House."

"The article says he was a representative from New Mexico," Lucinda noted, her nose literally in the paper because she had misplaced her reading glasses. "His sister is also in Congress; she's a representative from Connecticut. The paper says Juan was almost certain to be elected New Mexico's junior senator next year, and a few D.C. political savants have been talking about his becoming the first Hispanic U.S. president."

"Why did he stay in Cuba after the rest of the delegation went home?" I asked.

"According to the paper, to fly fish the next few days somewhere along the south coast near the infamous Bay of Pigs—*Bahía de Cochinos*. The paper says he stayed at a small hotel called the Playa Larga, near the entrance to the large Zapata Reserve wetlands. . . . Macduff, I thought you said fishing isn't a legitimate reason for getting a license to go to Cuba."

"It isn't. But Mendoza was different; he had a diplomatic passport and was on officially approved business, also called perks of politicians. . . . Did anyone see him in Zapata?"

"Yes, the man who took him fishing that day," she said. "His name is Nacho Gomez. When they got back from fishing, he dropped Mendoza off at the hotel. They were off early the next morning and fished a second day. One hotel staff member said Mendoza looked exhausted when they returned. He said he'd be in for dinner after a shower and then was going to bed. He planned a final third day fishing before he returned to D.C."

"I've read that the Zapata Reserve has some of the best fishing in all of Cuba. When you asked if we could go to Cuba, my thoughts turned to fishing on the flats off Zapata while you photographed in Havana and Cojímar. . . . I think in view of the most recent regulations for travel, we should apply for licenses."

"Do I go as a journalist?"

"Yes. You qualify as a free-lance journalist and need a record of publication, which should be satisfied by your work at the Murie Center program in Wyoming."

"My photos of the Laurance Rockefeller Preserve will be in the Jackson Hole magazine in three months. Plus, I can get a letter from the Canadian travel magazine that I'm to do a series of photos on Hemingway in Cuba."

"I think you'll pass the test. But *I* don't. I'm no longer active as a professor. But I have an idea."

"That worries me, but tell me."

"A friend who's a fly fishing guide in Key West and some other guides have joined to form the St. Peter the Fisherman church in Islamorada. Some of their fellow guides in Cuba have formed a similar church in Playa Larga, the town where Representative Mendoza was last seen. They use that church affiliation to justify fishing trips several times a year.

"Churches throughout the U.S. organize travel groups to go to Cuba. They charge enough to make a little money for the church in each country, mostly Cuba. The minister writes a letter that so-and-so is a member of the church. I know the minister of the Islamorada church; we've fished together. I think you and I both could go by joining the church. Our government's pretty liberal and looks the other way when it comes to religious travel. The President has enough trouble with church and state separation issues without adding a new debate."

"Macduff, I feel better applying as a journalist. You apply through the church. How long would you be fishing?"

"One day for us to travel to Havana and stay overnight. Another for me to get to Playa Larga in time to do some fishing. Two more full days of fishing and back to Havana for a night or two before we fly home. Let's plan on five or six nights. . . . Maybe you can get someone to drive you to Playa Larga after you finish your photos. You could fish one day with me. Catch your first bonefish, maybe catch a tarpon or even the elusive permit. Maybe all three—the 'grand slam' added to your fishing laurels."

The following morning I made some calls, and we began plans for a January or February trip. Lucinda's Canadian magazine was excited to help her; my guide contacts in Key West asked us to join their church group on an already scheduled and approved trip to meet with "fellow parishioners" at St. Peter the Fisherman in Playa Larga. Lucinda and I would join that church, but she also would obtain permission to travel as a journalist, allowing her to stay alone to photograph in Havana and Cojímar before she joined our group of "devout members" of the church of St. Peter the Fisherman.

6

INTERLUDE AT MILL CREEK

I HAD ONE MORE DAY OF GUIDING in Montana before we left for Florida for the winter and who knows what. Predictability is not part of our life. But as we were having dinner the prior evening, the phone rang.

"Macduff? This is Hank at the fly shop."

"About my float in the morning with the couple from Rhode Island?"

"Yep. The guy called me and canceled a few minutes ago. Sorry."

"Another client worried about the wicker man and mistletoe murders?"

"Maybe. But they said they both have the flu and don't think a day on a drift boat in mid-October is wise."

"Everyone seems to have the flu. If they're telling the truth, I understand. But a beautiful day with temperatures in the low seventies is the forecast. The browns are killing hoppers along the banks of the Yellowstone. Plus, I've just received a few 'petticoat' flies from my fly tying friend, Dave Johnson, in Indiana. The petticoat's a great fly on the salt flats in front of my cottage in Florida, and Dave says it should work when casting streamers here in the West."

"Tell me how they work for you," Hank said. "I may want to order some. For next year."

"I will. I'll stop by late tomorrow. Lucinda and I are leaving for Florida in a couple of days."

"Escaping our beautiful winters?"

"As fast as we can. We don't ski on snow, and we don't shovel snow. When the temperature drops below seventy, Lucinda begins to shiver. I can hold out until it's in the fifties."

"Two wimps! Some year you should stay the winter and learn it's not that bad."

"I stayed the winter my first year here. It *was* that bad. . . . I'll drop by late tomorrow afternoon."

When I closed the phone, Lucinda asked, "Are the wicker man murders last year hurting your floats?"

"I don't think so. For every float I've had canceled, someone else signs up. And invariably wants to talk about the gill net murders, the wicker man and mistletoe murders, the Shuttle Gal murders, or even the shootout on the Snake the first year I guided."

"Next year Hank should advertise your guide trips as celebrity floats."

"*I've* never killed a client on my boat."

"You came close the first year with Park Salisbury. I saved you."

"Don't remind me . . . again. I do wonder at times if clients know I have a loaded Glock in the guide box on my . . . *our* drift boat *Osprey*."

"If they do know that, I hope they don't know how bad you are shooting it."

"Can we change the subject? . . . What do you want to do tomorrow since we have a free day? Your choice."

"Let's fish by ourselves and leave *Osprey* home. We'll walk the shoreline of some creek or river. You can be my guide. We'll take Wuff."

"Where?"

"We've never been up the Boulder River," she said, thumbing through a guide to Southwestern Montana fly fishing. "It's not far. What's it like?"

"Lots of farms and endless menacing fences. Not much access until you're in the Gallatin National Forest. But I know a couple who own property along the river below the natural bridge state monument. The river corkscrews through their land. Good pools. Good riffles. Heavily wooded. The water won't be high; this is about the lowest time of the year."

"How do we fish?"

"There are big holes where we can throw streamers to deep trout. Dry flies may be OK, but the summer caddis hatches most likely are over. Maybe we'll use hoppers."

Two hours later we had driven through Livingston and were headed east on Interstate 90, closing in on Big Timber.

"What's in Big Timber?" Lucinda asked, juggling a road map of Southwestern Montana on her lap and fumbling for her reading glasses that she discovered in the refrigerator. I'm not mentioning *that*.

"Maybe 2,000 folk. And like everywhere around here, more people in the summer. There's a self-serve car wash that prefers clean cars; a sign says 'No mud or ice caked pickups. No trailers. No RVs. No cleaning farm vehicles.' And the town has a sure sign of civilization—a century old Carnegie Library! It has about ten books per resident."

"How many do you suppose have read their share?"

We turned off the interstate and started along the Boulder River Backcountry Drive, paved until a little after the one-time mining town of McLeod was built, fortuitously settled nearly twenty miles from where the interstate would be located. But maybe McLeod residents are envious of Big Timber's waterslide. More attractive to the wayfaring fly fisher is the Road Kill Bar & Café in McLeod, offering what has not yet come to most of the East—bison and elk burgers.

The road and river are parallel south for another thirty miles to Natural Falls. The river, like towns throughout the Northeast that assert "Washington Slept Here," claims fame because allegedly it was where scenes of fly fishing in *The River Runs Through It* were filmed. Washington must have slept two to three times the same night in beds in towns miles apart. And "the River" must have run through most of the states west of the Rockies.

Boulder River's Natural Falls are a unique combination of free flowing water roaring over the top during the spring high water and catheter-like dribbling through a tube in the rock during the dry season.

The thirty miles before Natural Falls was a ranch owned by a testy breeder of the other beef—the one that's caused cows to try to convince people to "Eat Mor Chikin." The ranch owner had been pleased a few years ago when I donated my guiding time to his favorite charity in Livingston. He gave me lifetime free access to the Boulder River, which does "run through it."

I drove through the private ranch slowly so my vehicle might be recognized and parked us by a picnic table that overlooked two bends in the river. At the head of the first, a gravel bar protruded into the river, leaving a promising-looking pool on the downstream side. Lucinda was anxious, and before I sorted through my flies to find the petticoat, she had her rod assembled, reel added, and was sitting, holding the tippet toward me and smiling.

"Macduff, a petticoat if you please." she said.

The petticoat fly is a mass of white fluffy marabou hair. I tied it on Lucinda's tippet with a loop knot intended to increase the fly's movement. She soon was off across the gravel and small boulders that a year ago formed similar bars further upstream, before the spring surge of snow-melt from the mountains rousted them and sent them rolling along their way, ultimately to join the Yellowstone River near Big Timber.

Before she found a place to stop and set her feet, Lucinda sent her fly across the pool below the bar, slipped on a round rock, and went down ungraciously.

"Your parents should have named you Grace," I called. I think that's called a 'sitting cast.' You did it beautifully."

"Don't bother me," she said, sitting in six inches of water, no longer smiling, and turning toward me as something took and quickly threw off her fly. "Damn it, Macduff! You caused me to lose a fish. Is that how you treat clients?"

"Not the ones who give me big tips. . . . Pay attention to your fishing," I said.

After Lucinda turned, did one false cast to gain some distance, set the fly nicely at the downstream edge of the pool, stripped line to pull the fly back, and this time firmly set the hook, something deep in the water struck.

"First two casts, two hits. Pretty good for a girl," I called.

"Don't distract me," she yelled looking back over her shoulder. "If you make me lose this one, we will have had a short marriage."

"Promise?" I called out.

She turned toward the fish as it rose and rolled on the surface and disappeared from sight, turning and slashing upstream to offer the line some slack and turn the odds against a landing in its favor. The glistening colored trout rolled and caught a patch of sun flashing its namesake—a rainbow. Its side showed it had dined richly over the summer.

"Come and help, Macduff," she called.

"You can't yell for help every time you hook on to a fish. I promised to love and cherish you, not to pamper you."

"You're awful. If only I could turn back the clock eight years and not let you in my house for dinner that Thanksgiving evening."

"You would have had eight more years of the same dull work—investment advice in Manhattan. . . . No adventure."

"And no scars or bullet wounds. No being tied to a drift boat, wearing a wicker man and mistletoe—waiting to be blown into little pieces. No more walking into a cabin rigged to blow up. No more. . . ."

"You loved every minute of it. Or you never would have come back from New York and married me."

"Now I've lost my fish! I'm skunked because of you."

"Please be quiet. I have a brown on *my* line. Also on a petticoat fly. I'll talk to you after it's in my net."

Out of the corner of my eye, I saw Lucinda bend down, pick up a round stone, and throw it at my fish. I was distracted and lost the fish.

"You threw that at me! You could have killed me."

"Now I've missed three times today," she exclaimed, smiling as I brought in my line with the petticoat intact. At least I didn't lose my fly. "And I didn't throw it at *you*," she added. "Anyway, it was a big rock, as hard as your head."

She waded over to me with a broad smile, dropped her rod on the gravel bar, took my rod and dropped it next to hers, and wrapped her arms around my neck and squeezed.

"Hey, you two," came a voice from the tractor that had been turning soil in the field across the river west of us. "I only gave you permission to fish, Macduff. No spawning in my river!"

"Damn," Lucinda responded, "it was just starting to be fun."

"Do you have any sisters?" the man called to Lucinda as the tractor disappeared over a small rise.

"Now look what you've done to my reputation," I said to her.

"When we get home, I'll do a lot more," she answered.

7

THE FALL MOVE FROM MONTANA TO FLORIDA

LUCINDA AND I WOKE EVERY MORNING to see burnished leaves from the aspens that during the night had silently floated down to add to the golden carpet that would soon fade and decompose, merging with the rich soil of the forest. The turning of the leaves was especially late this year, but we were determined to risk some snow and not miss any part of a season of endless color scattered across the mountains that frame Paradise Valley.

Our Montana cabin had beckoned after the gill net murders were history, Lucinda and I tied the knot, and we luxuriated for a week on Captiva. We could only stay at Mill Creek six weeks before our migration back east to Florida for the winter. The time demanded by the gill net murders over the past half-year meant I had to do some fall floats to retain credibility as a guide. I could count my summer floats this season on two hands.

Lucinda and I each had left a few belongings at my cabin at the end of our separate brief visits to Montana during our time apart. My new SUV, without pampering, faced a Montana winter sitting unsheltered in my yard next to the garage that protected only my two drift boats.

When it was time to head east, with Wuff sprawled in the back of the SUV and the help of Sirius radio, we completed the monotonous drive across the U.S. from Montana to Florida—from *our* Mill Creek cabin to *our* St. Augustine cottage—in record time. We swapped hours at the wheel and drove from sunrise to a half-hour after sunset, avoiding the drudgery and danger of the interstates.

Three days after closing the gate to our cabin on Mill Creek, we pulled into our cottage driveway in Florida. My irreplaceable housekeeper, Jen, had prepared the cottage. Two bottles sat on the kitchen table, with large glasses. One was Gentleman Jack, the other Montana Roughstock Whiskey.

Our focus when we arrived in St. Augustine would be on the trip to Cuba. Our honeymoon and idyllic brief time in Montana were stored in our memory box.

Four days after we arrived at the cottage, a vehicle drove in at 8:00 a.m., honked a few times, and parked. Before the door opened, I knew it was my daughter, Elsbeth, in her Jeep Wrangler newly decorated with University of Florida Gator symbols. Elsbeth had left Little Palm Island Resort immediately after she finished her 4 p.m. to midnight shift managing the check-in desk. She and her friend Sue, who had stayed in the Keys to work, had two months left until Christmas and the end of their employment. They had already completed spring term registration to begin in January at UF in Gainesville.

"You drove through the night?" I asked as we hugged. "What's so important?"

"You two. And I brought my laundry. Plus, I'll mooch some free meals. Am I too late?"

"Not at all. You can share my breakfast. In fact, you may have it all."

"That must mean Lucinda tried out a new breakfast on you."

"Sort of. She made huevos rancheros."

"I love them. Sue and I had them last summer in Jackson. *You* actually eat them?"

"I'd like them better if we put them in the blender and substituted Gentleman Jack for Monterrey Jack."

"Leave mine out of the blender, and I'll keep the Monterrey Jack. . . . What's new with you two?" she asked.

"Not much. We're an old married couple now, going on two months, and she hasn't left me."

"Don't think I haven't thought of it," came Lucinda's voice as she joined us and warmly embraced Elsbeth. "If he complains once more about a meal, I'm going to. . . ."

Thankfully my cellphone interrupted her in mid-sentence.

"Macduff here."

"This is Elena Mendoza, Mr. Brooks. The summer before last you took me and my brother Juan fly fishing on the Deadman's Bar to Moose section of the Snake River in Wyoming."

I put my hand over the speaker and quietly said to Elsbeth and Lucinda, "It's Representative Juan Mendoza's sister. He's the one who's missing in Cuba. She's also a U.S. Representative."

"I remember the day, Elena. In your other life as a fly fisher, you caught one of the best browns of all my clients that year, about where Cottonwood Creek joins the Snake a little above Moose. You used a Dave's Hopper. . . . You represent Connecticut if I recall."

"Good memory," she replied. "Juan often has mentioned that trip."

"If I remember," I said, "You two were siblings who graduated from high school in Miami, left for different colleges outside of Florida, and never turned back."

"To the consternation of our parents, although they encouraged us to think of universities outside Florida. The result was that neither Juan nor I decided to settle in Florida, however unusual that is for Miami Cubans. . . . Mr. Brooks," she said, her voice breaking, "Juan went to Cuba and is missing."

"We read about it in Montana before we drove here," I said. "Lucinda had asked me if we could go to Cuba; she has been commissioned to take photographs of Hemingway-related places in and around Havana. It's for a Canadian travel magazine. . . . When she opened the daily paper, we learned about your brother. Any news?"

"*Are* you going to go to Cuba?" Mendoza asked.

"I checked the laws. I think Lucinda can get a license, but I can't. I. . . ."

"Yes, you can," she interrupted.

"What do you mean?"

"If I endorse your application, Treasury will give you a license. . . . You might be able to help me find Juan. He went to a town named Playa Larga on the south coast at the Bay of Pigs. He planned to stay in Cuba and fly fish for three days after a meeting in Havana discussing further trade between the U.S. and Cuba. He went missing after the second day he fished. . . . When you guided me, we talked about *your* hope to fly fish in Cuba."

"I remember. I wanted to fish near Playa Larga where your brother went missing."

43

"You'd be better than me in trying to find out what happened to Juan. As a House member going to search for her brother—not only a House member but maybe in the Senate in another couple of years—I would draw more attention than you. Attention of both the Cuban authorities and foreign journalists."

"What would my license say about my purpose?"

"That you're going to fly fishing locations to look into opportunities to open lodges once the U.S. has better relations with Cuba. To sort of 'test the waters.' You must know that an increasing number of people from other countries fish in Cuba legally."

"I do. Along with many U.S. citizens who go illegally by way of Canada or the Bahamas or some other nation."

"Let's not talk about that. Will you help?"

"My thinking of going was because of Lucinda's interest to photograph. Can you get her a license? She's really entitled to one as a certified journalist."

"Not a problem. . . . Macduff, I have a committee hearing in ten minutes. Talk to Lucinda and think about it. I'll call you soon."

"I'll have an answer for you."

Lucinda and Elsbeth had heard only my end of the conversation. It was enough to cause them both to ask me what Elena was saying about going to Cuba.

8

NOVEMBER AT THE ST. AUGUSTINE COTTAGE

THE BROOKS QUARTET—Elsbeth, Lucinda, me, and
Wuff trailing along with a slight limp from a gunshot
wound several years ago, were engaged in the invigorating salt-
flecked air, walking along the beach at nearby Summer Haven.
We had been to St. Augustine to pick up a book Lucinda wanted to give Elsbeth.

Elsbeth began to say something but seeing that Lucinda
was about to speak to me, nodded at her.

"How soon do we leave for Cuba, Macduff?" Lucinda
asked.

"Are you sure it's a good idea?" I replied. "We might irri-
tate the early exiles in Miami."

"Now that we're an inseparable duo, we can take on anyone."

"Except *becoming* separable because we're in different prison cells. In Cuba or the U.S."

"We'd be safer if you'd practice using your Glock," she
urged. "But on second thought you might try to draw it from
its holster and shoot yourself in a foot or put a hole in the bottom of *Osprey*."

"With you by my side, I don't need to be armed." I said.

"With me by your side, *I'm* in danger," she responded.

"Dad, go!" Elsbeth interjected. "You won't need guns. You'll get to fly fish for bonefish and tarpon *and* be helping your country without having to assassinate anyone! . . . Plus, Lucinda will be able take the photographs she wants. What's keeping you? Don't be a wimp, Dad. Go!" she exclaimed, stepping in front and facing me with an exasperated look.

Elsbeth's two days with us passed too quickly for me, except when she and Lucinda, joined by Wuff, ganged up to form a ruling triumvirate. When she drove off, headed back to the Keys, Lucinda and I began outlining our uncertain Cuban trip. An hour after Elsbeth left, Elena called again.

"Macduff, at Lucinda's urgings I've talked to some of our Treasury Department people—the office that controls travel to Cuba. They have a backlog of applications. But you've been bumped to the head of the line. It will be late January or early February when you go. By that time Juan should have been found. . . . Or his body," she said as her voice broke. "If there's no word about him, the trip will be all the more important.

"You'll get a call soon for some information about the two of you that Treasury needs for the licenses. . . . I'm sending you as much as I could find about Juan's trip and disappearance. . . . Oh! Damn! Macduff, I didn't want Juan to go in the first place. I *begged* him not to go. Castro holds grudges, and our name isn't well liked by him or his followers. I am *so* worried about Juan."

The phone was quiet for a few moments. I didn't want to say anything until she regained her composure.

"You OK?" I finally asked.

"Yes."

"You said you had information for us?"

"Yes. It includes contact info about Juan's guide, Nacho Gomez. You'll have a reservation at the Playa Larga, where Juan stayed. Not fancy, but it's clean and the food's good. . . . If you can think of anything more, call me. Someone's walked into my office I need to talk to. Bye."

"Lucinda," I asked, setting the phone down, "have *you* urged anyone else to help us? The Secretary of State? The President?"

"I called the Secretary of State, but he wasn't in. I don't especially like the President."

"What else have you arranged?" I asked

"I've arranged for me to be driven to Playa Larga to join you after I'm finished photographing. I get to fish a day with you. I really meant 'outfish' you, but I was being kind. We'll be driven back to Havana and stay overnight for two nights at the Hotel Nacional. Elena and I thought you and I might want to see the city together. We'll be shown around Havana and after our second night be taken to the airport."

"You're good, Lucinda. Maybe in addition to being in charge of our nutrition, you'd like to take over our clandestine operations?"

"I already have. Remember that I'm better than you with a Glock."

"Anything more I ought to know, to the extent you feel you can share it without compromising us?" I asked.

"There is. We'll fly both directions, using the Miami airport. Elena said we may get hassled a bit—going and coming home—because the U.S. TSA staff includes a number of Cuban exiles; some are not pleased about *any* travel to Cuba by *anyone* and for *any* reason. . . . By the way, since we arrive back in Miami in late afternoon, too late to drive to St. Augustine in day-light, we have a reservation at the restored 1950's Fon-tainebleau Hotel on Collins Avenue in Miami Beach—an area called 'Millionaires' Row.'"

"Whose paying for all this?"

"You are. I don't want to be seen using public money to help someone fish."

"Did you arrange for us to fly first class?"

"Not a chance. You'll have to rough it for the forty-five minute flight. When we finish taking off, we'll start preparing to land."

"Elena didn't say exactly what we're supposed to do," I noted.

"She did say, Macduff. *We're to bring Juan home.*"

9

THE HOLIDAYS

A WORRIED ELENA DIDN'T SAY "DEAD OR ALIVE," but as each day and week passed without word about Juan, it became increasingly apparent that dead was more likely. The information she gave me wasn't encouraging.

"Macduff," she said on a call in mid-December, "the Cuban government has been evasive talking about what they have been doing to find Juan. One official said little more than that Juan shouldn't have been 'nosing around' the Bay of Pigs, where the Cubans in 1961 turned back the *Brigada de Gusanos*, continuing government reference to Cubans who left the island as being 'worms.'"

The holidays arrived. So did Elsbeth. It was far better than a year ago when she had to choose *between* visiting me and visiting Lucinda.

We went to Lucinda's New York City apartment two days before Christmas and stayed until January 2nd. Early on Christmas Eve four inches of snow blanketed Manhattan. We were like kids. Dressed in our warmest assortment of non-matching clothes, we hiked through drifting snow to Rockefeller Center, throwing snowballs at one another. The snow had discouraged most folks from going outside except for the ice skaters of every skill level who raced, circled, and pirouetted on "the Rink." The annual imported Christmas tree sparkled and high above on window ledges where snow was piling up in ridges.

The cold crept through our hats, scarves, jackets, and pants, chasing us inside where we rode the elevator seventy stories to the Top of the Rock observation deck. The snow stopped, and we watched the whitened city darken and be consumed by millions of tiny lights reflected on the new snow. Elsbeth put an arm through mine on one side and Lucinda did the same on the other. Christmas bliss!

"Dad, are you going to feed us?" Elsbeth asked as we got off the elevator and left the building.

"Sure. There's a stand across the street on the corner selling roasted chestnuts. 'Tis the season. Remember *The Christmas Song?* I can sing it for you."

Chestnuts roasting on an open fire,

"We may roast you on an open fire," threatened Lucinda, looking at me as though I needed therapy.

Jack Frost nipping on your nose,

"Anywhere you want to go?" I asked. "Sardi's, 21 Club, Russian Tea Room, Carnegie Deli. Name it."

Yuletide carols being sung by a choir,

"I know where I want to go," said Elsbeth.

And folks dressed up like Eskimos.

"Where?" I asked.

They know that Santa's on his way,

"Nathan's!" responded Elsbeth.

He's loaded lots of toys and goodies on his sleigh.

"Nathan's?" exclaimed Lucinda.

And every mother's child is going to spy,
"Nathan's. In Penn Station," Elsbeth added.
To see if reindeer really know how to fly.
"Elsbeth," said Lucinda, "I'm beginning to think you inherited some strange genes."
And so I'm offering this simply phrase,
"Why Nathan's?" Lucinda asked.
To kids from one to ninety-two,
"It's a favorite of Dad's. He told me he's had more meals at Nathan's in Manhattan than any other restaurant."
Although it's been said many times, many ways,
"Don't blame me for his eating quirks," Lucinda said, turning to Elsbeth and then back to me and adding with a raised voice, "And stop that off key singing! It's worse than when you play your oboe."
A very Merry Christmas to you.

"Merry Christmas to you both," I said, finished with my song, bowing, and doffing my hat. Before I could put it back on, a homeless man walked over, put a quarter in the hat, mumbled "nice song," and walked away.

"How about a cab to Penn Station?" I asked. "Dinner at Nathan's and a walk back to the apartment through Times Square, up to Central Park, maybe a carriage ride, and then home."

"Dad, that's brilliant. Now I know why Lucinda married you. You're so romantic."

"Elsbeth," interjected Lucinda, "Your dad has separation anxiety mixed with urban agoraphobia. You haven't taken psychology yet at UF. When you do, you'll learn that's the technical language to describe Macduff. Basically, it means he's nuts."

We took the cab. Three of us sitting in the back. I was between the two people I most loved in the world.

"Dad, why Nathan's? There must be a story."

"When I was growing up in Farmington, Connecticut, my parents began to let me come here to Manhattan when I was about fifteen. But with strict rules. My high school best friend had to go as well. His name was Jim Brooks. He died of cancer the year before I chose to use his name. I miss him.

"My dad would make a reservation at a safe hotel, near Carnegie Hall where we'll walk by later. Jim and I walked and walked and walked some more. Once we walked from our hotel all the way south to a restaurant in Greenwich Village called Bianchi & Margarita. Everyone who worked there sang opera. Jim and I loved opera, mainly because our parents let us out on a school night if we went to a cultural event.

"We became very cultural event oriented; we went to dozens of operas, plays, and symphonies in Hartford. . . . Elsbeth, I'll tell you more later. The quick ending is that to save money Jim and I ate almost every meal at the Nathan's in Grand Central Station. It's long closed, but there's one where we're going—Penn Station."

We ate grandly on a bench at Penn Station, the abomination that rose from the ashes when the *Beaux Arts* masterpiece was demolished in 1963. The station we ate in was in the basement of America's basketball and boxing arena—Madison Square Garden.

"This was good," I mused, grinning, and throwing away the hot dog wrapper.

"You ate two," noticed Lucinda.

"Twice my budget in the 50's."

"What's for dessert?" asked Elsbeth.

"Times Square," I said, "a visual smorgasbord. Christmas lights. Millions of Christmas lights."

Elsbeth was awed by the discordant and riotous color of Times Square. We walked through a dozen blocks of garish ads in lights emphasized by strobes. North of the Square, the lights moderated, and snow on the sidewalks quieted the streets. We enjoyed being together and walking arm-in-arm so much so that we decided against the carriage ride in Central Park and walked along 57th from Carnegie Hall to Park Avenue and then north ten blocks along the edge of the park to Lucinda's street.

When we walked into the lobby of her apartment building, the doorman smiled at Lucinda and Elsbeth and stepped in front of me.

"Miss Lang," he said, turning to Lucinda, "do you want this man to come in. I encountered him some years ago when I thought he was coming to steal your silver."

"I remember and appreciate your concern, Alfred, but for better or for worse, I'm married to this man. I'm now Mrs. Brooks."

"Sorry," he said, meaning either he was sorry for making a mistake or sorry she married me. I didn't ask for clarification.

The next morning became afternoon by the time we arose and made breakfast.

"I'm looking forward to Christmas dinner," I said, sipping on my coffee. "Roast turkey, dressing—lots of dressing, maybe Yorkshire Pudding."

"I was thinking of Nathan's again," Lucinda said. "I wouldn't have to cook."

"You mean on our very first Christmas together, and with Elsbeth present, there's to be no Christmas dinner? I could have stayed in St. Augustine with Wuff. She's being served regular meals by Jen."

"Stop complaining," Lucinda ordered. "There is to be a Christmas dinner, but not here, nor at Nathan's."

"I wouldn't try to guess," I said, slumping in my seat in utter defeat.

'Would you accept corned beef hash for your meal?"

"Only if we're at the Carne . . . my gosh, we passed it last night! We're going to the Carnegie Delicatessen!"

"That's right. It's listed as number two on your most visited restaurants in Manhattan."

The corned beef hash we had at the Carnegie was enough to feed us as much as we could consume on site, plus a full "doggie" box to take back and put in Lucinda's refrigerator for several future meals. . . . After all the beef, I wondered what corned bison would taste like. It might become the state meal of Montana.

The rest of our New York interlude passed quickly, with never a single word spoken about Juan Mendoza or Cuba. We walked back to Times Square to join thousands to watch the new year come in and the following morning flew south to Florida.

Elsbeth left for Gainesville the next day for a week of getting settled at her Golf View rented house before beginning her first classes at UF.

It was time for Lucinda and me to get serious about Cuba.

10

TO HAVANA

O N THE DAY OF OUR FLIGHT TO HAVANA, Lu-
cinda and I locked the gate to our St. Augustine cottage
at 5 a.m. and drove to Miami, reaching the airport at noon.
Considering the language and looks of other passengers, it
should be called the Aeropuerto Internacional de la Ciudad de
Miami.

The public area outside the terminal was filled with people
waving placards opposing travel to Cuba. A few said "DON'T
DO IT." I assumed they had just come from picketing some
abortion clinic.

When we reached the terminal where all flights to Cuba are
processed, we quickly learned that patience is a mandate for
such travel. Check-in was at 12:30 p.m. for a 4:10 p.m. forty-
five-minute flight to Havana on American Airlines. We might
have gone quicker by raft.

The delay allowed time for a thorough search to confiscate
items like aspirins or hand soap that might be intended as gifts
to Cubans but nevertheless are considered illegal trade.

Check-in was slow. Because so many people were waiting for flights, we wondered if the travel ban might have been lifted overnight. That proved not to be the case. There were simply hundreds of people taking advantage of looser rules applying to family members going to Cuba. Or maybe they were all devout members of the St. Peter the Fisherman church.

The check-in agent looked Hispanic; I heard her Spanish accent when she spoke to the person in front of me. She was a formidable, bulky lady; what she lacked in height she made up in width. Her nametag read Ariana Vazquez.

She stared at me for long enough to convince me she was an important person and possible roadblock in my quest to be approved for passage to the next check-in stage. Then she looked at my papers for an equally long time and finally back again at me. Never any trace of a smile. She must practice at home in front of a mirror. This went on for ten minutes before she said a word. She had shifted her focus to the two three-feet-long rod cases next to my bag.

"What's in those round tubes?" she asked.

"Rods."

"Clothing rods? Curtain rods? What *kind* of rods?"

"Fishing."

"What is the purpose of your trip?" she frowned.

"People-to-People exchange," I replied. That was true. Elena Mendoza had thought that was a good purpose to put on my license.

"Do you need fishing rods to meet local people?" she next inquired. She was not through with me.

"They're gifts."

"To who?"

"People. I'll give them rods in exchange for their giving me local crafts and meals. That's called People-to-People."

"Don't get smart. That sounds like trade to me. Trade with Cuba is not permitted," she said emphatically.

"But we're one of Cuba's major trading partners despite the ban," I said, knowing that fact would not be well received.

"Well, that fact's not my concern. We shouldn't be trading *at all* with those *communists*."

"I guess we have to follow *our* U.S. law, Agent Vazquez, which is moving toward the day when all the Cubans who fled the island in the 60's are resting in peace in Miami cemeteries and no one will give a damn about Cuba anymore. It will just be a suburb of greater Miami." I immediately knew that was not a wise opinion to have expressed. Lucinda, next to me, dug her elbow into my side and showed me her looks-could-kill face.

Vazquez muttered something in Spanish I couldn't and probably didn't want to comprehend, then scowled at me and continued her inquisition.

"Do you plan to fish?" she asked.

"It depends on what our Cuban hosts want us to do. We are their guests and owe them the respect they deserve."

Lucinda jabbed me again, concerned that I was shifting from combativeness to a surreptitious condescension that would be no less welcome.

"Do you know traveling to Cuba to fish isn't permitted?" the agent asked.

"I'm traveling to meet *people*. I really can't tell you what they plan for me."

"Then why are you carrying fishing rods?"

"As I said, they're gifts."

"I don't think you should go to Cuba."

If this is what Cubans on the island are like, I thought, I'm not sure I want to go.

"I have a license," I responded, staring her down. "Unless you have some authority to *reject* my travel permit, please give me my tickets."

I didn't understand what she mumbled, but she handed me my tickets with a scowl that made me think I wouldn't like to be next in line, immediately realizing that would be Lucinda. But she smiled, said little, and was promptly given her flight ticket. Of course, I was carrying her fishing rods.

My license from Treasury had no stipulations about what I could take to or do in Cuba. But our airport agents apparently needed to have their Warhol cliché: "fifteen minutes of fame." I assumed the more severe challenge would come at the airport in Havana.

Two hours of sitting and waiting for the flight to be called followed. When it was, the agent at the gate looked at my ticket and then my rod tubes, and with a smile and in quiet voice whispered, "Hope you get the grand slam. I came close in Belize, but I lost a permit." The grand slam is catching a bonefish, a tarpon, and a permit. The permit's the most difficult to catch and the usual barrier to the grand slam.

I opened a small bag, took out a fly, and handed it to him. "Try this the next time you fish. I've hooked my only permit on a fly like it." He took the fly, smiled, touched his brow, and handed me my boarding pass.

The flight departed more or less on time, which meant adding about thirty minutes from gate to lift off. At cruising altitude a few minutes later, the pilot announced that we could unfasten our seat belts. Five minutes more and he made another announcement—to fasten our seat belts for our landing at the Havana José Martí airport. The flight consumed forty-seven minutes.

If Martí could see Havana today, he'd weep.

The airport was as busy as it was disorganized. Lucinda and I expected a long entry process, until a woman approached with a sign: "Mr. & Mrs. Brooks." I nodded when she looked my way.

"I'm Celeste Jones. I work with the embassy or, rather more properly, the U.S. Interests Section. Be prepared; we might be here for hours. But we'll try something," she said, ushering us to a customs agent who was processing air crews and a few others.

The agent saw her, nodded, and waved us to his line, and said, "Buenas dias, Señorita Jones."

Without asking why, we became part of the "few others" being processed and quickly were given stamped entry cards that would not mar our passports with any reference to our visit to forbidden Cuba.

At the baggage inspection the agents passed Lucinda through without asking that she open her single bag carrying clothing and photo equipment, their efforts diverted to leering at her. I was not leered at even once but briskly was told to open my bags. I assumed more questions were about to begin about the fly rods. But with our greeter from the Interests Section standing next to me, they pawed briefly and gently at my belongings and said to go. I've had more hassles entering Atlanta.

A car and driver were waiting. When we were settled, Ms. Jones turned from the front passenger seat and said, "Welcome to Cuba. I'm the Public Affairs Officer. I've been with the U.S. Foreign Service for fourteen years in five different countries, including Italy and Portugal. This is the best assignment yet and might end up being the highlight of my career."

"What makes it so attractive?" asked Lucinda.

"It's a country of anomalies," Jones answered. "For example, Cuba recently changed the rules for selling cars. There's a Peugeot dealership that opened not far from here in the center of Havana. Prices range from a minimum of about $91,000 up to $262,000 for the 508 model. Used cars at the Peugeot dealer start at about $25,000. Even with *free* housing, *free* education, *free* health care, and ultimately *free* burial, Cubans can't pay anything close to those car prices. The average monthly wage in Cuba is about $20. Cuban officials apparently have never heard about U.S. economist Milton Friedman's comment that 'there's no such thing as a free lunch.'

"The government employs eighty percent of the workforce and purportedly provides everything the Cuban people need. The caveat is there's a shortage of everything. Except prostitutes. Prostitution allegedly was wiped out forever in the 1960's, but now there's one or more *jineteras* on every block.

"The government artificially raises the value of its currency more often than Argentina does, but the Cuban peso keeps decreasing in purchasing power. Cubans are allegedly free to buy whatever they want, but for goods like the foreign cars, the prices are out-of-sight. I don't have to tell you that the people are not content with their economy.

"The Cuban government, deceitfully trying to soften the blow of involuntary socialism, blames the U.S. trade embargo for Cubans' lacking what they need and want. The truth is that they *don't* have the means to pay for what they lack—if they did, they could buy whatever they want from dozens of other countries that are delighted to trade with Cuba, but usually do *not* extend credit to Cubans. Most are too poor to shop in the Cuban 'dollar' stores that no longer accept the banned dollar."

"So the dollars we brought are useless?" Lucinda asked.

"Not really. There are two official currencies in Cuba, the regular Cuban peso and the convertible Cuban peso. The former is the currency of compensation but not of choice. It's what Cubans use mostly to buy a few basic staples. The latter peso was created to replace the dollar. You're supposed to exchange any dollars you have for convertible pesos—but not at a one to one rate. The government declared that one convertible peso is worth about eight percent more than a dollar.

"And, you also pay a ten percent surcharge when you turn over your dollars. The surcharge doesn't apply to exchanging such currencies as the euro or Canadian dollar. Castro doesn't like the U.S. dollar. The government insists that its two kinds of pesos are of equal value; those who trade Cuban currency say the convertible peso is worth about twenty-five times more."

"Do I *have* to exchange my dollars? Can't I give tips in dollars?" I asked.

"First, you're not likely to use the useless regular pesos. Sometimes people will try to give you change in the regular peso after you've handed over payment in a hard currency such as the euro. Don't accept regular pesos as change; insist on convertible pesos.

"As for tips, *never* give a tip in regular pesos. Remember that they're worth a fraction of convertible pesos. Give the tip in convertible pesos or hard currencies. If you do use dollars, they are required to be turned in and be subjected to the surcharge. But they are still used. If you gave a Cuban who guided you around the city for a few days $100 U.S. dollars, it will be worth something like eighty convertible pesos. That has the purchasing power of about 2,000 regular pesos."

"When will Cuba use a single currency and let it float?" Lucinda asked.

"When it snows in Havana. . . . Actually, not until the post-Castro era."

"Wouldn't Cubans prefer a market economy?" Lucinda continued, her economics background increasing her curiosity.

"It depends on who you are. Likely most Cubans would like a *little more* capitalism, but probably not as much as in the U.S. Our hiring this driver illustrates the problem. We pay the Cuban government about $870 per month for a driver; they assign us the driver and pay him $20 a month, of course in mostly worthless Cuban pesos. We also give him a generous amount under the table, of course in convertible pesos or a hard currency. A bellhop in your hotel makes more than a doctor. . . . I could go on and on. It's often humorous but very tragic."

The ride to the hotel was brief; there were numerous vehicles on the roads—a few new cars, a fair number of junk cars left over from the Soviet days, and a fleet of the much valued and cherished U.S. cars from the 1950's. The traffic wasn't close to the gridlock of a large city in the U.S. or any major city in most nations, including—surprisingly—Vietnam.

Lucinda and I checked into the Inglaterra Hotel in Old Havana, built nearly a century-and-a-half ago and now a national monument. The exterior has a neoclassical façade and the interior an Arabic opulence with thousands of wall tiles. Guide books give the hotel four stars, one more than it deserves on any international standard. But on any international standard it's a five-star *experience*.

Across from the Inglaterra through the Parque Central and a further short block away is one of Hemingway's favorite bars—El Floridita. Lucinda will be able to walk from the hotel and photograph several Hemingway-favored places. She may be whistled at, but she'll be safe. Criminals do not go unpunished in Cuba.

We opened our bags, freshened up, and walked downstairs to the main Colonial restaurant, filled with soaring archways, decorated plaster ceilings, wrought iron, and tile. We sat and ate traditional oxtail soup (*rabo encendido*) and shredded beef (*ropa vieja*). I didn't ask for Gentleman Jack. Lucinda didn't ask for Montana Roughstock Whiskey. We both drank mojitos made with real Havana Club Rum. The mojito essentially is a mint julep with rum replacing bourbon. And enhanced by a dash of lime juice.

I didn't follow-up by smoking a cigar, but put several in a pocket for friends so inclined in Florida, if the contraband cigars made it through Miami customs. The mere thought of our drinking Havana Club Rum and smoking Cohiba cigars gives sleepless nights to the early exiles in Miami.

After dinner we joined locals and tourists and promenaded through the park and beyond for several blocks, taking in the sights and sounds of this country, which the U.S. Congress designated threatening and disfavored. Before we knew it, we saw another Hemingway haunt—La Bodeguita del Medio. It was expensive but on our list of places to visit. Hemingway wrote on one wall: "My mojito in La Bodeguita, my daiquiri in El Floridita." We both had another mojito; the daiquiri would come another day at El Floridita.

"What are you going to photograph tomorrow?" I asked Lucinda on the walk back to the Inglaterra.

"I have a list of places. I'll start around here, with Hemingway's favorite lodging—the Hotel Ambos Mundos. Then the bars—Bodeguita and Floridita."

"Can I trust you alone in the bars?" I asked.

"Can I trust you alone on the beaches?" she answered.

"Depends on who I meet."

"Same here."

11

THE FOLLOWING MORNING

Lucinda was ready at 6:00 a.m. to start photographing. I wanted breakfast.

"If I leave you, what are you going to have for breakfast?" she asked.

"Bacon, eggs, sausage, a couple of croissants. Maybe vanilla flan. That's the national breakfast here."

"Flan's a dessert, not part of a Cuban breakfast. I'm staying. I'm still your nutritionist."

"No."

"No?"

"Your jurisdiction doesn't extend to Cuba."

"Says who?"

"You don't want to violate social norms of Cuba. Much less U.S. trade policy. Do you?"

"What social norms?"

"This is a patriarchal country. *Men* rule. I'm the man."

"Mac," she said, switching the subject and using my shortened name showing concern for something, "what if Mendoza is dead? Missing often ends up meaning dead."

"At least Elena will have closure."

"But that doesn't solve who was behind Mendoza's death, if it were murder rather than accidental."

"I'm going to start with the idea that it was an accident and go from there," I responded, with no basis for assuming Mendoza was in an accident rather than a victim of murder.

"If it were murder, who would have done it? Did Mendoza have enemies?"

"Elena said no, but that's a sister speaking about a younger brother she loved dearly."

"Have you given thought to who might have wanted Mendoza dead?" she asked.

"Some, but I could focus more if his body were found or if there were at least some evidence of how he died. There may be several people who wished him dead."

"Who?"

"To start, aged early exiles in Miami who remain intolerant of anyone disagreeing with their belief that the only way to deal with Cuba is to roll the clock back to the 1950's. Those were not good years for anyone who disagreed with President Batista. La Cabaña political prison was filled. Some who experienced a stay there must now live in Miami. They have good reason to be angry. But murder?"

"Any specific group of the early exiles in Miami that is particularly troublesome?" she asked.

"Maybe those who donate substantial sums to keep Senator Jorge García García in office. He's clever. He knows how to do two things as well as any member of Congress. In his view his goal is clear—keep getting elected and enjoy the perks of office. He was elected in 1972 at about twenty-eight. He's held office for more than forty years and shows no sign of retiring."

"What else is he good at?"

"Keeping the U.S. trade boycott of Cuba alive. It's had some shaky times, under Carter and Clinton, but García García is conniving. He trades his votes for anything his colleagues from other states want—needless dams, bridges to nowhere, retaining obsolete and unneeded military bases, or granting unregulated mining or grazing permits.

"He's known by other senators as the most reliable ally *as long as* you don't agree to end—or even reduce—the Cuban trade boycott. García García will agree to anything to extend the life of the boycott. Remember that Cuba is irrelevant to most of the U.S. But not in Miami."

"Why would García García be a threat to Mendoza?"

"Mendoza may soon be in the Senate, representing New Mexico. If he is, he'll be a threat to García García. Mendoza is a Cuban-American who wants the trade embargo ended. And who is talked about as a presidential candidate in a few years."

"Would García García go to the extreme of murder?

"If he could get away with it, maybe. He's ruthless. If Mendoza was killed, the murder took place in Cuba. The Cuban authorities probably wouldn't do much of an investigation, and they certainly wouldn't cooperate with the U.S."

"Is Mendoza liked in Cuba?"

"Yes, by those who want the trade boycott ended. But there are Cubans who don't, especially those in government. They use the boycott as the reason for Cuba's troubles, hiding the fact that it's a failed economy regardless of the boycott."

"Macduff, what's the argument that García García is *not* likely responsible if Mendoza was murdered?"

"Prestige and security. He likes the perks of federal office. He milks the country with his needless travel at government expense. García García always carries his golf clubs and takes along his two pit bulls. He has access to a government jet. He's content. He could retire anytime and make loads of money on some boards of directors, especially companies like big U.S. sugar producers that benefit from keeping Cuba non-competitive."

"Which side are you on, Macduff? Do you think he killed Mendoza, if Mendoza was murdered?"

"No. I suspect García García is not losing sleep over the thought that Mendoza is dead. But I don't believe he was directly involved."

"Would anyone else in U.S. government want Mendoza dead?"

"Certainly there are some House of Representative wannabees in state government in New Mexico. I don't know enough to speculate."

"Outside of some politicians, who do *you* think might like to see Mendoza dead?" she asked, narrowing her focus.

"Cubans in Cuba who benefit from keeping the status quo. Like high ranking government officials who live comfortably. Angry exiles living anywhere, especially Miami, who don't want more trade or tourism with Cuba.

"Maybe even Montana cattle ranchers who are happy with what they sell to Cuba, but don't want Cuba to become a cattle *exporting* nation. The same for other exporters who have current contracts with Cuba. We could go on and on. It could be that a *group* of Cubans and Americans are involved.

"Politicians make enemies; it could be someone and something unrelated to Cuba that Mendoza had tangled with. Maybe a U.S. rancher who doesn't sell beef to Cuba and is content with making big money grazing his cattle on public lands. I remember Elena telling me that her brother introduced a bill in the House to stop all grazing on federal lands. Some Western ranchers went ballistic.

"Also, Mendoza was from New Mexico. Ted Turner owns a huge spread for raising bison in Northeast New Mexico and Southern Colorado—the Vermejo Park Ranch. Bison ranchers like Turner are not popular with some cattle ranchers. Mendoza voted yes on several bills that encouraged raising bison."

"Macduff, I shouldn't be interfering with what you have to do. I'm trying to tell you just be careful. You came here for one reason—to find Mendoza. If he's dead, that's all you promised to learn. You didn't agree to solve his killing. If he's alive and in Cuba, you may want to meet him and find out why he disappeared. Nothing more. I don't want to leave you thinking I expect you to play detective. Don't! Promise?"

"I guess so. I don't want to do anything more than find out about Mendoza and then fly fish for bones and tarpon. And fish some more when you join me."

"Three days here photographing, and I'll see you in Playa Larga." She finished her coffee, grabbed her bag, and was headed for the hotel front door before I could say another word, especially any words that might be construed as qualifying my promise not to play detective.

She was sure to attract attention as she walked toward the park across from the hotel. It would be a hot day; she wore white crinkled cotton pants that were slit for twelve inches from the bottom, each slit fastened by three large buttons. Her top was a French blue jersey with a slightly scooped neckline. She looked more like a fashion model than a photographer.

Thirty minutes later I was in a two-tone green and white 1954 Chevy that didn't have a rattle, a sway, or bad shocks, testimony to the endurance of the U.S. cars of that era and to the Cubans who became mechanics of necessity. And to the U.S. Interest Section's access to spare parts from the U.S.

12

ARRIVAL AT PLAYA LARGA - DAY ONE ON THE FLATS

Luis Ferrara was my driver, employed by the U.S. Interests Section and driving the Section-owned '54 Chevy that would not draw attention. The car qualified as an antique under Florida law and looked like a hybrid of a couple of popular American models. Under the rusted hood was a three-year-old engine yet to reach 30,000 miles. The brakes, shocks, muffler, and other critical parts had all been replaced. The car's dents and fading paint were a disguise; no one we passed so much as turned a head.

The drive took us southeast from Havana, ninety miles on the central highway, to Jagüey Grande, Cuba's citrus production center. Leaving Havana, we passed dozens hitchhiking, a common method of traveling in a country where few own cars and gas is scarce even with Venezuelan subsidies. Turning south, we drove through the curiously named town of Central Australia, where Luis pointed out the old sugar refinery that became the headquarters of the Cuban Armed Forces during the Bay of Pigs conflict. Another fifteen miles, and we arrived in Playa Larga.

Luis left me at the Hotel Playa Larga and headed to Cienfuegos where he would stay with some family until he returned
and picked up Lucinda and me at the end of the three days.

The hotel put me in a two-bedroom one-story concrete
block bungalow which, like Joseph's "amazing technicolor
dreamcoat," had a coat of many colors.

Outside on a cracked and mold-stained concrete porch
under a brightly painted overhang sat two rocking chairs. Inside
was plain but had been carefully cleaned. The toilet flushed,
taking its own time, but only from 7:00 a.m. until sundown
when the water was shut off for the night.

I reminded the bell boy I would need a second set of tow-
els when Lucinda arrived. He nodded and said that beach tow-
els, as well as beach chairs, came for an extra fee to be paid in
convertible pesos like all charges at the hotel. However modest
the facilities proved, the hotel's food was good, the menu was
pleasantly repetitive with fresh fish caught each day, and the
staff members were uniformly gracious and responsive to requests.

I left my bags in the bungalow and walked to the hotel restaurant for lunch, enjoying the refreshing smell of the salt air
off the bay. I ate *robalo*, which in Florida is snook. Our numbers
of snook off Florida have dropped drastically, and the delicate
flavored prize has been removed from restaurants menus, but
not in Cuba.

The Playa Larga's guests appeared exclusively foreign; a
half-dozen Canadians and a few British had come to fish and
two German couples to bird-watch. They were excited by an
early morning sighting of both a Cuban Pigmy Owl and the
tiny, rare *zunzuncito*, the world's smallest hummingbird. An Italian duo sat with their backs to the wall in a corner away for the
others; the men looked as though they were Mafia hiding from

other Mafia. While most guests wore short sleeve shirts, the two Italians always appeared with long sleeved shirts but no ties, and suit coats with a bulge under the left arms. The guns were obviously not for shooting Pigmy Owls or rare humming-birds.

Nearly finished with my meal, I looked up to see approaching a thin man of indeterminate age, wearing long baggy pants, shirtless and showing every rib on a deeply suntanned stomach inadequately active, and a Panama hat. He came directly to my table.

"Are you Señor Brooks?"

"Yes."

"I am your guide. My name is Nacho."

He didn't look like a fishing guide. Years in the sun had sped his process of going from youth to advanced age.

Nacho sat down, put his hat on an empty chair, and quietly asked, "Why you staying here? There are more better places than Playa Larga, like the Hostal Mayito or the Casa Frank?"

"This is where a friend stayed," I answered, not wanting to mention Juan Mendoza by name. "I don't think he was aware of the other places. He. . . ."

"Excuse me, Señor Brooks. I just arrive. Need to use rest room." With that, abruptly he rose and left, leaving his hat on his chair."

A waiter came over and asked, "Will Nacho be joining you for lunch?"

"Yes. Do you know him?"

"He's the best guide in Playa Larga and even the whole Zapata Reserve."

Nacho returned and sat. "My whole name Ignacio Hernandez Gomez," he said, "but better just Nacho. . . . That look like *robalo* you eat. You want fish for snook?"

"Only if we can't catch bonefish, tarpon, or permit. I don't think I've ever gone out fishing and put snook *last* on the choice of four fish we might catch."

"We catch many bonefish and hook many tarpon. Whether we get one permit is God's will."

"What's on tap for today?" I asked and then realized the use of diction such as "on tap" is often confusing to foreigners. "Where are we going to fish?" I rephrased my question.

"You finish eating, and we go in car ten miles in Zapata Reserve and go from Salinas on a single skiff boat. Days short this time of the year."

"Single skiff? Is that a flats boat?"

"Yes. For bones I use only my single skiff. One guide—that's me—and one angler. There are two-angler skiffs, but I don't like fish with two people for bones."

"Why? Worried about two people casting fly lines from the same boat?"

"Maybe. But I best like stalk big bones one-by-one."

"How big is big for a bone?"

"Ten pounds, maybe twelve. I think record about sixteen."

"That means three feet long. That's a huge bone! Two feet is big."

"No promises about weight and length, but you gonna catch bonefish until arm says 'enough.'"

We soon reached Salinas on the coast of the Reserve. Nacho's single skiff, made in the U.S. and brought to Cuba from Mexico, was tied to the small dock. After loading rods, reels, flies, some water on ice in an old Igloo, and little else, Nacho left the motor tilted and began to pole us west from the dock, barely rocking the light, tiny skiff.

No more than fifty feet off the dock, he said quietly, "Cast, señor, two dozen bonefish thirty feet in front of us."

I cast blindly into the sun, using two false casts and then setting the tiny pink fly into the calm water with enough splashes to scare any Florida Keys bonefish. But not the aggressive school in front of us. My 9' 8-weight rod bent as a bone immediately took the fly and headed west, a single spray from the line rising an inch or two above the surface like a Lilliputian jet boat. I felt clumsy and late doing what I ought to do instinctively. But no measure of my incompetence benefited this bone.

In less than five minutes, a slim fifteen incher was in Nacho's net. It lay quietly, showing the missile-like shape that allows it to appear or disappear in a matter of seconds. The slender body begins with a nose—long and cone-like with an overlapping upper jaw that looks weak—and only a modest line of small teeth. The dorsal fin is large and elegant like the tail fin. A bonefish is silvery, not unlike tarpon and barracuda, but appears greenish or bluish along the back. It's the Ferrari of the sportfishing world.

Three hours later the sun convinced us to turn toward the dock, no more than a mile away. I rubbed a sore right shoulder that had worn down from casting and landing three dozen bones. I may need Tommy John surgery or for a fisherman more aptly called Joan Wulff or Lefty Kreh surgery.

We had landed mostly bones that were similar in size to the first fifteen incher, but there was one that Nacho stretched to full length against a measurement marker scribbled on the edge of the port rail. It was twenty-seven inches long. Nacho estimated it at eleven pounds, by far my biggest caught over the years on a few dozen days spent on good bonefish waters.

"Nacho, you didn't use a lip-gripping device to weigh that bone? Why not? You have one in your equipment bag?"

"Those things destroy bonefish mouth. I got weight-to-length table in my brain. Bones don't change much in weight for length. But my table ends at thirty inches for fifteen pounder. I've caught only half dozen longer than twenty-five inches in twenty years guiding. None longer than thirty-two. World record is little over sixteen pounds. My thirty-two inch bone may be better than that. Cuban fishing not like U.S. No way to get a potential record certified."

Our skiff touched the dock within moments of the sun touching the western horizon. An hour later at the hotel, I bought Nacho a Cuba Libre and a refreshing mojito for myself. After our third drinks and a few *empanadas de pollo,* I thought I might extract some information about Juan Mendoza from Nacho.

"Good day, no?" Nacho asked, setting down his empty glass.

"Do days on the water come any better?" I replied.

"No, señor," Nacho said. "It *was* good. They come worse. Last week other guide and me took out two skiffs and two men from Texas. When we pick them up at Casa Frank at 8:00 a.m., six empty daiquiri glasses sit on table. They drink last ones down as we left.

"I thought they good friends; they arrived together and shared a bathroom at their bungalow. But they argued from the beginning over everything—politics, religion, wives, mistresses, and fish.

"They fish OK once we got them separated, but until the other guide and I got skiffs far enough apart so they couldn't hear each other, they messed up casts, didn't set hooks, and lost most what they hook. My client fell off the boat, and for a moment I wanted to chum for sharks. Are all people from Texas bad like that?"

"They often try to be. But not all of them. Nobody's nicer than an eighty-year-old gal from Texas I have as a client every year in Montana. But sometimes I wonder what big money from new oil does to a man. You apparently saw the worst with those two guys."

"Señor, how you got permission to fish in Cuba?" asked Nacho, with some hesitation that his question might be too personal. "You flew from Miami, but you not one of many Americans who come through Bahamas or Mexico *without* a U.S. permit to travel to Cuba."

"I came as my wife's assistant," I fudged. "She's photographing Hemmingway's favorite places in Havana and Cojímar for a Canadian magazine. She qualified as a journalist. She'll be here the day after tomorrow to get in a day with us on the flats. Bones again and maybe permit and snook." I left it at that, not having answered his question.

"You heard about the U.S. government guy who went missing from here?" he asked.

"I have. Melendez or something like that?"

"*Mendoza*. Juan Mendoza. From New Mexico. Nice guy."

"Did you meet him?" I asked.

"I was his guide. After meetings in Havana, he took a couple of days to fish here."

"Did he go missing from here?"

"Yeah. He stay where you are, here at Hotel Playa Larga. We fish same flats you and I do today, and next day Mendoza and me fish where we go tomorrow, the Rio Hatiguanico."

"Did he just walk away from the hotel?"

"Don't know. Word is he taken from this hotel and killed."

"Who do you think in Playa Larga might have been mad at him?" I asked.

"No one. . . . He go fishing with me one hour after he get here. I was in Havana at my sister's apartment night before and bring car back here. Señor Mendoza is waiting. He put his bags in his room, got his rods, and we go, all within forty minutes. He was not outside my sight all afternoon.

"We all through and come back here time for dinner. I pick him up early next morning, and we fish Hatiguanico. He not out of my sight. We get back here about 6:30. After one drink, I leave. He completely tired. Not here when I come next morning at 8:00. One hotel person go to bungalow and knock for few minutes. Then go into room. Rum bottle half-empty on table and half of stubbed out cigar in ashtray. Nothing else touched. Fishing gear inside by door, ready go fishing. A maid told me all other things in room taken by the police."

"Who called the police?"

"Someone here. When I arrived, police were removing things from Señor Mendoza's room."

"Did they have the room blocked off as a crime scene?"

"No. I saw one policeman walking out of the room with Señor Mendoza's fishing gear bag in one hand and the rum bottle in the other. The policeman wasn't wearing gloves. His fingerprints have to be all over bottle. When I look into the room, other policeman throw cigar stub into waste basket.

"Police gone in ten minutes. They not ask me or any hotel workers nothing."

"Did that seem strange to you?"

"Yes. Policeman I talk to say no sign of fight."

"Then why would they have taken things from his room? He could have already gone off with you for another day of fishing."

"Police want to clean out his room as soon as they got here. I don't talk with police; in Cuba they are not trusted."

"Is there anyone on the hotel staff who'd tell the truth?" I asked.

"Why all questions? You ask more than police do."

"Mendoza was from my country and was a prominent member of our Congress. He grew up in my state, the second child in a very wealthy and successful family that had fled Cuba in 1960. . . . Have any people from the U.S. Interests Section in Havana been here investigating?"

"Not I know about. I not here every day. My clients stay at different places. You talk Celia Bustamante; she manage this hotel. Very honest. . . . Señor Brooks, I must go home. Is 8:00 a.m. tomorrow OK?"

"I'll be ready. Tarpon?"

"Tarpon. At tarpon nursery. Bring heavy weight fly rod."

When Nacho disappeared in his sixty-plus-year-old red and white Chevy, I went inside to the hotel registration desk and asked a young man coming from an office marked *Manager*, "Is Celia Bustamante here?"

"She is on the phone. She may be a few minutes. I'm her assistant. May I help you?" He seemed outgoing and pleasant.

"I'm staying here for a few nights. To fish. I was talking to my guide; he mentioned this is where the American representative disappeared recently. Have they found him?"

His expression and attitude changed abruptly. "I don't know anything about it. You'd have to talk to the police, but they won't tell you anything. And don't waste Señora Bustamante's time. It's a matter for Cuban police and not any of your business. Enjoy your time here as a guest." With that he turned and left.

On the chance that Celia Bustamante might be willing to talk, I remained within sight of her door. It opened twenty minutes later and a medium height, black haired, fortyish woman came out. She wore light cottons of soft coordinated colors. She walked my way and smiled. As she passed I asked, "Señora Bustamante?"

"Yes, I'm Celia. May I help you?"

As we stood in the hallway, in as few words as possible I told her who I was, that I was here fishing for a few days, that my wife Lucinda would join me, that we had left our daughter Elsbeth in Florida at the university, that my guide Nacho Gomez had mentioned the disappearance of an American guest who was fishing and staying here, and that I was curious about the disappearance of a fellow American—originally from my state—whom I once briefly met. She didn't react the way her assistant had.

"Señor Brooks, my staff and I know little about the disappearance of Representative Mendoza. He may not have disappeared from the hotel; he may have already left to fish. When I arrived at my office, he was gone. His room was empty. He left nothing. I assumed he rose and left early."

"Did anyone see him leave?"

"Not that I've been told about."

"My guide Nacho told me he came here early to meet Mendoza to go fishing, and the police were loading all of Mendoza's personal belongings into a police car."

"That's very strange. I wasn't told that," she replied, obviously concerned. "I want to talk to Nacho. He's a good man."

"We'll be fishing together tomorrow on the Hatiguanico River, then a day off Salinas, and then my wife joins me for a final day on the flats before we return to Florida. If you wish, I'll ask Nacho to stop by here when he has some time in the next few days."

"Please do. I should be told more about what goes on at my hotel. But I am scared to talk to the police."

I went back to my bungalow and sat in a rocking chair on the porch and wished I could talk to Lucinda. She's good at sorting out conflicting facts. I wondered how her day had gone in Havana. Tomorrow she would be going to Hemingway's house—Finca Vigía—for most of the day.

13

LUCINDA'S FIRST DAY PHOTOGRAPHING IN HAVANA

L UCINDA LEFT ME AT THE INGLATERRA, and I watched her walk across the Parque Central. She looked as enticing from the back as she did from the front. When she entered the park, a young man who couldn't yet be twenty approached her. He was good looking, trim, and dressed in Nikes, khakis, and a pale blue guayabera. He wore stylish sunglasses beneath a tan Panama hat. Lucinda turned away, not knowing what the young man wanted. He called out to her as she stepped off the curb and slipped between two waiting taxis to avoid the man. I knew she could handle him.

"Mrs. Brooks, I am Francisco Sandoval. Celeste Jones from the U.S. Interests Section sent me. Please read this letter of introduction." He removed his sunglasses, handed Lucinda a letter in a sealed envelope, and stepped back. She opened what appeared to be an official envelope and glanced at the letter, written on what looked to be Jone's stationary. Then she read the brief letter slowly.

Lucinda, this will introduce Francisco Sandoval. He is a student at Cuba's Instituto Superior de Arte, the most prestigious art school in the country, located on the former Havana Golf Club grounds. Golf was a sport of the rich in the view of Castro, and the club gave way to the art institute.

Francisco is studying art with a special interest in architectural photography. His mother is Christina Sandoval, the Cuban Minister of the Interior and a very powerful figure in the Castro government. Francisco and his mother disagree on many social and political issues in Cuba. We are trying to get Francisco into the U.S. for a year of graduate study at Virginia in Charlottesville.

Francisco said he would be very pleased to take you to the various Hemingway places. He is an avid Hemingway reader.

I hope we have a chance to meet again before you and your husband return to Florida.

Celeste Jones

When Lucinda finished, she turned her head and smiled back at me, her left hand in the air with a thumbs up signal. She turned again to the waiting Francisco and smiled at him.

"May I call you Francisco?" she asked.

"Yes, please do, Mrs. Brooks."

"If we're going to work together for a few days, please call me Lucinda. . . . I was on my way to the Ambos Mundo hotel."

"Ah! Your first Hemingway stop. My mother knows the manager there, and I've met him," Francisco mentioned. "I have read everything Hemingway wrote while he lived in Havana and probably most of what he wrote elsewhere.

"I should tell you that my mother and I do not always get along well philosophically. She is close to Raul Castro because her ministry is in charge of national security. But I am my mother' son and using her name and letting people know who I am opens a lot of doors. You'll see. It's like dropping Hitler's name in 1930's Berlin. . . . My mother would not be pleased if she heard me say that."

Ambos Mundos was crowded with tourists. One tour group after another dropped off new visitors for a ten-minute stay. It seemed impossible to take photographs to show where Hemingway spent many of his days in Havana; the hoard of travelers obscured the peace that made Hemingway favor the hotel.

"Francisco! This is impossible. I wish I could get photos with only a few Cubans present. Wearing long pants and guay-aberas. Not Russians and Canadians wearing shorts and tank tops."

"I'll see what I can do. Wait for me." He disappeared into the manager's office. In fifteen minutes he came out and said, "Buy me a café Cubano. We need to be back at noon."

"Why noon?" Lucinda asked.

"The manager is going to have Hemingway's favorite ref-uge, room 511, where he is said to have written much of *For Whom the Bell Tolls*, locked 'for cleaning' from noon until one. The room will look much as it did when Hemingway wrote there often during the 1930's, before he bought Finca Vigía in 1939."

"*What* did you say to the manager?"

"Not much. I told him who I was and said I would have *mami* tell Raul how much the manager believes Raul is leading the country in the right direction. I didn't indicate what direc-tion that was."

Lucinda and Francisco returned at noon. A sign on the front door of the hotel expressed regrets that someone had been ill in the lobby and the staff was cleaning. Only hotel guests were permitted to enter. It would be ready for tourists at about 1:00 p.m.

Francisco introduced Lucinda to the manager, which made him even more cooperative. Especially when she asked him to pose with Francisco. She used the full hour to take dozens of photos and thought the one that would be used in the magazine showed Hemingway's bed and the table where he wrote. On the table was his 1929 Underwood typewriter; next to it was a replica of the first pages of *For Whom the Bell Tolls*.

Leaving the hotel, Lucinda took Francisco's arm, stopped him, and said, "I don't believe what's happened."

"Then you'll be pleased with what the manager did. He told me while you were taking photos that he had contacted the managers of both La Bodeguita and El Floridita about your interest in photographing Hemingway's two favorite bars. Can we be at Floridita at 10:00 a.m. tomorrow?"

"Of course! What did you do?"

"Floridita opens for business at 11:00. When we get there, the manager will have a half-dozen Cubans sitting at the bar dressed as though it were the 1930's. At the end of the bar—leaning on it—there's a bronze life-size statue of Hemingway."

"Drinking a mojito?"

"No, a daiquiri. When we finish, we'll head the few blocks to Bodeguita, where he drank mojitos. We need to be there at 11:00; it opens for tourists at noon. You can photograph the wall where he wrote about his preference for drinking his mojitos in La Bodeguita and his daiquiris in El Floridita. There will be some different Cubans at La Bodeguita, also dressed in 1930's clothing."

"Didn't Hemingway's presence at the two bars attract some famous people?"

"Yes. Dozens, including Marlene Dietrich, Graham Greene, John Dos Passos, and a favorite of mine who recorded an album in Spanish here in Cuba—Nat King Cole."

"I won't ask what you promised the two bar managers."

"Much the same as at Ambos Mundos. Who you are and who you know helps in Cuba."

Lucinda and Francisco were on schedule in the morning. They arrived at El Floridita at 10:00 a.m. At that moment I was with Nacho, fighting a twenty-pound tarpon on the Hatiguanico River in the Zapata Reserve.

14

MACDUFF'S SECOND DAY IN PLAYA LARGA

NACHO HAD MET ME AT 8:00 a.m. in the hotel parking area for our day of chasing tarpon on the Hatiguanico River. Although it's in the Zapata Reserve, the access is different from the approach to the flats off Salinas. We headed north out of Playa Larga past Central Australia and joined the central highway at Jagüey Grande. A few miles west on the highway, we turned back south.

"Do you know where you're going?" I asked Nacho, only half-kidding. "I didn't see a sign."

"Sign's down. There's no real town in the reserve, maybe couple of thousand people here and there. I lived there to avoid being got by the Army and sent to Angola."

"How far is the river?" I asked.

"We go about nine miles into the reserve, to springs at the beginning of the Hatiguanico and its main tributaries, the Guareiras and Gonzola rivers. We have boat at the Santo Tomas Ditch. Go downstream toward Hatiguanico's mouth—the Boca de Hatiguanico—and won't see many people. A couple of other foreigners with local guides and once a day maybe small tour boat—if enough sign up."

Our boat was sixteen feet long with a deeper draft than the flats skiff we used the previous day at Salinas. It was something like a jon boat in the U.S. Ours was wood and, from the looks of the hull, was last painted before the Revolution. The motor was an old hand-starting 25 hp Johnson with the cover missing.

The boat and motor looked like the cars of Cuba. Both were maintained with the same care, meaning lots of jury rigging and salvaged parts. I tried not to think of motor failure and spending a night on the river. We would run out of mosquito repellant far sooner than the Cuban Hatuey beer Nacho brought. I passed on the Hatuey, preferring even something Bud makes. Rumors question whether the strong and often odorous Hatuey justifies being called beer.

Nacho told me to be ready soon after we pushed off in the upper portion of the river where there was barely room for two boats to pass, and he had the boat at the motor's top speed. I could envision someday fiberglass twenty-footers with 100 hp Hondas racing along the curving Cuban river, like forty-five-foot Cigarette muscle-boats rocketed by 2,000+ hp Mercedes engines that terrorize the narrow Intracoastal Waterway in South Florida.

I had brought both my 9' 8-weight and 10-weight rods. The 10-weight for larger tarpon, the 8-weight for small tarpon, bones and, if we struck gold, a permit. Two hundred yards of backing was about the minimum I added for tarpon and permit. A little less backing—150 yards on my 8-weight—had been enough for the bones we caught the first day. A sixty pound mono shock tip helped when tarpon started jumping.

For flies, I brought a bunch of Clousers and Lefty's Deceivers, both as useful in Cuba as in Florida. As I tied on a chartreuse Clouser, I realized it was the same one I had used eight months ago fishing with Florida State Attorney Grace Justice on the flats next to my Florida cottage. With my wife Lucinda now with me, those times with Grace are days I want placed in the darkest corners of my memory bank holding subjects best forgotten.

Nacho slowed and said, "Now we start seeing tarpon. Small ones, to about twenty pounds."

"Twenty pounds for small ones! If I said that when guiding for trout on the Yellowstone River in Montana, my client would know something had scrambled my brain."

The motor went silent. Nacho said in little more than a whisper, "Look ahead at right, under hanging trees. There are young tarpon rolling. . . . They roll and gulp air and fill their air bladder. This water no got much dissolved oxygen. Even when the water got oxygen, older tarpon still roll. Some think because they rolled to survive as young tarpon. I think because they're happy."

"Any idea what they feed on?" I asked.

"Small crustaceans. Worms. As they get older, they add crabs, shrimp, and fish. Even the biggest tarpon will chase small crabs no more than an inch or two wide."

"It's different than in our West," I commented to Nacho, not knowing if he was listening while concentrating on the tarpon. "Rainbow and brown trout in a place I like to fish in New Mexico—the San Juan River—gorge on tiny midge larvae that tied as flies are only size 22 to 24. Check the stomach of a 14- to 18- inch rainbow, and you couldn't begin to count larvae."

"Señor Brooks," he said interrupting, "can you make cast under those trees?" He hadn't been listening about rainbows and browns.

"I'll try sidearm. It's about forty feet."

I tried, but my low back cast hung the fly on a branch. It pulled free, and I tried again, dropping the fly short of the fish.

"Leave it," Nacho said. "Tarpon moving this way. Current taking fly to them."

It was like fishing in a gothic cathedral: trees arched across to touch and form a tunnel. Sunlight occasionally burst through the trees to dance and sparkle in the water, like rays between passing clouds, streaking through a stained glass window.

It wasn't a matter of picking out a tarpon to sight fish; these were hungry, aggressive young fish.

Nacho was right. The tarpon and fly converged, and one edged out two others and took the fly.

"Keep rod tip close to water on one side."

The tarpon had its own plan. Although a juvenile, it was strong enough for a jump that took it over a hanging branch where the fly caught and my tippet broke. As we drifted by the branch, I retrieved the hanging fly.

A half-dozen more young tarpon rolled while I replaced the tippet and fly.

Nacho looked at me and smiled. To ease my embarrassment he said, "Ditch widens pretty soon and becomes bigger, curving river. We don't land many in this narrow section. That was about a seven pounder."

In the wider portion of the river, the tarpon were slightly bigger, more in number and no less hungry.

"Where should I look?" I asked.

"Stay away from trees," he said. "Look ahead. I see something. I go toward it and turn off motor. We coast to casting distance—about fifty feet. OK?"

It wasn't more than three or four minutes later that we saw several tarpon in mid-river. I piled some line on the deck in front of me, took a single back cast, and dropped the fly ten feet in front of the tarpon. No sooner than I had reeled in the slack, the water surface around the fly exploded in spray as a small tarpon hit the fly and immediately took off skyward, its body twisting as the limpid tail dragged along the frothing surface.

The fish landed with the expectation that it had thrown the hook, but this time that was not to be. It jumped twice more, a signal it could do battle with me above or below the surface. No trout had ever been so persistent on being free of me. I was determined that this fish would not join others that succeeded. Seconds that seemed like minutes caused pulsations of fear of losing another battle, but finally the tarpon was alongside.

For every foot of line I had retrieved during the contest, Nacho had taken in another foot by moving the boat closer to the tarpon. When it was alongside the boat, he showed that catch and release does not end with adopting barbless hooks. He more certainly assured that the young tarpon had a life ahead by using wet hands to hold it and slide the hook from its mouth. Never lifting it free of the surface, he turned the tarpon so its mouth faced upstream and the water flowed freely through its gills.

Any fish exhausted from a battle and lying on its side after being tossed back into the water is a target of predators from above and below the surface. This tarpon would not have that disadvantage; it quickly swam off and disappeared.

We never reached the mouth of the river. The tarpon we hooked were a bit upriver in what endearingly is called the tarpon nursery. The day's take was reflective of this little visited tarpon fishery. I had something like sixty takes, hooked half, and boated a dozen. Not one was larger than ten pounds, but each one I hooked was larger than any trout I had ever taken. When it seemed that the mosquitos were larger than the tarpon, we called it a day.

Nacho and I drove into the Playa Larga grounds at 6:00 p.m., ten hours after we left. He declined dinner but stayed for a drink, ordering a daiquiri while I stayed with the mojito. Daiquiris are readily available in the U.S.; a request for a mojito, however, often brings a "what's that?" stare.

"Tomorrow we look for permit?" I asked, more to confirm than to debate.

"Yes. . . . No guarantees. No good guide ever guarantees catching permit. Especially not landing it. *Maybe* hooking up with one, but nothing more."

"Is that because there are fewer permit than bonefish, tarpon, snook, and most everything else?"

"Like pompano—a relative—the permit is a delicacy. *More* than snook. Tarpon and bonefish don't worry about being food; they're full of strength for running and leaping, but not flesh for eating. Cuban people keep permit to eat."

"There isn't very much fishing along the coast here," I observed. "The permit population is not decimated like pompano and snook have been in Florida."

"You're right. There's no much recreational fishing here—yet. But starting. For every person who ignores U.S. law and fishes in Cuba, there are couple of dozen fly fishermen from nations we got good relations with. When U.S. allows citizens to come here to fish, we gonna have too many fishermen.

"There's already talk on island 'bout limiting and licensing number of guides can work, requiring catch and release—especially for permit and snook—and use only barbless hooks. We use barbless hooks the past two days, but not all Cuban guides do that.

"It's not just fishing that will be filled with tourists when the U.S. takes away rules. Places like bars Hemingway drink at already got too many tourists, including many, many Chinese. If they like fly fishing, I retire soon, either because I got lots of money or there no more fish."

"You're right," I said. "Wealthy U.S. northeasterners a century ago discovered that the New York mountains had big numbers of trout. Many fishermen went to that region and quickly the trout numbers went down drastically. Then the fishermen discovered Maine, moved fishing there and soon that population dropped off. Now, with transportation easy to the Mountain West and more wealth in many other nations allowing time and money to fish, the numbers have dropped in some of the once great Western rivers. Lewis and Clark caught all the fish they wanted whenever they wanted them. No longer."

"We gonna have a problem in Cuba," Nacho added. "When more private business and more Americans come, our socialist rules can make us avoid having sport fishing be only for rich people. And especially the *foreign* rich. Something like golf that was played here before the Revolution. If that happens, fish numbers go down quick."

Before we knew it, the sun had been replaced by a full moon that glistened on the small wavelets of the bay visible in front of the hotel. The dusk was quiet. Light and sound together faded.

Only two of the other bungalows were occupied. I could hear music coming from a private engagement party next door. An older male voice carried our way, singing *Dos Gardenias*:

Dos gardenias para tí
Con ellas quiero decir:
Te quiero, te adoro, mi vida
Ponle toda tu atención
Porque son tu corazón y el mio

[Two Gardenias for you
With these I mean to say:
I love, I adore you, my life
Look after them because
They are your heart and mine.]

I missed Lucinda and hoped her days were going well. She comes the day after tomorrow.

15

LUCINDA'S SECOND DAY PHOTOGRAPHING IN HAVANA

LUCINDA AND FRANCISCO MET in the lobby of the Ingleterra at 9:30 a.m. and walked the few blocks to Calle Obispo for their 10:00 appointment at El Floridita. Even in walking flats Lucinda was an inch taller than Francisco. But it was not her height that made people stare at them but how attractive they were together. Francisco's skin was Caribbean caramel; his hair was coal black. Lucinda's skin was Northern European white; her hair was shoulder length, soft, and tousled. His black hair was slick and combed straight back with every strand in the place assigned. Her burnt auburn hair expressed a lively motion where every lock found its own place.

The Floridita owner and manager expected the two. Tourists were lining up in the street to visit, small groups led by middle-age Cuban women holding variously colored identity flags high above their heads, as though they were leading their national team into the Olympic stadium. But the tourists would have to be patient another hour.

Wanting to impress Francisco, the bar owner had found six locals to wear 1930's dress and sit at the bar, all attentive with eyes fixed on the life-size bronze of Hemingway resting on the end seat.

"Francisco, this is incredible! It's *perfect* for photographs. I won't ask what you promised the hotel and bar managers."

"Wait until this afternoon at Finca Vigía."

Lucinda was entranced by her treatment at El Floridita and thrilled with one photograph she took of the red-coated bartender placing a daiquiri in front of the bronze Hemingway and next to three empty glasses that had held his earlier rounds—one tipped over on one side like the slouching Hemingway bronze.

An hour later they walked into La Bodeguita del Medio on the narrow Calle Empedrado. Lucinda photographed a single Cuban male who had dressed in the same period style clothing as at Floridita, sitting at the bar having boiled rice, black beans, pork shank, toasted fried plantains, and a mojito. On the wall was the handwriting of Hemingway's ode to his preference for mojitos in La Bodeguita and daiquiris in El Floridita.

When they finished at noon, Lucinda asked Francisco, "Shall we stay and have lunch here in La Bodeguita's restaurant? That meal I photographed looked awfully good."

"Let's not. The place is crowded; the food is expensive and is *not* very good."

"Where would you like to go for lunch?" she asked.

"I'll show you. Close by in Miramar. Near where I live. The restaurant is called El Aljibe."

"What do you recommend?"

"Roast chicken, black beans and rice, and fried plantains."

"What's your second choice?"

"Try roast chicken, black beans and rice, and fried plantains."

"And third?"

"Nothing other than roast chicken, black beans and rice, and fried plantains."

"It must be good. I guess I know what I'll have," said Lucinda.

After a mojito next door at Dos Gardenias, the El Aljibe served her the best roast chicken, black beans and rice, and fried plantains she ever tasted.

Francisco had arranged for a car and driver that picked up the two at 2:00 p.m. at El Aljibe and drove ten miles east of Havana to the small town of San Francisco de Paula, where Hemingway had lived at his Finca Vigía. After first visiting Cuba in 1928, he returned in 1932 and used the Hotel Ambos Mundos for nearly a decade as a writing haven.

Fleeing Key West and his second marriage in 1939, Hemingway rented and then—in 1940, for $12,500—bought Finca Vigía, where amid a clutter of items, acquired not as souvenirs but as objects of memories, he finished *For Whom the Bell Tolls* and wrote *The Old Man and the Sea* and *A Movable Feast* as well as several less remembered short stories.

"Don't forget," noted Francisco, "that Hemingway lived in Cuba for some thirty years, two-thirds of his productive life."

"Francisco," asked Lucinda, "when did he leave the house? I know he owned it when Castro took over."

"He lived there when Castro rolled triumphantly into Havana in 1959. Hemingway was sympathetic to Castro's revolution, as were many who detested corrupt former president Batista. Hemingway met Castro only once, in 1960, during a fishing contest that Castro won."

Francisco left out some facts. As Castro's policies unfolded, the U.S. government urged Hemingway to leave. He departed Cuba for good in late 1960, but retained the house. But the house was seized by the Cuban government soon after the April 1961 failed U.S. invasion at the Bay of Pigs. A perfect storm had formed around Hemingway's life: depression over where Castro was leading the country, declining health, and the distractions from an increasing surge of strangers who insisted on visiting the house.

Fortunately for Hemingway, his most significant piece of art—Miró's *The Farm*—acquired in 1925 in Paris, was removed from Finca Vigía in February, 1959, barely a month after Castro assumed power. It now is in the collection of the National Gallery in D.C. Much more was removed from the house by Hemingway's fourth and last wife, Mary, who shipped loads of Ernest's possessions to the U.S., leaving books and those records she didn't burn in the yard.

Rather than living out his life at Finca Vigía—perhaps another twenty years—within a year Hemingway was in his grave, the result of a self-inflicted shotgun blast at his isolated home in Ketchum, Idaho. A Pulitzer Prize winner and a Nobel Laureate, he attended to his writing and his drinking but not to his physical or mental health. He fretted over and recorded—on a wall in Finca Vigía—his high blood pressure readings and weight fluctuations from a trim 190 pounds to a corpulent 240. He was only 63 when he ended his life.

When Lucinda and Francisco turned into the driveway, they were stopped by a guard, a gate, and a sign indicating that, due to some emergency repairs, the property would be closed for the afternoon. Francisco said something to the guard who nodded, opened the gate, and directed the two to the house.

On the sloping drive they passed planted mango and palm trees, and Mary Hemingway's gardening efforts—hibiscus, jasmine, and bougainvillea. And orchids hanging in the trees. The Finca Vigía Museum director, Dariana Castillo, met them at the front door. They saw no sign of anyone working on repairs.

The property—as Lucinda and Francisco saw it—was not the same as during the 1940's and 1950's, when Hemingway and his fourth wife, Mary, called it home. After Cuba asserted ownership in the early 1960's, deterioration began, accelerated by the tropics. The house slid into death throes as the trees, shrubbery, and vines began to consume what they had been intended to enhance.

A half-century passed before an uncommon association began to restore the house. Hemingway's affection from thousands of Cubans and Americans drew donations, overruling the intransigence of the remnants of the early exiles, many of whom had deteriorated much faster than Finca Vigía.

Director Castillo showed the two through the building and grounds so Lucinda would have an overview and decide what she wanted to photograph. When Castillo left to attend to some office work, Francisco turned to Lucinda and said, "Do you know you were humming while we walked through the rooms?"

"I was. . . . What impressions of Hemingway did *you* gain from the walk-through?" Lucinda asked, without looking directly at Francisco.

"Lots of heads from his African hunting. Bull fighting posters. He was very macho."

"A macho man?" queried Lucinda.

"Yes."

"I was humming the music to the Village People's song: 'macho, macho man. I've got to be a macho man.'"

"Hemingway would not have appreciated that kind of association," interjected Francisco.

"But macho was what he tried to be. And was successful. . . . What *else* impressed you?"

"His books. Thousands of books," Francisco said. "And they looked read. There were hundreds of slips of paper written on and inserted in the pages. He was truly a man of literature."

"I want to make that impression with my photographs. . . . Do you think he was boasting?" she asked.

"No, his fixation on machismo was embedded. Put that aside and the house was light and airy. It was a house of 5,000 books and hundreds of records—a place of comfort and relaxation. Remember that he moved here to be in a small village and to get away from the increasing bustle at Ambos Mundos. But two decades later at the time of the Revolution, it was also where he was deteriorating in health and mental capacity, even though he produced *The Old Man and the Sea* and one of my favorites, his memories of Paris in *A Moveable Feast*."

Lucinda seemed at ease as she photographed the places where Hemingway wrote and sat relaxing. One photo of his working instruments—bunches of sharpened number 3 pencils; another photo showing relaxation time instruments—the collection of absinthe, wine, vodka, whiskey, and rum bottles next to his chair.

Finca Vigía had the same effect on Lucinda as it had had on Hemingway; she was visibly more relaxed at Finca Vigía than in the hotel and bars in Havana. She could imagine being with Hemingway, sitting in the living room with a glass in hand, listening to the sounds of Gershwin flowing from the old record player. But she knew she couldn't have done any better living with him than had any of his four wives.

"Francisco, one more thing. I want to see his walnut hulled boat, *Pilar,* crafted for him by one of America's premier boatworks—Wheeler. It may have been his favorite companion. Hemingway never divorced *Pilar.*"

"*Pilar* is outside," said Francisco, starting for the door. "It nearly did not survive. When Hemingway died, Mary had his shotgun dismantled and buried. She wanted to take *Pilar* to sea and scuttle it. She changed her mind. It sat for years by the house until it was restored and now rests on blocks under the old and no-longer-played-upon tennis court. Like golf, tennis is not a proper sport for a committed revolutionary."

The drive back to Havana coincided with people returning home from work. The few cars on the road were filled. Bus stop lines were lengthy. There were few smiles.

At the Parque Central, Francisco hopped out quickly and opened Lucinda's door. He reminded her, "Tomorrow at 9:00 a.m. I'll be here with the driver. We'll go to Cojímar for the morning and have lunch at Hemingway's favorite bar, La Terraza. In the afternoon a surprise—I'm taking you to Playa Larga so you can join Mr. Brooks and get an early start the next day fishing on the flats. Please check out of the hotel in the morning. . . . You'll come back to Havana with Mr. Brooks and stay at the Nacional for two nights before you both return to Florida."

"Thank you, Francisco, for all you've done. I want to live at Finca Vigía; it looks so much like it must have when Hemingway was here."

"A product of the Revolution, Lucinda. Hemingway left Cuba suddenly. An unhappy man. But not with the Revolution—with his health. His clothes still hang in the closets. Some of the things he liked to have around remain—scrapbooks, galley proofs, art, fishing rods, typewriters, and photographs."

"It's a shame the trade boycott has hurt the restoration efforts," Lucinda commented.

"It is. But the Cubans who left the island soon after the Revolution never were much involved with Hemingway. While his legacy to Cuba began to die from the poor relationship the Miami Cubans have imposed on your government, his name gained such fame that he is often referred to as 'the *Cuban* writer.'"

"But others claim him," said Lucinda. "Spain and France and Italy and, of course, we do as well. He *was* American. . . . I wonder what *he* would say he was."

Lucinda was overjoyed with the day and the plans for the next as she walked into the Inglaterra. She had dinner sitting alone in the hotel's restaurant at a table by a window, making notes of the day's visits. Afterwards, she went upstairs, showered, packed her bags, and was asleep by 9:30.

16

THIRD DAY AT PLAYA LARGA

M Y THIRD MORNING AT PLAYA LARGA began with the same frizzling sun heating all within its view the moment it broke free of the horizon. In the time since Lucinda and I landed in Havana three days earlier, there had not been a drop of rain; the tense and heavy air was draped above Playa Larga. My clothes smelled like day-old fish carcasses—the hotel guest washing machine had broken the morning I arrived and would not be repaired for a week. There was no hot water. It seemed futile to shower.

I thought out loud, "It's time for me to give my clothes to the chambermaid for washing, before even she refuses to touch them. Lucinda is due tomorrow, and I don't want to present her with any excuse to avoid my clutches."

The hotel's pressurized expresso machines were working, and I downed two shots of Café Cubano made from a dark roast. It was like a direct injection of caffeine into a vein.

Breakfast might be my last chance to enjoy eggs and bacon—Lucinda could arrive before I ordered the next morning.

"Bacon and scrambled eggs," I asked for.

"We're out of both," he answered.

"Sausage? Ham?"

"Out of those, too."

"You must have fish; I can see the water from here."

"It's too early," the waiter responded. "Fresh fish will be delivered in mid-morning in time for lunch."

"What do you suggest?"

"Vegetarian," he offered.

I settled for an assortment of fresh papaya, avocado, mango, pineapple, and guava. Plus two slices of toasted locally baked bread. Lucinda would be pleased.

While I was sipping the last of my coffee, Nacho walked in wearing clothes that were far shabbier than mine, but unlike mine his were fresh and clean. I would try to fish downwind of him on the boat.

"Where to today, Nacho?" I asked.

"Go again to Salinas. This time use bigger 16' skiff and go south off coast three miles to the Bocas. It's where keys sit on edge of flats and the bottom drops off into deep water on the Bocas' Caribbean side. . . . It gets rough on reef's edge for small boat like ours. If there's no much wind, we fish drop-off and see what we find. Who knows? Snook, mahi mahi, cubera snapper, barracuda, shark, and. . . ."

"That's enough," I interrupted. "Hold the shark and the barracuda. I don't eat either."

"We catch what we catch," he noted. "Barracuda got to eat. Besides, this is barracuda country. *Grande* barracudas! As many as five feet long. A research place in Playa Larga has dozens—maybe hundreds—of barracudas in pens," commented Nacho. "I never try to go there. They don't have a good sign, and guide friends have been turned back when they tried to enter. People who work there not good people. Do nothing to help Playa Larga."

"Leave the barracudas to their research," I suggested. . . . "You didn't mention catching permit."

"We saving best permit grounds for tomorrow, when your wife come. I talk with guide friend last night; he tell me where he catch permit past few days. They not always in schools; some permit are loners. We look for both."

We fished the reefs off the Bocas, catching and releasing more bonefish and tarpon, as well as a half-dozen other fish. No sharks and only one harmless-looking 12" barracuda. Small barracudas are cute, all silvery, playful in their movements, and harmless. Big barracudas are ugly, blotchy, deceptive in their movements, and threatening. We never saw a permit.

My mind was distracted, focused on tomorrow and seeing Lucinda, and having her share this spectacular part of Cuba. Nacho sensed I was tired and no longer focused, and we broke off from fishing and went back an hour early.

"Nacho," I said as we arrived at the hotel, "join me for a drink, and you can tell me what's planned for tomorrow when my wife has arrived."

"You spoil me, Señor Brooks. Usually, I not asked to join my client for drink after guiding. I happy to sit with you and have a mojito. . . . I have important thing to tell you, but is maybe only local rumors."

Nacho didn't get to tell me about the local rumors. Lucinda unexpectedly arrived.

17

LUCINDA VISITS COJÍMAR

CHECKING OUT OF THE INGLATERRA, Lucinda allowed a tear to roll down her cheek. She quickly had come to love being in Old Havana and intended to read some of Hemingway's later writings when she returned to Florida. The bookshelves in their cabin in Montana held a dozen of Hemingway's novels, plus a few of the many biographies of his life, such as his years in Paris and Key West before he settled at Finca Vigía. Unfortunately, little biography had been produced about his time in Cuba.

Francisco and Lucinda met at 9:00 a.m. for a quick coffee in the park under the shade of some trees. Their driver was on time and drove them through the deteriorating tunnel under the mouth of Havana Harbor and followed the coast east, reaching the small fishing village of Cojímar within the hour. The car was not air conditioned, and when they were dropped off at the modest 17th-century stone fort, they welcomed the breeze from the north off the Florida straits which link the Gulf of Mexico to the Atlantic. The driver promised to pick them up after lunch at the nearby La Terraza bar and restaurant.

Facing none of the crowds of Havana for the next three hours, under a layer of sunscreen and wearing wide-brimmed straw hats, they strolled about the town and then returned to the harbor and sat on the sea wall, awed by the rough surface of the Straits stirred by the Gulf Stream's ferocious surge northward. It wasn't a propitious day for disillusioned Cubans to launch a raft and set off in search of Florida.

"Hemingway kept his boat *Pilar* at a wooden pier—long since rotted away—that thrust into the harbor off the cement dock by the fort," explained Francisco. "It was here in Cojímar that he crafted his character Santiago in *The Old Man and the Sea.* He began his venture to hook a marlin but returned with nothing more than a few pieces after it was decimated by sharks—leaving Santiago barely enough to authenticate his catch while locals shared his disappointment at being unable to fend off the beasts.

"It's this village of Cojímar," Francisco continued, "where Hemingway met Castro during a marlin fishing tournament. It was the only time the two ever met; truthfully, neither had much in common with the other. Hemingway didn't understand our glorious Revolution. . . . La Terraza bar and restaurant was Hemingway's favorite drinking oasis in Cojímar. It's where we're headed."

La Terraza, like the Hemingway hangouts in Havana, offered overpriced drinks and underwhelming food. Two framed faded photos of Hemingway with Castro decorated one wall. And like La Bodeguita and El Floridita, La Terraza bar had herds of tourists.

A bus filled with persons speaking some Slavic language was unloading as Francisco and Lucinda walked past them into La Terraza to sit down to a lunch of fresh broiled fish and beer. Afterwards, they walked back alongside the fort that clutched the edge of the harbor. They wanted to see the bust of Hemingway on a pedestal overlooking the water he fished and loved.

"Francisco, this bust looks like the head portion of the life-size bronze Hemingway on the bar stool in Ambos Mundos in Havana. Is it a copy?" asked Lucinda.

"Yes, but not fully bronze. It was dedicated soon after Hemingway's death, made from a variety of metals donated by Cojímar fishermen. They gave old cleats, propellers, blocks, tools, anchors, and whatever would melt."

No such monument exists to Gregorio Fuentes, Hemingway's boat captain and the likely inspiration for his fictional Santiago in *The Old Man and the Sea*. Fuentes lived on in Cojímar another four decades after Hemingway died. Not long after his death, the *Pilar*, on which the two friends spent so many happy hours, was confiscated by the Cuban government and began a lonely natural demise from inattention. Only because of foreign donations was it restored years later. It sat where we saw it on the tennis court at Finca Vigía.

Lucinda took her last photo of that final bronze tribute of the locals to their friend.

The ride south carried Lucinda and Francisco to the Central Highway, described by Hemingway in *Islands in the Stream* as being a combination of "poverty, dirt, four-hundred year old dust, the nose-snot of children, the shuffle of untreated syphilis, sewage in the old beds of brooks, . . . and the smell of old women." They went on through Jagüey Grande and turned south to Playa Larga. Lucinda was as surprised as Macduff had been to pass through the oddly named town of Central Australia.

Francisco began to ask Lucinda questions that she was hesitant to answer until she was assured and satisfied that their driver understood no English.

"Mrs. Brooks," Francisco asked, returning to the formality he had exchanged for "Lucinda" the first day, "why did your husband not join us for the past few days?"

"He is a fan of Hemingway, Francisco, but he's even more devoted to bonefish. And tarpon. And permit and most every other fish there is. He frequently fishes in fresh water in our Mountain West rivers, where he guides. He has some Montana and Wyoming friends who have fished here and encouraged him to come. My assignment for the Canadian magazine was what got the trip started."

"Why did he choose to fish out of Playa Larga?"

"I don't really know. He didn't want to go too far from Havana."

"Does he know anybody in Playa Larga?"

"Not a soul."

"Who's his guide?"

"I don't know."

"Does the name Ignacio Gomez mean anything to you?"

"No."

"He is a man not to be trusted."

"Is he a danger to my husband? Why do you say he is not to be trusted?"

"He was disloyal to the Revolution. Without permission, he moved to Playa Larga to avoid military service."

"Was he caught?"

"No. But we know where he is. We can arrest him any time."

"I thought you were an art student. You're talking as though you're a prosecutor or police investigator."

"We all must do our best to protect the ideals of the Revolution. Those who are against our choice of governance are a continual threat. Gomez is friends with too many foreigners. He and others personally profit from the economic changes that Cuba has permitted."

"By fishing?"

"Yes."

"I don't understand. I believe my husband is paying several hundred dollars a day to fish, and Gomez is paid only the usual monthly amount of about $20. The government must take the difference."

"We know Gomez receives generous tips in convertible pesos or hard currency, such as Euros or Canadian dollars."

"I have been told that many Cubans receive such tips or money from relatives abroad. It helps them survive."

"Those are lies your government spreads. Look at me. I am in school. I'm healthy. I eat well. I have access to a car."

"And your mother is an important government minister who often travels abroad at government expense." As soon as Lucinda said it she realized she had made a mistake.

Francisco was becoming more irritated each minute. Lucinda knew she had to end the conversation that had turned into an interrogation. But Francisco persisted.

"How long has Mr. Brooks known Juan Mendoza?" he asked.

"Juan Mendoza?"

"Mendoza was a U.S. House of Representatives member from New Mexico. He was fishing out of Playa Larga about a month ago. He's missing."

"That's a long time to be missing," she suggested, seeing an opportunity to learn something that might help Macduff. "I never met or talked to a Juan Mendoza. . . . What was he doing in Playa Larga?"

"Other than fishing, our government doesn't know. Mendoza had been at a trade meeting in Havana. When it was over, he went directly to Playa Larga."

"That makes sense. He was finished with his business and apparently stayed to fish."

"He stayed to *spy* on our country. Just like your husband!"

"*Macduff is not a spy!* Your government *allowed* my husband to go to Playa Larga to fish. You *know* that fishing is encouraged because it brings in hard currency."

Lucinda was aghast at Francisco's change in attitude from the past few days of being such a gentleman. "How would Macduff spy by fishing?" she asked quietly.

"He was with Nacho Gomez."

"I think you are mistaken. My husband came to Cuba with *me*. He has no history with Cuba and frankly no interest in Cuba beyond fishing and a fondness for Hemingway."

"You are wrong, señora. Several decades ago, a man named Maxwell Hunt attempted to enter Cuba with the help of your CIA."

Lucinda choked on hearing the name "Maxwell Hunt." She struggled to retain her composure but feared she failed miserably.

"I . . . I don't understand. Who is this Hunt person?"

"We are investigating."

Francisco continued with accusations Lucinda was astounded to hear.

"Maxwell Hunt flew from Gainesville, Florida, to Miami and then to Mexico City where he spent a week—mornings at the U.S. embassy, conspiring with the CIA mission, and afternoons at our embassy, lying to our people to gain an entry visa.

"Hunt was fingerprinted as part of the routine process to obtain a visa to enter Cuba. His fingerprints were retained in our records. When Cuba issued an entry visa a few weeks ago in the name of Macduff Brooks, his fingerprints were recorded, and there was a routine check to see if they matched *any* prior prints on record in Cuba. They did.

"What we do not understand is that the prints in Mexico were the prints of one Maxwell Hunt, who our investigation affirms was a law professor at the University of Florida. We did some further checking. Hunt reportedly died of a stroke several years later after a trip to Guatemala. How do you suppose it is possible that two people have identical fingerprints?"

Lucinda was stunned. "I think there is a mistake in your records," she offered as an explanation.

"You will have to do better than that. Why don't we ask your husband?" he suggested, as they entered the grounds of the Playa Larga hotel and stepped out of the car.

18

EVENING IN PLAYA LARGA

NACHO GOMEZ AND I WERE SITTING in the Playa Larga bar debating—Lucinda would say lying—about the length and weight of fish we had caught. I assumed he would leave soon, and I would go to bed, anxious over Lucinda's arrival in the morning. I did not expect what happened.

Behind Nacho, *Lucinda* was walking into the hotel toward us with a young man accompanying her. It was the same young man who three days ago approached and walked off with her in Havana's Parque Central. She looked as though she had just been told that my body had been found washed up on the flats off Salinas.

"How did you get here?" I asked, hugging her and feeling her trembling. "I thought you were coming tomorrow. Are you OK?"

"This young man is Francisco Sandoval," she said, pointing but not looking at Francisco as she stepped away from him. "Celeste Jones at the U.S. Interests Section arranged for him to help me with my work. He was indispensable in my being given time to photograph free of tourists in each of Hemingway's favorite places, from Havana to Cojímar. I have wonderful pictures; the Canadian magazine will be thrilled."

"Thank you for helping my wife," I said turning to face Sandoval, "and for driving her here. Sit with us and have something. I assume you face a drive in the dark back to Havana. . . . I also want you both to meet Nacho Gomez, my guide for the perfect past three days."

Francisco was gracious, a remarkably mature young man. I was pleased Lucinda had the benefit of his company. I would soon learn that this young man was not as he appeared.

"I must have my driver soon take me back to Havana," Francisco said, turning toward me, "but he can wait. My conversation with Mrs. Brooks left some questions I asked unanswered. Maybe you can help."

Lucinda again appeared tense and remained so as Sandoval related his conservation with her. When he asked for my opinion why my fingerprints from my entry permit a few days ago matched those of Maxwell Hunt taken decades ago, I joined Lucinda in fear that we had become more deeply involved than I expected in the disappearance of Representative Juan Mendoza.

"Mr. Sandoval, your story about the matching fingerprints is quite incredible. And, I assure you, something more for fiction than reality. I have never been to Mexico."

"Where were you at the time Hunt was in Mexico?" he demanded more than asked.

There was no way I could make up a convincing story on such short notice. Lucinda knew that as Professor Maxwell Hunt I had traveled several times to Mexico long before we met and before I assumed the name Macduff Brooks and shed the Hunt name I had carried since birth. I don't recall ever telling Lucinda that on one of my early foreign trips I had tried to go to Cuba by way of Mexico, mainly to meet with some Cuban law faculty and discuss a book I had then recently authored that dealt with the Cuban expropriation of foreign property soon after Castro assumed power.

"I think you will find that there have been some errors with the way Cuba matches fingerprints," I said, ignoring his question about where I had been when Hunt was in Mexico. "I welcome your checking when you return to Havana and informing me when we arrive there tomorrow that you indeed realized you were wrong."

"And if I discover I was right?"

"Please let me know whatever you discover. Lucinda and I have a reservation for two nights at the Hotel Nacional. Leave a message, and I will call you immediately."

"I must say the print matching sounds implausible," admitted Francisco, suddenly more relaxed, "but I have to follow-up to set our records straight."

Turning to Nacho, who he had ignored since his arrival, he added, "Make sure Mr. and Mrs. Brooks safely return from fishing tomorrow. I don't want anything to happen to them."

When Sandoval and his driver left, I wanted to talk to Lucinda without Nacho present. But Nacho might have to help us with getting out of Cuba before someone in the interior ministry concluded that the prints were identical and that I would be detained to answer their questions.

"Nacho, please don't leave. I want to talk to Lucinda for a few minutes. Then we can continue our drinks together."

Nacho ordered another mojito and took it down to the water's edge where he sat on a piece of driftwood and sipped while he watched the sun lose its earlier scorching authority.

"Mac," Lucinda said. "I know you went to Mexico before we met. But you've never told me why."

"I went to Mexico because I couldn't fly directly to Cuba. I expected to obtain my entry permit at the Cuban embassy in Mexico. My plan was to speak to several Havana law professors about the accuracy of some of the suppositions in my book. The U.S. was willing to give me a visa to travel to Cuba, and I agreed to talk with some disenfranchised Cubans the State Department knew had information useful to our foreign relations. Remember that those were years when our dealings with Cuba were tempestuous."

"Would Cuba want to revisit that earlier time?" she asked. "A few conversations with people now undoubtedly retired and possibly dead don't seem to me to be important enough to cause you trouble two decades later."

"They have good reason to revisit that time. I didn't know—when I agreed with our CIA staff in Mexico to meet with specific Cubans in Havana—that the CIA people were planning something I couldn't have dreamed was possible . . . assassinating Fidel Castro. If the current Cuban government decides I was involved, I will not be permitted to leave the island."

"Should we call Celeste Jones at the Interests Section in Havana? She's sending a car for us tomorrow."

"Would you do that? I'll be close by if she wants to talk to me. I'm going to call Dan Wilson in D.C. I'll call Celeste and have her patch me through to Dan.

After I got through to Dan, Lucinda used her phone to call Celeste and explain our predicament to Celeste.

"Macduff Brooks," Dan said, answering my ring. "What brings you into my life again? Someone shot in your boat?"

"My boat is in Montana. I'm in Cuba."

"Cuba? Not because of anyone in this office—I hope."

"I'm here for several reasons. One, Lucinda is photographing places where Hemingway lived or ate or drank. It's for a Canadian travel magazine. She finished today. It went well; she has wonderful photos."

"What's *your* reason? You don't photograph."

"I'm tarpon and bone fishing off the south coast. A place called Playa Larga. Lucinda and I are there now."

"Sounds like all play, which you should know is not permitted under whatever license you have."

Diverting the subject, I asked, "Do you know about the disappearance of a U.S. House member from New Mexico named Juan Mendoza?"

"Where did he disappear?"

"Here, at Playa Larga. He went missing maybe a month ago. I was called by his sister, Elena, also a House member but representing Connecticut. I once took Elena and Juan fly fishing in Montana. Our only contact for the past half-dozen years has been receiving formal Christmas cards from their Washington offices showing the Capitol in the snow.

"Elena told me about Juan's disappearance and about the hostility towards both of them by some of the early exiles in Miami. Juan and Elena have wanted to see trade and tourism with Cuba fully restored. That position hasn't endeared them to one of the senators from Florida, Miamian Jorge García García. People joke that he represents *only* the Cuban exiles in Miami who back the trade boycott and only those who also keep sending him money for his re-election campaigns. His kind are losing power and running scared. They'd like to see—before they pass on—both Castro brothers dead and Cuba restored to the way it was in 1958."

"Are you involved with Mendoza's disappearance?" Dan asked.

"Indirectly. I promised Elena I would ask around here and see if I could collect any more information about Juan. The Cuban government in Havana doesn't want to talk about it. You would think they would support Juan, but there are many in the government who prefer the status quo. They use the trade and tourism restrictions to justify to the Cuban people why they live so poorly. Except, of course, those in the government who are doing quite well the way things work right now. . . . Let me tell you why Lucinda and I are not doing so well."

I repeated to Dan each of Francisco's questions about my fingerprints.

"Mac, are they going to be able to connect your fingerprints?"

"Yes. It's only a matter of time, maybe days, maybe hours, before they conclude they're right."

"You'll be considered to have been involved in trying to assassinate Castro. You need to get out of Cuba," Dan urged. "When are you *scheduled* to leave?"

"Tomorrow evening Lucinda and I are returning to Havana. The Interests Section is sending a car to pick us up and take us back to Havana where we're due to stay for two nights at the Hotel Nacional. Then we fly to Miami. That's three more nights in Cuba, including tonight."

"That's three too many. I'll call Celeste. I want her to get that car to you right now and get you out of Playa Larga."

"Where do we drive? There's no bridge to Florida. No car ferry."

"You could go to the Interests Section in Havana. But you might be there for days or months before the Cubans would allow you safe passage to the airport to get a flight home. . . . I need to think. I'll call you right back. Go pack your bags. I'll call Celeste and get the car on its way to you. I want you both to be prepared to leave your hotel in two hours."

"We'll be ready."

19

THE ESCAPE TO FLORIDA

IT WAS NEARLY MIDNIGHT WHEN THE DRIVER who brought me to Playa Larga—Luis Ferrara—arrived at the hotel, driving the same 1956 Ford. Lucinda and I had checked out earlier and told the desk people we would be leaving to fish early in the morning and then head directly to Havana from the Zapata Reserve.

"Señor Brooks, are you ready?" asked Luis. "We have an easy hundred miles to drive. We want to reach our destination before dawn."

"What's our destination?" I asked, not certain that Luis would tell me.

"A place in the north, along the Matanzas Coast at El Mamey Beach."

"That doesn't make sense, Luis. You intend to drop us off on some beach? Are we rafting to Florida?"

"Not on the beach. At a very historic location, 'though not so in the minds of our leaders. It's the location of one of the most embarrassing moments in our Castro era."

"I don't understand," declared Lucinda, who was exhausted from her taxing day.

"Have you ever heard of Major Orestes Lorenzo?" asked Luis.

"Not that I can remember," I replied. Lucinda shook her head.

"Lorenzo was a major in our air force. He was trained in the USSR, served in Angola, and was flying MiG-23s."

"Nice story. But?" I asked.

"Lorenzo became increasingly disenchanted with the Castro regime and finally decided he didn't want his children to suffer the indoctrination he had received all his life. On a spring day in 1991, he climbed into the cockpit of his MiG for what was to be a routine training flight in Cuba, took off, and immediately dropped down to nearly wave-top level and aimed for Key West. Cuban radar missed the boat, and although U.S. radar picked him up and scrambled fighters, Lorenzo landed at the Naval Air Station at Key West to the surprise and dismay of those defending our nation."

"Did the U.S. keep him," Lucinda asked.

"Yes, but sent the MiG back."

"What about his family, those children he didn't want to live under Cuba's communism?"

"That was the next problem. Cuba wouldn't let them out unless they denounced Lorenzo as a traitor. They refused."

"Are they still in Cuba," I asked.

"No."

"Are they in the U.S.?"

"Yes."

"How did they get there?"

"In a Cessna, the same way you're going to Florida."

"A Cessna? That's ridiculous. What have you been drinking, Luis?"

"I talked to a man named Dan Wilson just before I arrived to pick you up. He told me how you're getting home. I knew it was the same way Lorenzo did with his family."

"Tell us more?" pleaded Lucinda.

"Wilson called me from D.C. and instructed me to take you to the highway between Matanzas and Varadero at 4:00 a.m. and drop you at a place near Mamey Beach. It will still be dark. A Cessna will land there."

"Is there an airport there?"

"A big one, but we're not going there. We have a special airport—called the Circuito Norte. It's sort of a runway," commented Luis quietly, hoping we wouldn't ask more.

"What's 'sort of'?"

"The runway is normally used as a highway."

"*A highway?* Busy?"

"Not at four in the morning."

"Can you take us back to Playa Larga?" asked Lucinda, not fully in jest.

"No. I will have you at the highway, and you'll be standing by the side of that road at 4:00 a.m. Whether or not you get on the plane is your decision. As soon as I drop you, I'm off to Havana."

"What kind of plane is coming for us? I thought I heard Cessna, but that can't be right."

"I *said* a Cessna. No 747. Or F-14. Wait and see. I've told you all I know. I suggest you both take a nap."

"What kind of a Cessna?"

"I wasn't told. Probably old like my car."

"We'll be there by 1:00 a.m. What do we do until four?"

"If anything's open when we pass through Cárdenas, I'll bring you coffee and whatever."

Lucinda and I looked at each other, mouths open, eyes squinting, and brains in overdrive, trying to understand what was going on.

The drive was uneventful but anxious. The time passed while Lucinda and I dozed against each other in the back seat, her fragrance reassuring me. We reached Cárdenas a little after midnight. A few places were open, and Luis brought us coffee and two-day-old flan. We didn't want to get to the pickup spot too early because over a three-to-four-hour period there was a good chance of having a police vehicle see us and stop. Luis found a secluded nook to park near Mamey Beach.

The next few hours passed slowly. We woke at the slightest bit of noise. Luis's head popped up over the back of the front seat.

"You two awake? It's 3:30. We'd best get going. The plane could be here anytime. Fifteen minutes either side of 4:00."

Luis drove slowly along the highway. We watched a fishing boat glide through the swells offshore, dropping out of sight one moment, then ascending to the top of the next swell.

Luis turned his head and said, "The weather's perfect: some wind blowing north, which will make your flight brief, about an hour. We're five minutes at most from the pickup spot. We should see a large billboard on the southwest side of the highway. The same as the one in Havana across from the Interests Section."

"I'll look for it. What does it say?" asked Lucinda.

"It's in Spanish and shows a Cuban soldier carrying a gun and shouting across the Florida Straits at a cowering Uncle

Sam. It says 'Dear Imperialists. We have absolutely no fear of you.'"

"How is the plane going to find us?"

"The sign is one of the only things lighted between Matanzas and Varadero. It's there so that foreign tourists who've been visiting Matanzas for the day will see it as they head back to their hotels at Varadero."

"So tonight it's a beacon! What about landing lights?" I asked.

"Nothing much on the ground. I have three flashlights. There's a half moon—that will help. The plane will likely fly low along the highway, looking for the sign and the car."

"The plane should have landing lights. You said something about flashlights."

"Three. We're the ground crew," said Luis, smiling.

"If we have two of us on the roadside and the third fifty yards down the highway standing in the middle, the pilot will have a target," Lucinda suggested.

"Smart lady," said Luis.

"Do you think the plane will have its wing lights on?" asked Lucinda. "Those ones that flash red and green."

"Not likely. It will be flying low and dark."

At 4:10 we heard noise of distant motor coming from the north. Lucinda and Luis took up positions on opposite sides of the road. Because there was a slight breeze from the southeast, I ran about fifty yards south along the road, flashlight ready. Only one vehicle had passed us on the road.

"That sounds like a plane," called Luis.

"I think so. He may come in along the shoreline and fly low looking for us."

Minutes later the plane came into view in the moonlight, moving directly over the road and dropping down to no more than seventy-five feet.

"He put his wing flaps down," I called to Lucinda. "He wants to land at as slow a speed as he can safely. About sixty with full flaps. The wind is no more than five to ten knots, so he's going to land doing something like fifty-five."

In a moment the plane was over us, waving its wings when we turned on our flashlights and turning on its bright landing lights. As soon as it passed, it dropped and touched down, taxied until it could turn and come back, rolled to a stop slightly off the highway, and turned off the engine."

I was amazed at how well the pilot handled the plane. The touchdown was picture perfect. The plane looked like a Cessna, but it wasn't painted, and there were no numbers on the wings or fuselage.

"You're on your own, you two," said Luis, walking toward his car. "Maybe I'll see you again here in Cuba."

"Don't count on it, but thanks," Lucinda answered.

The plane's door opened on the left side and a voice said, "Care for a ride?"

"Where to?" Lucinda asked.

"How about America?"

"Sounds good."

"Get in. One in back, one up with me. Either of you fly?"

"A long time ago," I answered. "In a Cessna 150. This looks like a 172."

"It is. You're my co-pilot. Right front seat. Let's hurry."

When we were settled in and the door shut, I turned to the pilot and said, "Thanks, guy."

"I'm Baker. Navy Air Lieutenant Commander *Nan* Baker at your service," the voice said over the noise of the engine.

"A woman! *You* fly?" I asked realizing my male assumption was a poor choice."

"Usually F-14s. This Cessna is my hobby. We didn't think it wise to use a fighter jet. Ready?"

"What about being shot down by a ground to air missile?"

"Been there, done that. I was shot down in Afghanistan. I'm still flying. This is fun, running the wave tops. About missiles? Cuba's defenses are so outmoded we will be out past twelve miles and in international waters in a few minutes. They didn't pick me up on radar on the way here and apparently they haven't yet. They need fifteen minutes from when they spot the plane until they can launch a missile. We're safe."

We were moving faster to take off. I looked at the instrument panel to see what our speed was. There was only a hole where the airspeed indicator was supposed to be."

"We'll fly visual; the lights on the panel aren't working," Commander Baker said. "We're flying by moonlight."

"Very romantic," mumbled Lucinda from the rear.

"I'm replacing most of the panel," Baker explained. "We're flying without much help. No airspeed indicator, no altimeter, no attitude indicator, no directional indicator, no vertical speed indicator, and no trim and slip indicator. I guess you could say I'm flying by the seat of my pants. Or for me by the seat of my dress," she looked at me, smiling. "It's not what you'd call an instrument flight. But the night's clear, and I can already see the glow over Key West."

"Do you have a fuel gauge? Macduff drives our cars until the near empty light comes on."

"I topped it off before I left."

"Oil pressure gauge?" I asked.

"I install it tomorrow. I checked the oil before I left."

"Lights?"

"Got those. Put new ones in last weekend. Strobes, a light on each wing tip, and dual landing lights on the forward edge of the wings, which you saw me use as I landed. We need lights to identify us when we approach Key West. I'll have them *all* on."

"When will you call the base tower?"

"Can't. All the radio gear should be here in a week. But the folks at the base know what's going on. We may have a welcoming committee."

"We don't want that."

"The base commander's pretty savvy. He won't have the press around."

"You do all the work on the plane yourself?"

"I don't do engines. . . . We're at 2,000 feet now. We stayed low for the first dozen miles off Cuba. . . . That's Key West off to the left. The Naval Air Station's at Boca Chica Key about three miles from Key West. If you look carefully, you can see the runway lights. The wind's still a little from the southwest. We're going to sweep around and land heading more or less south, into the wind."

"I hate to mention it, commander, but there's a fighter plane out my window."

"They're my guys. There's one off my side as well. They're about to drop off so we can land. . . . Macduff, since you said you fly, put on about ten degrees of flaps."

"Are you sure you've got flaps? Most everything else is missing."

"Don't be so nervous. We have all the parts we need. Flaps down."

I did as she ordered, and we touched down a couple of minutes later. Two fire engines guided us to the hanger. Only one person was there, standing to the side in the shadows of the hanger. Baker turned off the engine, and we all hopped out. The ground didn't move and felt good. The person came out from the shadows.

"Welcome to America. Enjoy your ride? Let's go into the officers' club. I've got a bottle of Moët & Chandon Champagne. I'm Bill Westwood, commander of this little base."

We walked to the club. The breakfast crew was drifting in. Only one person was in the bar.

Dan Wilson.

20

LUCINDA AND MACDUFF GO HOME TO ST. AUGUSTINE

"DAN, I TOLD YOU ABOUT my conversation with Francisco that led to this rescue."

"My best reading is that the Cuban authorities learned you were in the country not to fish but to find out about Juan Mendoza's whereabouts. That made you a spy and cast blame also on Lucinda. But the serious concern is the matching fingerprints. It could mean your former identity is known and your cover is gone. . . . But, maybe . . ."

"It may not matter," I interrupted. "The Cubans have no reason to take the matter outside Cuba. They will likely list both names with the passport control people and ask them to hold anyone who has either name. But I didn't do anything that should cause the Cubans to lodge a complaint with the U.S."

"If fact," Lucinda interjected, "they don't want to embarrass themselves and admit we departed successfully. They messed up. Their radar system missed us. No planes ever left the ground to check on us. Luis said Cuba doesn't have enough funds even to buy bullets.

"Castro has turned over some tourist facilities to military battalions and told them to earn the money they need to maintain their weapons," Dan added.

"That explains a sign on a hotel being built in Cojímar," commented Lucinda. "It said something like 'This new luxury resort is being brought to you by the 3rd battalion of the First Army of Cuba.'"

"Did you two learn anything about Juan Mendoza that might point to who did what to him?"

"No. I did sense yesterday in Playa Larga, having drinks before Lucinda and Francisco Sandoval arrived, that my guide, Nacho Gomez, wanted to tell me something. He said he was going to tell me the substance of what he referred to as 'maybe only a local rumor.' He didn't get to tell me anything because Lucinda arrived with Francisco and Nacho never uttered another word other than goodbye."

"So the link that Sandoval mentioned—the matching fingerprints—is probably going to be nothing more than a footnote to his report to his mother about you?"

"Correct," I responded. "But maybe there won't even be a report. Francisco may believe he won't be punished if he doesn't pursue the fingerprint issue."

"Macduff, does it really matter? Juan Pablo Herzog in Guatemala *knows* that Maxwell Hunt didn't die, but survived and is living somewhere."

"True, but he doesn't know where Hunt's living and, most importantly, he doesn't know that Macduff Brooks is the name Maxwell Hunt chose as part of his new identity."

"At least Isfahani is gone. That half of your pursuers is no longer alive."

"But the other half—Herzog—is perfectly capable of eliminating me all by himself. And he carries more hatred for me because he blames me for killing both his niece and nephew."

"Your demise is unlikely to happen in the near future," Dan explained. "The polls in Guatemala show the new president is not liked and Juan Pablo will probably win the presidency at the next election."

"By then, Macduff," Lucinda added, "you'll be too old to be a concern to him."

"Thanks. . . . But *you* won't be."

The next afternoon after a morning of a little extended sleep and a lot of debriefing, Dan had his jet drop us at the Miami airport to pick up our car and drive home. Because it was too late to drive to St. Augustine, his office called the Miami Beach Fontainebleau Hotel and changed our earlier reservation.

In the evening we strolled leisurely long the garish South Beach waterfront, watching barely clad women promenading, artificial breasts sagging at the same pace as their drooping facial uplifts. Try as we may, we never determined the gender of more than a few twosomes.

*W*e were overdressed, not in style but to the extent that our clothes covered body parts normally unexposed. Abundant and unreadable tattoos on almost everyone under fifty, tiny sparkling diamonds were everywhere but on ring fingers, and various metals—implanted or dangling—reinforced Miami Beach's image as a surreal carnival.

Despite the lavish glitz, the ocean was as I remembered it from years ago, except that the beach in front of the hotel had shrunk. Florida was sinking into the ocean. Or rather the ocean was rising. Scientists estimate it may rise as much as six feet in the next fifty years, covering Miami, which now sits a mere five feet above high water. Some consider that idea a blessing. Most Miamians will have to move inland or plea to the Dutch for help building dikes.

The following day we joined the surge of unpredictable I-95 traffic, driving north toward St. Augustine. After a half hour absent of conversation, Lucinda, who was driving, turned her head, put her hand on my arm, and asked, "Are you troubled by our experience in Cuba?"

"I'm disappointed. I promised Elena Mendoza I would try to learn what happened to her brother. I asked my guide, Nacho Gomez, questions and posed a few more to the Playa Larga hotel manager, Celia Bustamante.

"The only other thing I did was walk around Playa Larga town. I wanted to see the St. Peter the Fisherman church in case I came back to fish again. Small, cement block painted white, and topped with a signature churchly steeple, I saw the building only from the street.

"Moreover, I stumbled upon the nearly obscured and mostly unmarked dirt road to the barracuda research center but, when I started to walk along the entry road, was stopped by two disagreeable looking men and gruffly told it was private and I was to immediately turn around and leave. . . . Lucinda, did *you* talk to Francisco about Mendoza's disappearance during your time photographing or driving to Playa Larga to meet me?"

"Not a word. I thought I shouldn't be the one who raised the subject. I wish *he* had."

"No one other than Nacho saw Mendoza and admits it. Someone must have waited on him in the restaurant at Playa Larga. Or maybe a chambermaid brought him something. Or someone was waiting with the skiff at Salinas. No one came forward with any information. Were they afraid? Or didn't they know anything? If we hadn't had to leave suddenly, we might have met someone our final day who was willing to talk. "

"Do you want to talk to Elena?"

"Not really, but I owe her a call; she doesn't know we're back." I found her number and tapped it on Lucinda's cell phone.

"Representative Elena Mendoza's office," a soft female voice said without a trace of a Spanish accent.

"This is Macduff Brooks. I've returned from Cuba and would like . . ."

"Elena is anxious to talk to you," the voice interrupted. "I'll transfer you; she's at a meeting."

I waited no more than a few seconds. "Macduff, it's Elena. I'm glad you're back. I tried your number an hour ago. You didn't answer. What happened? You're not calling from the usual number."

"I left my cell phone in Cuba, fortunately at the Interests Section. Lucinda and I departed in a hurry. Have you talked to anyone? Celeste in Havana?"

"No. Are you two OK? Do you have any news about Juan? Why did you leave so fast?"

How much should I tell her, I wondered. She did make it possible for us to go to Cuba in the first place. And I made a promise I didn't keep.

"Do you have a minute?"

"I'll make time. I'm walking out of a meeting as we speak. . . . Tell me the whole story."

I told her nearly every detail. Lucinda interrupted me a couple of times and added something. But I intentionally omitted the issue critical to our departure: that of the alleged matching fingerprints.

"I still don't understand why you had to leave so abruptly," Elena commented, "especially the way you got out of Cuba. You're leaving something out. Please tell me."

I decided to tell her more but not mention names. "In Playa Larga I learned that a trip I tried to make from Mexico to Havana for the State Department three decades ago was somehow rejuvenated by the Cuban government. I thought that attempt was history. Someone in Cuba wants to learn more about what my plans were at that time. It was a sensitive era; I didn't know then that the CIA was planning to assassinate Castro."

"You were involved with an assassination attempt? You should have told me."

"I wasn't involved. I was going to Havana to meet with a couple of professors. I was writing a book on Cuba. Our CIA people in Mexico tried to use me to obtain sensitive information from some contacts in Havana. I never received a visa from Cuba and returned home from Mexico. Two days ago was the first time in decades anyone has mentioned that aborted trip. I never talk about it."

"This doesn't help with finding Juan. Is there *anything* else that might help?"

"My brief conversation with the manager of the Playa Larga hotel left me wondering why Juan's room was cleared out by the police so quickly, why there appeared to be no investigation, and why the manager knew absolutely nothing. It's as though any staff member that might have had information was told not to speak about it. But that's not very much to go on."

"It's better than nothing. Can I call you again? I should get back to my meeting."

"Call when you're free."

Lucinda's cell phone speaker had been on. She was listening and occasionally making notes with one hand and steering with the other.

"I didn't know about your conversation with the hotel manager, Macduff. Her denial that she knew anything about how Juan left or why the police cleaned out his room so abruptly and surreptitiously doesn't make sense."

"I was scheduled to talk to her the next morning before you arrived. Circumstances prevented that. I'd give anything to talk to her again; she was not pleased with how Juan's disappearance was handled. . . . But I doubt you and I will see Cuba again."

"I'd like to go back," Lucinda added. "Francisco Sandoval was studying art in Havana. He briefly showed me the art college on the grounds of the former Havana country club. It has some unusual 1960's architecture I'd like to photograph. . . . But I agree . . . we won't go back, at least not until the Castro regime is history."

"That may be years," I said. "And it may never occur all at once. There's no reason Cuba won't change like Vietnam or China, keeping the substance of a communist government that oversees a controlled private market economy."

"Where does that leave the early exiles in the U.S.?"

"Very unhappy. On the outside looking in. Not in control in Cuba as many of them expect and demand. Significant restitution of expropriated property is inconceivable after a half century. Plus, there isn't enough money for meaningful compensation. It's not like Iran, which paid a lot of U.S. claims only because Iran had huge sums that we blocked in U.S. banks."

"Lucinda, you were scribbling on a pad while we were talking to Elena. Any ideas?"

"I was thinking of last year's gill net murders in Florida. It wasn't the work of one killer. Six families from Oyster Bay and Apalachicola participated. Could Juan's death be the result of a number of people?"

"You're better at this than I am. What are you thinking?"

"Juan strongly and publically opposed the trade and tourism boycott. Who stands to benefit in both countries if the boycott remains in place?"

"Start with Senator García García," I answered. "His career has depended on keeping the boycott in place. Why? He thinks he's a hero among the exiles. Within a dying group he is. Not many others in the U.S. want to keep the boycott. It stays in place because of two things. One is when advocating preserving the boycott might give a presidential candidate the edge in gaining Florida's electoral votes. The other is the way supporters of the boycott in Congress trade votes with other states' delegates. You vote for the boycott, and I'll vote for your bridge-to-nowhere."

What about public support of the boycott?"

"Cuba is *de minimus* to most people outside South Florida. Who in Tennessee or Idaho cares much about Cuba?"

"Maybe people would like to visit Cuba and are angry they can't," she answered. "To sunbathe at Varadero or see Old Havana. Or go bonefishing."

"Potential tourists aren't organized. Miami Cubans promoted both the wet-foot/dry-foot immigration policy and the liberal family visit rules. Recreational fishing advocates, like general tourists, have not promoted anything. Besides, the reality is that almost anyone in the U.S. can go to Cuba. If you want to go join a church that promotes exchanges. Or go with a group like the League of Women Voters. Or sign up for a People-to-People tour. Or even go through the Bahamas or Mexico or Canada and on returning to the U.S. face the not very severe or even enforced sanctions."

"Macduff, have you thought about the commercial traders in the U.S. who sell to Cuba? I've pulled up some figures on my cell phone. A year or so ago U.S. businesses sold over $500 million in food products to Cuba. Archer Daniels Midland alone has about half the food trade of the U.S. with Cuba. If they thought they had an advantage that wouldn't last if the trade boycott ended, they would be quietly supporting its continuation."

"Isn't that offset by other companies that want to trade with Cuba, but can't because of the boycott?"

"To some extent, yes, but Cuba is small. It's not like opening trade with China or Russia. There's no question that trade would increase and possibly much of it would be brokered by exiles in South Florida. But keep in mind that Cuba is broke. The goods they need are available, but Cuba doesn't have the means to pay."

"Are you saying that there are more votes on any level for keeping the boycott than for ending it?" I asked Lucinda.

"Probably not. There are some current traders who like the status quo. Opening up trade would bring competition those traders would prefer to avoid. Most of the U.S. companies that engage in international trade don't care about Cuba. It's too small a market."

"Why isn't there more pressure *in* Cuba to end the boycott? If you talk to people in Cuba, as both of us did, they invariably blame their poor status on the U.S. boycott."

"Could that be because the *Cuban government* doesn't want the boycott ended?" asked Lucinda. "They can blame the U.S. for their poverty, and they don't have to take any action to smooth relations and end the trade restraints."

"Over the past twenty years, starting a few years after the Russians pulled out, the Castro brothers adopted some market economy characteristics, especially allowing very small businesses to exist. But not in many areas. What if they asked U.S. contractors to build condos in Havana? Would they allow a Cuban exile-owned firm in South Florida to be awarded the contract? Would they allow Cuban exiles from Miami to buy the condos? I have doubts."

"Are you saying that Cuba might slowly open but *prevent* the exiles from participating?" she asked.

"Yes. . . . But we're looking for reasons that Juan might have been abducted and whether he's dead or being held somewhere. The Cuban government hasn't been responsive to U.S. requests to talk about Juan's case. That points to something Cuba feels it will *gain* by not helping and that means the U.S. not wanting to discuss ending the boycott."

"Macduff, we're in over our heads. Don't we want to stay out of this? You did what you could for Elena. I did some photographs, and you did some fishing. Can't we call it a day?"

"Something else surfaces every time I think of staying involved—the risk to you and Elsbeth. But you're right; we should back off."

"Good. I agree with you."

"We'll call it a day. No more talk of Cuba. For tomorrow and tomorrow."

21

SPRING AT THE COTTAGE IN FLORIDA

BACK OFF IS WHAT WE DID. March and April were quiet times at the cottage. Lucinda's photographs were a hit at the magazine in Toronto; she's begun her next assignment for a U.S. conservation magazine—a spread of aerial photos of the threatened salt marshes of Northeast Florida.

We visited Gainesville twice to see Elsbeth, and she brought her friend and housemate Sue to the cottage for Spring Break. Elsbeth thought Lucinda and I had been to Cuba only for Lucinda to photograph and for me to fish. We left it at that. But Elsbeth had another idea about Cuba.

"Dad, what do you think of student foreign exchange programs?" she asked during the break.

"They're usually good. Where are you thinking of going, Europe, Latin America, Asia?"

"*Cuba*, in late summer the week before fall term classes begin at UF," she answered with the firmness of a decision already made.

"Why Cuba?" Lucinda asked, suddenly interested in the conversation.

"You and Dad liked it. Sue and I have been reading Hemingway in our English lit course. We'd like to see some of the places you photographed. You showed us the photos."

"For example?"

"Finca Vigía."

"And?" I asked, interrupting.

"Whatever."

"El Floridita? "

"Maybe."

"La Bodeguita?"

"Maybe."

"Ambos Mundos?"

"Maybe."

"Any others?

"*Maybe* La Terraza at Cojímar."

"That's five places, four of which are bars. And you can't drink until you're 21."

"That's in Florida," Elsbeth said.

"And in Wyoming," added Sue. "But it's something like 16 in Cuba, and most resorts don't check."

"You're scaring me. Why are you really going to Cuba?"

"Dad, we won't be in Havana bars. Truthfully, we won't even be in Havana. We want to meet some university students and compare university life in Cuba and here."

"You know it's risky. Cuba has very different attitudes towards foreign visitors who make negative comments about the country."

"We'll be careful."

"Elsbeth," I said, nodding, "Lucinda and I haven't told you everything about our trip to Cuba."

"You fished; Lucinda took photos."

"That's true, but those weren't the only reasons we went. I was sent to Cuba to look for a missing U.S. House member from the state of New Mexico named Juan Mendoza. I took him fishing once in Montana. Before Lucinda and I went to Cuba, Mendoza was there at a trade meeting and stayed to fish for a few days. He disappeared overnight. Our trip was urged by the State Department, working with Mendoza's sister, Elena, who is also in the House, representing Connecticut. Lucinda's photographs and my fishing were covers for my investigation."

"That all sounds exciting. But how will it affect Sue and me?"

"We had some trouble. The Cuban government thought I was there for a reason other than fishing: to search for Mendoza."

"Did they have any proof? You seemed pretty occupied with your own fishing."

"I was, but I stayed at the same Playa Larga hotel where Mendoza had stayed. And I hired the same fishing guide."

"Is there more?" she asked.

"Yes." After pausing to consider what she had a right to know, I told her about my trip to Cuba years ago as Professor Hunt and that my fingerprints recently taken for an entry visa as Macduff Brooks matched earlier prints of Maxwell Hunt.

"A person with some link to the government—his mother is the Minister of the Interior—asked us to explain the fingerprints. We put him off," Lucinda added.

"What did you tell him?" Sue asked.

"That Cuban customs officials made a mistake. We didn't try to explain what we couldn't explain. . . . We were worried and called Dan in D.C. He shared our concern and wanted us to get out immediately."

"We did," Lucinda added, saying no more about our departure.

"So, you're certain it's not safe for Sue and me to go?"

"My first thought is it's not safe," I responded slowly. "But your trip is almost four months away. Let Lucinda and me talk about it more on our drive to Montana."

I had one idea that might work, but I needed to do some checking.

22

CROSS COUNTRY TO MONTANA

L ATE APRIL WEATHER IN MONTANA AND WYO-MING arrived unseasonably warm. Heavy snows in February had extended into March. Entering April, the snow pack was far higher than normal, but the weather shifted abruptly, and the days warmed ten degrees above the norm for the month. The larger than usual snow pack meeting the higher than usual thawing temperatures produced unseemly amounts of run-off, tumbling helter-skelter from the mountains and disobeying the boundaries of the streams, creeks, and rivers.

The surging water of the Snake River poured into Jackson Lake and brought the level behind the dam to a depth marker untouched for decades. Water-use conflicts involving power companies, ranches, communities, riverfront homeowners, and recreational interests were all placed on the back burner for another year, avoiding decisions on the inevitable long-term allocations of this increasingly scarce resource.

The same issues were present along the Yellowstone River in Paradise Valley, modified partly by the absence of dams and their staccato effect on the natural flows.

Lucinda and I were not free of concern even on Mill Creek—well away from the Yellowstone—about the daily increases in this menacing turbulence, talked about in terms of cubic feet per second or *cfs*.

Our Mill Creek properties were re-contoured by the strength of flow, which cascaded down the mountainside carrying silt and gravel and rocks from tiny stones to hundred-pound boulders. On the steeper runs the water dug out deeper channels, and when the creek flowed across more level ground, the boulders and larger rocks came to rest to form new pools.

There were other casualties of the comfort of being for years a part of a defined riverbed. As the water rose, it loosened the roots of *flora* that usually rose to become tiny wild flowers and towering cottonwoods and aspens. Torn from their anchorages, their remnants floated downstream until they wedged under rocks or sank from saturated weight.

On Mill Creek the rushing water created new trout habitat. Along the edge of Mill Creek at the parking area for Passage Creek Trail, the rushing water dislodged thick brush that tumbled downstream to form new habitat. Lucinda would never catch the trout, which last year had rejected every offering she presented, in the pool beneath the brush near the parking area. This year the trout would take up new residence, perhaps at the ranch a mile downstream or at our cabin another mile further.

The noise from the surge increased daily, ignoring the silence of a late summer when the water's movement was obscured by other forest sounds—wind blowing up the canyon, songs of a dozen species of resident birds, and undefinable murmurs of the season.

"Macduff," Lucinda turned toward me, lifting her head from the *Bozeman News,* and asked, "did you know *Montana* sells goods to Cuba?"

"Yes, Miss Ph.D. economist, but not what goods or why Montana. Explain it to me and don't use the unintelligible theories of economics. I won't understand things like elasticity of demand or game theory."

"I'm glad I was never one of your teachers."

"But you've taught me all sorts of things, especially at night."

"Macduff! Do you want me to continue with Montana and Cuba or not?"

"Please go on, teacher."

"Trade with Cuba is growing. A few years ago sales were only $2 million to $9 million a year. By opening 'humanitarian' sales of food and medicine, they quickly grew to $145 million and one year even to $700 million. Sales leveled off at about $300 million to $400 million a year.

"Our Montana congressional delegation has supported opening up far more trade with Cuba, recently announcing that they would sign a trade agreement on behalf of Montana to sell more goods."

"That's a different attitude from what the Florida congressional delegation prefers," I commented.

"All the trade has been *export* trade," she added. "We don't import anything from Cuba, except the hundred or so *Cohiba* cigars you snuck out when we came back."

"I didn't sneak them out; I brought them back in my bag. But we never had to go through customs coming home to Key West. . . . You didn't mention the bottle of *Havana Club Máximo Extra Añejo* rum *you* brought back."

"That doesn't count. By the time we reached our cottage, we had finished it."

"*What* does Cuba buy from *Montana?*" I asked.

"The article says that next year they expect to buy 100,000 head of cattle. Montana and Wyoming cattle ranchers have their foot in the front door. A couple of them went to Cuba a few months ago with our House rep and one of our senators. The two ranchers signed tentative agreements to sell an estimated 30,000 cattle to Cuba."

"Is Cuba interested in products other than beef?"

"Apparently so," Lucinda answered, looking back in the article for comments. "Here it is. Cuba also wants dairy cattle, wheat, malt barley, and beans."

"Maybe we could have gone to Cuba from Montana as part of a trade delegation. Rather than going from Florida."

"We never thought about that," she said. "The newspaper article says the Montana Chamber of Commerce has sponsored two trips to Cuba and that they were not only trade trips but also recreational trips open to anyone."

My new cell phone rang as Lucinda put down the paper. She flipped open the phone and turned on the speaker.

"This is Lucinda *Brooks*," she said with an emphasis on the Brooks.

"So Macduff has a personal secretary now. This is Hank Benson at Angler's West in Emigrant. Are you booking Macduff's guide trips?"

"I am, and I negotiate the terms of his guiding contracts."

"Give me that phone," I said. "I'll never get another guide trip. . . . This is Macduff, Hank. My personal secretary has just been fired. I'm booking my own trips. Got a float for me? The Yellowstone's not too good a choice these days."

"Agreed, it's blown out. It'll be well into June before it clears. I want you to float the Madison with a guy from Billings. You choose what section, but it's fishing pretty well on the lower Madison. The water's a bit off color; the east side of the river is fishing pretty good. Best for nymphing. If you fish late in the afternoon, try some streamers off the banks."

"What section of the lower Madison?" I asked.

"You could do Warm Springs to Black's Ford. That's only about four miles, which isn't far with the water moving. Or maybe run Black's Ford all the way to Blackbird at Three Forks. That's a long twenty-one miles, and you'd want to be on the water early and not dally along the way, unless you and your client like night fishing."

"Twenty-one miles is too much," I answered. "Maybe with an old friend. But not with a new client you don't know. Being with him for twelve hours! . . . How are the accesses at Grey Cliff and Cobblestone this year?"

"Cobblestone is still walk-in, so that's out. And it's seventeen versus twenty-one miles from Black's Ford. That's not much difference. Pulling out at Grey Cliff drops the trip to about four miles, similar to drifting from Warm Springs to Black's Ford. I prefer starting at Warm Springs. The rafters and tubers won't be out yet to take over the river."

"You and your client decide, Macduff."

"Where do we meet?"

"Here at the shop. The client is staying with friends up Tom Miner Road. He'll be here at 7:30."

"Who is the client?"

"Some Montana cattle rancher. I forget his name."

"I'll be there fifteen minutes early to pick out some flies."

23

FLOATING THE LOWER MADISON RIVER

M Y CLIENT WAS CLIFF CAMERON, a name I'd
heard but couldn't place. He arrived early and was picking through the flies at Angler's West when I walked in. He was
in well-worn creased jeans and a pale gray shirt with Western
yokes and pearlized snaps. His tan Stetson had long embedded
sweat stains seeping above the band. Cameron seemed pleasant
enough, but for some reason I thought to myself that I was
glad we were doing a short four-mile float rather than a long
twenty-one miles.

We settled the day's charges with Hank, and Cameron
joined me in the front of my SUV. I was towing my ClackaCraft drift boat, which is a functional vessel but not compara-
ble in looks and lacks the character of my mahogany, ash, and
oak wooden drift boat, *Osprey*.

I bought the plastic boat my second year of guiding on the
day after a client from New Orleans named Joe Quinn left cigarette burns on *Osprey's* oak and mahogany crosspieces that are
for leaning against, not serving as ash trays. Plus, he showed up
wearing wading boots with metal studs that don't respect wood.
But the worst was the consequence of his bringing aboard a

dozen cans of Bud Lite and consuming all of them by mid-afternoon. After his sixth can only two hours into the float, he didn't catch a thing because his coordination had departed with the beer cans he tossed over and that I rowed back and netted before they filled and sank.

One might think that would have been enough dumb conduct to discourage me from ever guiding again. But it didn't, nor did Quinn's *coup de gras* after he consumed the last beer—turning toward me with signs of *mal de mare* and throwing up in the boat. Fortunately he dumped his stomach contents to the side of him, but only managed to get half overboard. Had he turned around and gotten me, there would have been one more homicide on my boat.

After pressure washing *Osprey* at the Emigrant car wash, I towed the boat home and drove to Bozeman where I bought a three-year-old ClackaCraft. *Osprey*, burn marks refinished, the floor repainted, and the front repeatedly drenched with disinfectant, in the post-Quinn era has been reserved for clients I know, including three-dozen annual repeat clients who have become friends.

"Where are we floating?" Cameron asked, as I pulled out of Emigrant, glanced at the blinking light, rolled through the intersection, and headed north.

"At this time of year, we almost have to float the Madison, including for maybe another week only a section of the *lower* Madison."

"Why not the Yellowstone?"

"Too fast and too dirty. We had a couple of weeks—the last of April and first of May—when we caught as much as we could hope for on the Yellowstone. But it's blown out now; the *cfs* flow has been increasing the way you'd like to watch the stock market perform. The river was about 4,000 *cfs* a week ago, and in five days it's increased to 14,000. Plus, the clarity has gone from an off-green—but still one to two feet of visibility—to brown, brown, and more brown—and no visibility. We won't be floating the Yellowstone until mid-June if were lucky, mid-July if the big snow pack hasn't melted."

"So that leaves the Madison?"

"Yes. From Enis Lake downstream past the town of Enis to Quake Lake is what we call the 50-Mile Riffle. It doesn't open to floating for another week. We'll go to the lower Madison, which is fishing very good right now, and should stay fishable until the water temperature rises in June. Now and late fall we fish the lower Madison. In between those times the river has too much warm water and too many tubes and rafts filled with happy but noisy and often sottish young folk."

"What's being caught on the lower Madison?"

"Well, rainbows have come back from having whirling disease in the mid-90s, and browns patrol under the riverbanks."

"Can we use dry flies?"

"Sure. We might see part of the Mother's Day baetis hatch. If we do, we'll try Parachute Adams—as small as #20, but #16 and #18 work well. A variety of baetis nymph patterns should also be good. We might have an afternoon caddis hatch. I like Elk Hair in anything from #10 to #20. Nymphing, we'll use some pretty well-known flies—Copper Johns are good. So are transplants from the San Juan River in New Mexico—variations of the famous San Juan Worm."

"Will we throw any streamers or stoneflies?"

"We will. Along the banks and behind boulders, even in mid-stream, we'll try brown or black rubberlegs and olive stoneflies. Streamers work nearly anytime of the season, mostly wooly buggers in a variety of colors—olive, black, brown, yellow, and orange. Occasionally I add what I use often in salt water in Florida—Clouser Minnows, especially chartreuse."

After an hour's drive we put in at Warm Springs, vying for room at the ramp with a half-dozen other drift boats. Cameron was standing by the water's edge, watching some clouds moving in from the southwest.

"The weather looks good, Cliff. Cloudy, but probably no rain. Not a wisp of wind. Kinda damp feeling. I like days like this. A lot of clients think the better the weather—meaning clear and bright sun—the better the fishing. Not in my experience."

The Warm Springs launch area had looked crowded when we arrived, but by the time we shoved off, only a couple of boats were in view on the river ahead of us, and the one launched after *Osprey* was more than fifty yards behind.

I checked Cameron's rod. His leader had a half-dozen wind knots, not caused by any wind but because his casts needed work, tighter loops without a tailing loop. He was likely dropping the rod tip near the end of his forward cast. I replaced his leader with a 9' 5X nylon leader I favored for floating Western rivers. A #8 brown rubberlegs was my best guess for the fly to start the day—it's an easy-to-tie stonefly imitation made up with little more than a medium brown chenille body and flexi-floss antenna, legs, and tail.

We floated thirty-five to forty feet off the east bank along the inside of a long bend. Cameron flubbed an easy cast when I suggested he drop the fly two feet off the bank. The cast was short, and he failed to mend the line upstream. The current was slightly slower by the bank, and the middle of the line moved faster than the fly. An upstream mend would have given more time before the fly dragged. My keeping the boat close to the pace of the current made possible a decent drift, but we needed to start the drift with the fly dropped in a better spot.

After Cameron had struggled with a dozen wobbly casts, not one followed by an attempted mend, I offered my first instruction of the day, which would tell me if Cameron was a listener and a learner.

"Cliff, can you do a reach cast?"

"Meaning?"

"Notice when you cast straight, if you try to mend *after* the fly lands, the little flip to one side that makes the mend pulls the line back. Your fly lands close to the bank and then your mend pulls it away. We want the fly to stay and drift closer to the bank."

"And a reach cast will help?"

"Yes. It's one of the best casts to use whether you're floating or wading and a mend is needed. Let me describe the reach cast. I want you to start a normal cast, and then when your rod is moving forward, about when you're beginning to lower the tip, move the rod upstream to the right."

He tried it and didn't move the tip in time. The fly landed on the bank and flopped back into the water.

"Try it again and be deliberate when you move the rod right for your mend."

Proving to be a good learner, after about ten casts, he tossed one that mended in the air after he moved the rod tip right and dropped the fly ten inches from the bank with a mend already in the line.

"That's a great cast. Practice it at home. Look online, for example, at 'reach casts.' You'll get a bunch of websites by casting instructors and fly shops. There are probably a dozen YouTube videos of reach casts that are yours for the asking."

"What should I work on?"

"Roll casts and reach casts for special purposes. But work mostly on the old standard cast so you have loops the way you want them and you're not doing what I call the wind knot cast, which is to good casting what a whitefish is to a native trout."

"I'll work on. . . . Got one!"

While talking, I had moved us out by a large boulder near the middle of the river, thinking there might be something on the downstream side. The rush of water from upstream was broken into two parts when it hit the rock, each part rushing past the rock and coming back to rejoin on the downstream side. But it didn't come back *hugging* the rock; the water was moving downstream and left a back eddy next to the rock, which meant a pool of comparatively quiet water, where trout rested and watched what came around the rock.

Cameron's fish had left the safety of the rock and taken the large rubberlegs. The trout had nowhere to go to hide and break off the fly—such as brush along a bank or a bridge piling.

From the flash when it came to the surface and rolled in some quiet water behind the rock, I was certain it was a rainbow. The fish was not pleased by the hook in its mouth attached to something foreign that pulled just enough to keep it from going where the reward was safety.

In five minutes I netted Cameron's first fish of the day, a color-laden 19" rainbow. Prolifically dark spotted on its silver skin, each fin, and the tail, the rainbow had tiny scales tinted blue and green along the back. But it was the solitary pink stripe along each side that identified the fish as a rainbow.

The barbless hook slid out quickly, and I held the fish carefully alongside the boat, facing its head upstream to let the current be carried through its mouth and gills. Within five seconds it jerked . . . and vanished. Humane handling after catching a trout on a barbless hook means the only harm to the fish is a temporary setback to its ego.

The rainbow was the first of a dozen fish the day produced. No hatch occurred, and we tried unsuccessfully to encourage rises by tossing dry flies. When we went back to the brown rubberlegs or to one in black or olive and concentrated on the edges and pools, the rainbows struck again, one after the other. Nothing larger than the first, mostly around 17". A small red Copper John drew a 14" brown from near the bottom two feet away from the bank, but that same fly set down nicely again and again in the same area further along the float produced not a single take.

Four miles in six hours does not excite an Olympic runner. That's an hour and a half per mile or a leisurely speed of two-thirds of a mile per hour. But we were not racing. My role was actually to slow us down, drop the speed from the current slightly to drift slower than the current and control the boat.

We stopped often, more than during a ten-mile float. Enticing locations for fish—behind boulders or under banks—were good places to anchor and get out and fish more intensively than when passing by in the boat.

Half the boats we launched with had disappeared downstream, either shortening their day on the water or pushing ahead for the long drift to Grey Cliff.

When we pulled to the bank at Black's Ford and cranked the boat onto the trailer, Cameron asked to sit for a few minutes and enjoy a beer. Our conversation changed from our fishing to small talk about "what do you do for a living?" and "do you have a family?" It was obvious what I did, at least dur-

ing the season, but I was curious about his work. He was intelligent, driven, and a little overbearing.

I opened the gate to exchanging information.

"Cliff. You fish well. Once we settled down, your casts
were fine. You judged distance and dropped flies where you
wanted. A drift boat is helpful. If I do my job, you don't need
to cast further than thirty-five to forty feet.

"What you need to work on are the nuances, reach casts,
pile casts, and gaining some distance. When we moved from
one shore and headed to a boulder in the middle, you had
trouble getting the fly near the boulder until we were within
forty-five to fifty feet. If you work on lengthening your cast so
you're comfortable casting seventy-five feet, you'll catch more
fish. . . . But like most clients I assume you have a job and can't
fish at will. You look to be mid-forties. Your tan suggests you
work outdoors. Doing what?"

"Chasing cows, Mac. I raise Angus cattle. Much of it goes
overseas."

"To where?"

"Canada, Mexico, mostly this hemisphere."

"Do you import any?"

"No. U.S. laws are pretty strict because of Bovine *spongi-
form encephalopathy.* You know it as mad cow disease or BSE. We
don't have any in Montana, and we don't want to start. Other
countries like our cattle because they're free of BSE. I was in
Cuba last month with two members of Congress from Montana and one other rancher from Wyoming."

"Cuba? Selling cows?"

"We signed a tentative agreement to sell 30,000 head, and
Cuba wants 70,000 more in the next year. It's a matter of Cuba
having hard currency to pay for them. We think we'll get approval soon for selling on credit. We want to get in on the mar-

ket before we open all trade with Cuba and every rancher will want some of the action. . . . You ever been to Cuba?"

I didn't want to answer. I certainly wasn't going to explain what happened two months ago. But I *could* admit to going to Cuba to fish.

"Yes, once," I said, not saying it was recent. "I went bonefishing."

"Bonefishing! Wouldn't I like to do that? We talked about it with our congressional folk, but they thought we ought to stick to business. . . . Where did you fish?"

"I was picked up in Havana and driven. I'm not sure where we went, the small town names go in one ear and out the other. But it proved to be nice water, flats amid some islands."

"Does the name Playa Larga sound familiar?"

"Larga? Playa Larga? I don't know; when we were along the beach area the name 'playa' seemed pretty common." Why would Cameron know about Playa Larga? I wondered.

"Macduff, how did you get permission to fish in Cuba? That's not one of the reasons the U.S. allows trips to Cuba."

"Don't ask. Actually, I have some friends in the Keys who belong to a church in Islamorada called St. Peter the Fisherman. They set up a church of the same name somewhere in Cuba. The two churches have exchange programs. If you want to fish in Cuba you pay $50 and become a member of the church. The pastor affirms that you're a member and off you go."

"That's great. Where is the church in Cuba?"

"I guess somewhere there's good fishing."

"That's a bit vague. . . . Does the name Nacho Gomez mean anything to you?"

"Who is he?" I asked. "Sounds Hispanic. Cuban?"

"He's a Cuban fishing guide in Playa Larga."

"Then he's one of dozens. Cuban fishing guides don't like their identity known because they make good money from tips. Probably twenty to fifty times what the state pays people, which means about $20 a month."

"Who was your guide?" Cameron asked.

"Cliff, I've been fishing with dozens of people whose last names I never got, and whose first names are long forgotten."

"Does the name Juan Mendoza mean anything to you?" he asked, changing the direction of his inquiry.

"Another Cuban fishing guide?" I responded.

"No," he responded, exasperated and giving a new edge to his voice. He was not pleased with my answers. "Juan Mendoza was a U.S. House of Representatives member from New Mexico. He went to Cuba a few months ago with a delegation of bleeding liberals who want to renew diplomatic relations with Cuba and open up trade. After their meetings he stayed on and went fishing. In the Zapata Reserve near Playa Larga. Nacho Gomez was Mendoza's guide. Mendoza's missing. You must have read about this?"

"In the *Livingston Weekly News*? Not likely."

"Damn, it was *in* the Billings paper."

"Billings is a lot larger than Livingston. The paper has more international news. When I'm guiding from sunrise to sunset, I don't get much time to read."

The drive back to Emigrant where Cameron had left his car was tense. Cameron leaned against his window, looking out and not saying much. But as we were in sight of the blinking light at Emigrant, he said, "I didn't mean to be hard on you."

Cameron wasn't merely *hard* on me. He scared the hell out of me.

24

THAT EVENING AT THE CABIN ON MILL CREEK

AFTER CAMERON LEFT, two other guides at Angler's West and I debated nymphs versus dry flies for a half an hour. It ended with an empty six pack of beer and no one budging from his initial views. I washed the boat across the way, picked up a few food items at the general store, and refilled the gas tank at a per gallon price that had jumped two cents for the second week in a row. If that persisted it would be a dollar per gallon rise every year!

Arriving at our cabin, I opened the SUV door and got out quietly, watching Lucinda completely absorbed in casting to a pool on Mill Creek. Wuff, purportedly our guard dog, was lying on her side facing the creek. Neither saw nor heard me coming—the rustling leaves on wind-blown trees and cascading water muffled my sounds.

The pool wasn't there when I built the cabin, but some judicious alterations of the largest river rocks I could move had created a haven for trout that one would never think had the hand of man in its evolution. During the spring run-off, the pool was especially productive as the oxygenated water raced down the creek to join the Yellowstone River. Trout were content to pause in that strenuous trip and idle in our pool.

By the time I walked within ten feet of Lucinda, she had hooked an 11" cutty with the signature red throat slash. I put my hand on her shoulder and she turned, jumped back, dropped her rod, landed on her rear, and yelled something she appropriately saved for special uses. The cutthroat easily slipped off the barbless hook before she could retrieve the rod and restore some line tension.

"Look what you've done!" she blurted, looking at me with restrained affection. "That was a beautiful fish!"

"At least you didn't lose the fly," I said, showing feigned relief. "I tied that Blue Wing Olive last evening for *me* to use today. No wonder I couldn't find it this morning. . . . I saw your fish. It *was* beautiful. But I was looking at something more beautiful."

"You're so sweet, Macduff. . . . I forgive you."

"Well, I really meant Wuff; the sun makes her coat sheen, her brown eyes entrancing."

"Macduff! Where do I fit in to your scheme?"

"Win, place, or show. Show isn't too bad."

"I need a dog that will attack you on command. Wuff just lies there, listening and watching, deciding who to side with."

"She's intelligent. She knows *I'm* about to get her dinner." After a pause and embrace, I asked, "Isn't this more fun than living in Manhattan like you did last year?"

"Don't ask. I was thinking about dining there."

"A couple of hot dogs at Nathan's?"

"Not again! I want dinner at Sardi's. Or somewhere else I could run up a big bill since you'd be treating me. Maybe taste some St. Emilion's $90- a-bottle *LaGaffeliere*. Of course, we'd need two bottles it's so good—such purity, such texture, such transparency. I can't wait."

"Enough! I'm sorry I scared you. But now you've scared me too. We're even."

After dinner we sat on the front porch, sharing a label-stained bottle of *Pinot Noir* from an Australian vineyard and aged four years beneath our cabin in the music room that Lucinda has been determined to convert to a wine cellar. We were entranced by the ebbing daylight unceasingly receding along the slopes of the Absarokas. It wasn't long before the night chill gathered around us and chased us inside.

Wine glasses in hand, before a small fire in the living room, I told Lucinda everything I could remember about my interrogation by Cliff Cameron.

"What do you make of his strange manner of questioning you, Macduff? It sounds aggressive; he had something in mind."

"I don't know what he was trying to achieve. I answered his questions in a way phrased to tell him nothing he might use to pry even more from me. And I never mentioned how we left Cuba. I'm glad our Cessna flight didn't make the papers or get much national TV coverage."

"What if you *had* told him you knew Nacho Gomez, that he was your guide for three days at Playa Larga, and that you had once guided Juan Mendoza here in Montana?"

"He would have wanted to know *why* I was at Playa Larga. Would I have gone there knowing about Mendoza? Did I have a choice where I went fishing? Obviously, I wouldn't have said a word about Francisco Sandoval's questions to us about the matching fingerprint issue."

"Cameron is worried about something," she declared. "He must think you're involved some way in U.S.-Cuban trade. He doesn't want anything to come between him and the Cuban government buying his cattle. . . . Why he would believe that a U.S. fishing guide could have any influence on U.S. trade is beyond me."

"He *does* want the trade boycott to continue. It was clear he disliked Mendoza for supporting ending the boycott, and he wouldn't be displeased to learn Mendoza was dead, if that's the case."

"I want to sleep on this, Macduff. Is Cameron capable of having killed Juan? Or Gomez? *Or you?* Maybe we ought to call Elena in the morning and see if there's anything new about her brother."

"If this gives you nightmares, don't wake me," I pleaded.

"If this gives me nightmares, I'll tuck myself under you. You promised to cherish me and take care of me," she whispered, grinning.

"I don't remember much about that ceremony. I recall that the day was rainy and gloomy. And I think you drugged me."

25

THE NEXT MORNING AT THE CABIN

LUCINDA DIDN'T SLEEP SOUNDLY, and her tossing and turning kept the bed squeaking and Wuff and me awake. All of our rest, relaxation, and engagement in normal daytime activities since our return from Cuba had become overwhelmed by troublesome dreams that included Minister of the Interior Christina Sandoval and her son Francisco, House members Juan and Elena Mendoza, fishing guide Nacho Gomez, and reliving our flight from Cuba in the old Cessna that had seen better days. But most of all we worried about Elsbeth.

My cell phone rang while Lucinda and I were at the small wooden table in what serves as our kitchen, having a third cup of high-altitude, shade-grown Antigua coffee. We downed the first two full voltage cups and turned to a mild decaf for the third. Lucinda had replaced her Beethoven's *Eroica* cell phone ring tone with Jimmy Buffett's *Havana Daydreamin'*. She was trying to tell me something about going back to Cuba.

"This is from a Connecticut area code," I said, looking placidly at the cell phone screen and smiling, but totally unaware who might be calling. "Maybe it's an old high school or college friend. More likely my university wanting a donation."

I turned on the phone's speaker and, still half-asleep, mumbled, "This is Macduff."

"It's Elena Mendoza. I'm calling from my Hartford office. Bad news from Cuba. Nacho Gomez is missing. It's as mysterious as Juan's disappearance."

"What happened?" I said loudly, now wide awake.

"About four days ago Gomez finished a guide trip in late afternoon. When he was back in Playa Larga, he stopped by the St. Peter the Fisherman church to ask about new fishing groups that might be coming from Florida and then, presumably, set out for home. His wife said he never arrived."

I wondered from whom Elena had gotten her information. "Are Cuban authorities investigating?"

"The manager of the Playa Larga hotel, Celia Bustamante, has helped us with the search for Juan since I can't do much from here in Connecticut. She said the police acted disinterested in any searching for Gomez. They accused him of fleeing Havana a couple of decades ago to avoid military service and assumed he was fleeing again, this time because he accepted but never reported hard currency tips from guiding. They suggested he'd probably turn up—using a different name—at some other fishing Xanadu, maybe on the northeast coast of the island. . . . Macduff, have you heard anything from your fishing friends in the Keys about Gomez?"

"I haven't talked recently to any guides who use the St. Peter the Fisherman churches in Islamorada and Playa Larga as a way to get licenses to fish in Cuba. As you know our trip ended traumatically, and we've avoided talking about it."

"Are you going to be in Montana for the next few months?" Elena asked.

"Until the first serious October snowfall sends us in flight across the country to Florida for the winter. I did a guide trip yesterday and have another the day after tomorrow. I'm spacing them so Lucinda and I can spend time together and because doing a float every day is getting to be too physically challenging."

"Let me change the subject," she decided. "Have you ever met someone named David Longstreet?"

"Do you mean the sole House member in D.C. from Montana?"

"That's him."

"I don't know him personally. I heard he visited Cuba with one of our senators and a couple of Montana and Wyoming ranchers. I believe Longstreet wants to end the trade boycott."

"Longstreet was *always* on TV," Elena continued, "speaking in favor of ending the trade boycott. Given any opportunity, he would speak at House sessions *against* keeping strict rules governing contact with Cuba. But Montana cattle rancher Cliff Cameron and some PAC largess may have convinced him to support the current restrictions. A big deposit from a Miami-based Super PAC was made in his name the day before he came back from Cuba. He did a complete flip-flop and began to *support* the restrictions now in place. . . . Another thing. Cameron is alleged to have promised Longstreet significant money for his next campaign."

"I guided Cliff Cameron yesterday—first time I've met him," I admitted.

"Rumors I hear in the House suggest that Cameron and Longstreet had a loud argument in the bar at their hotel in Cuba after they met with Cuban government trade officials. Cameron thought Longstreet pushed too much for a full opening of trade rather than limiting his support to the kind of contract Cameron signed to sell Cuba a lot of cattle. He is perfectly content with the boycott *if* it favors his own trade. Someone broke up their dispute and whispered to Longstreet. He suddenly changed his position. Now the two are in lock-step, both opposed to any change to our Cuban policy that currently allows limited trade. It's the motto of D.C.: Money talks."

"This is becoming too involved for me, Elena. You know more about what's going on in Cuba than I do. . . . I'm sorry I can't help."

"But I think you can. I want you to go back to Playa Larga," Elena pleaded.

"That doesn't make sense. I'm sure I'm wanted in Cuba. Lucinda as well for the way we left Cuba. We would be stopped at the Havana airport trying to enter Cuba, arrested, and taken to jail."

"I've done some investigating using contacts the CIA has in Havana," she replied. "One attractive female agent, purportedly an assistant economics officer at our Interests Section, but actually part of our CIA mission there, has dated Francisco Sandoval and picked up useful information about his mother's activities. There isn't *any* discussion or interest within the Cuban government in pursuing your dramatic exit. They're embarrassed about it. I loved seeing what little appeared about it on TV. I was surprised the coverage didn't show you or Lucinda."

"Cuba may not be pushing the issue because they can't reach us here. But if we went back, it would be a different case. Cuban prisons hold a number of Americans, some for months without a trial. Reports verify that the prisons are formidably unattractive places to reside. . . . *Please* don't ask us to go."

"I want you to think about it. We'll talk again in a couple of weeks."

"Elena, before you hang up, do you think you could arrange for me to meet with Representative Longstreet when he's here in Montana? He has an office in Bozeman. I could drive over to see him."

"I'll call him," she said. "I'm sure he'll meet with you. . . . Give Lucinda my best."

"Thanks," Lucinda called out, sitting at the end of the table, listening in on the conversation.

After Elena hung up, Lucinda and I sat quietly by the window, occasionally looking at each other without a word being spoken. A silent communication between us was confused by patriotism for the U.S., fondness for Cuba, concern for our own lives and that of Elsbeth, and a reconciliation to the fact that, try as we may, we two were somehow destined to become involved in trouble no matter where we went.

"Mac," she said softly, taking my hands in hers and not sure she wanted to speak and start something she couldn't hope to finish. But she leaned over and put her head against mine, and whispered, "Macduff, do we *have* to become involved?"

"I can't answer that with a clear 'no' because we don't know what hold our government has on us. Dan Wilson we know about, but where does Elena fit in? Is she any different than Juan. If *she* flip-flopped on Cuba or lied about Francisco Sandoval, it could be hard for us."

"There's no way she'll change her position," Lucinda guessed. . . . "Do you suppose she's working with Dan's office?"

165

"She must be having discussions with him. How else would he have helped us get out of Cuba? . . . Do you think I should call him?" I asked.

"Why not? Ask him outright what's going on between his office, our Interests Section in Havana, and Elena's and Juan's offices. And whether *Longstreet* is in any way involved."

"There's one more matter I have to tell you. I promised Elsbeth I wouldn't, but matters have changed with Nacho Gomez's death."

"What's that?"

"Elsbeth and her housemate Sue are going to Cuba in August on a ten-day student exchange UF has with the University of Santa Clara."

"Where's Santa Clara?"

"Not far from Playa Larga!"

26

CONVERSATION WITH DAN WILSON A WEEK LATER

D AN WILSON WASN'T ANSWERING QUESTIONS. He must have known details he wasn't sharing about both Juan Mendoza's and Nacho Gomez's disappearances. If we were to do anything more for Dan or Elena—especially agree with her that I alone or Lucinda and I both would return to Cuba— Dan had to tell us more than what he had shared to date. The best way to start seemed a simple phone call. But phone calls with Dan had proven more complex as the minutes unfolded. It was worth a try to call. But breakfast first.

Lucinda and I felt trapped inside our cabin, trying to see out of the large windows facing Mill Creek. Raindrops were splashing sideways against the windows despite the porch overhang. The fierce wind had given the rain a horizontal path we had never before experienced at the cabin.

Considering the run-off generated by the melting of an excessive snow pack this year, more water from rainstorms was unwelcome. Homeowners along the Yellowstone River were piling sandbags next to their houses, and some were evacuating as water crept higher each day by inches and was beginning to spread over the banks and threaten some dangerously sited luxury homes.

At first I was pleased that Lucinda finally was seeing *my way* preparing our breakfast. She served bacon and eggs. But I should have known better. The bacon didn't look like bacon and tasted strange. The eggs didn't look like eggs and tasted worse than the bacon. I looked at the wrappings left on the counter, which she should have hidden in the trash.

The eggs were not real, and the bacon was from the wrong animal. The eggs were called BeatenEggs and allegedly had been tested on laboratory rats. According to studies only half the rats that consumed BeatenEggs died. My impression was that rats eat most anything and survive. Those given real eggs grew fat and content.

As for the bacon, it came from a turkey. The label said that the turkey had been "mechanically-separated" into tiny parts too small to identify and then reshaped. The result looked like strips that were passed off as bacon.

"Lucinda," I asked, having finished choking on a bite of the egg, "did you order these bacon slices and eggs on eBay?"

"I was in a hurry, Macduff. Our local grocery store was out of low-fat hickory smoked bacon and free range eggs. I bought what was available. I assumed you'd eat anything that was labeled bacon and eggs. Your discerning response is surprising. Actually, you're not supposed to read labels on my food purchases."

"I thought I saw a black skull and crossed bones on the BeatenEggs container. I couldn't find any reference to eggs on the ingredients. I like turkey, but not when it's ground up particles masquerading as some other animal. At least you could serve bison bacon. . . . Why don't you call Dan while I clean up and make some oatmeal? Out of *real* oats. I'll listen in to your conversation with Dan."

Dan was having coffee in the CIA senior-staff lounge. He was debating the use of drones in Yemen to take out terrorists, whether or not they were U.S. citizens. He welcomed a diversion.

"What kind of trouble are you two calling about now?"

"I'm going to call Elena in her office at the House as soon as you and I are through. She wants me—and Lucinda—to go back to Cuba and search some more for Juan. Also to see what we can learn about the disappearance of Nacho Gomez. He guided for both Juan and me."

"It's your decision, Mac. How much support I can provide this time depends on how much trouble you stir up in Cuba. The Cessna's not available for another rescue. The pilot was transferred to the Naval Air Station at Ford Island in Hawaii."

"Are you working directly with Elena on Juan's case?" I asked.

"Well . . . yeah . . . sort of," Dan admitted.

"You're no help. I'll talk to you when Lucinda and I have made up our minds."

"Wait a moment. Give me *your* take on going back to Cuba. Do you two *want* to go?"

"First," I explained, "I'm not sure we'd have any luck getting new information, in view of how the locals in Playa Larga have clammed up and the cover-up by the Cuban police. They haven't done any investigation they want to talk about. Second, I suspect the Cubans have us on their watch list, in case we try to go back. They might block our entry by not issuing visas. Or give us visas and arrest us on arrival at the Havana airport. Or later, especially if we went to Playa Larga."

"We can get you and Lucinda diplomatic passports," Dan offered.

"What good would they do?"

"If you're arrested they have to release you. All they can do is send you back to the U.S."

"If they don't release us, what happens? You send gunboats into Havana harbor?"

"Don't I wish. . . . At most, we would expel some of their diplomats from the U.S."

"And then they do the same. A standoff. . . . I prefer staying right here. Lucinda's nodding agreement. Another question, Dan. What is Elena's reputation in D.C.?"

"She's known to be one of the few representatives who makes no promises she can't keep," Dan added. "And if she's made a decision, it's been well researched and won't be reversed by her being offered PAC or other donations."

"Does she have a family?"

"Yes. Her husband is an orthopedic surgeon. His name is Robert Macintosh. Obviously not Hispanic; his grandparents came from Scotland. Elena uses her maiden name. They have two kids, early teens."

"What are your thoughts about her views on Cuba?"

"She wants a different Cuba than currently exists. But she doesn't share with the early exiles the view that the Castro brothers have to be gone, communism or socialism rejected, or expropriation claims paid and properties returned. Her family lost property when Castro took over and her grandparents and parents fled. But she never has said she would try to reclaim their former properties. All she would like is to be able to buy a small house in the countryside or a condo in Havana to use for vacations or visits to relatives she's never met.

"Elena has talked publically and consistently about accepting a Cuba that's like Vietnam, where the government remains mostly communist, but there is a large private sector, and the government stays out of business. . . . That all means she's not popular in Miami among the early exiles."

"Dan, is there anything you can tell me about how much help Lucinda and I might receive from our Interests Section in Havana? We were impressed with the way Celeste Jones helped us get out. But I've heard she's due to be transferred."

"We think she's about to become Public Affairs Officer at our Paris embassy. A significant move for her. . . . Obviously, the Interests Section in Havana changes its focus with each new U.S. President. The Section exercises considerable discretion. So much so it sometimes seems contrary to the U.S. President's publically stated position.

"Our President can't only deal with *Cuban* officials; he has to meet with the South Florida group and increasingly with isolated individuals who have a stake in Cuba, such as the rancher you met in Montana. Plus, he doesn't control those members of Congress beholden to a PAC group that focuses on Cuba. The PAC passes out a lot of money around election time."

"How influential is the South Florida congressional delegation?" I asked.

"It's increasingly less powerful mainly because of the death of early exiles who once ran successful businesses in Cuba and usually had other assets, such as houses and bank accounts. Some of their offspring take the same rigid view about restoring Cuba to its 1950's glory, but many were young when they left Cuba or were born in the U.S., and they don't have the memories of Castro entering Havana and within a year and a half confiscating nearly all private property."

"What about Cameron and Longstreet. Do you worry about what they might do?"

"A little. Cameron is happy with the status quo because he has his foot in the door and permission to sell cattle. He doesn't give a damn about the Cuban people. If trade opens more, he knows how to compete when he has no other choice. The way he works means greasing some palms in Havana. That can be risky."

"And Longstreet?" I asked.

"I've checked up on Longstreet," Dan said. "He's totally untrustworthy. He'd sell his mother for a vote. If our Cuban policy changes—and he's a small cog in the wheel that makes that policy—he'll change with it. He's flip-flopped once and will have no qualms about doing it again, if it means remaining in office."

"That helps. I'm going to meet Longstreet in Bozeman in a couple of days. It should be interesting."

"Keep your backside to the wall."

27

THREE DAYS LATER IN BOZEMAN

DAVID LONGSTREET WAS WAITING FOR ME in his office in a restored 1920's brick building on Main Street in Bozeman. For years the building was a women's clothing store with large glass windows that displayed antique wooden mannequins wearing the latest New York fashions. Now the same windows displayed Representative Longstreet live and in person when he was in town to raise funds to stay in office. He was sitting at his desk facing the window and sidewalk when I walked up to his building, trying to look engrossed in issues of national importance.

I was five minutes early for our meeting. His secretary kept me waiting a half hour before she even told him I had arrived. He kept me waiting another forty minutes before his voice came over the speaker phone on his secretary's desk.

"If he's still here, send him in."

The secretary looked at me, mistrusting, and pointed at Longstreet's door. She didn't say a word or get up.

I walked into his office. The walls were lined with photos of him standing with people I assumed he concluded were important. I didn't recognize even one face. A few were autographed with comments like "to a swell guy," but most were not even signed. There also were some framed certificates on the wall, fading photocopies of the real ones that were likely in his Washington office, where more important people than a Montana fishing guide entered.

Longstreet didn't stand or even look at me and waved toward a chair in front of his desk as he turned his back and put a file in a drawer.

"I know you, Brooks. But only about your past decade, from the time when you arrived in Montana. You've been in a lot of trouble here and in Wyoming. Like murders on your boat. Where were you before you drifted into Bozeman?"

That wasn't anything I wanted to discuss. "Various jobs back East."

"College?"

"University. Followed by a marriage that ended; I don't talk about those years. And that's not why I'm here."

"You're here because I was willing to see you."

"I *am* one of your constituents."

"So, what do you want?"

"Your colleague in the House, Elena Mendoza, and her brother Juan, were fishing clients of mine on the Yellowstone a few years ago. I've read about his disappearance in Cuba and last week the disappearance of his fly fishing guide."

"That doesn't affect me," he said, turning his chair and looking out the window. "What's your reason to want to see me?"

"You know Cliff Cameron."

"I do. A fine man. One of my supporters."

"I fished with Cameron about ten days ago, floating the Madison. We talked about his trip to Cuba with you and the contract he signed to sell cattle to Cuba. When you returned from Cuba, you abruptly reversed your position on Cuba. Before, you were in favor of removing all trade barriers between the two countries. But a few days after you returned from Cuba, you announced that you now favored retention of the current restrictions. Why?"

"I'm not here to be interrogated, Brooks."

"As one of your constituents, I would assume you answer questions and explain your position on important matters."

"If it's any of your business, I was convinced while in Cuba that we shouldn't give in to any of their demands, including granting them credit to buy U.S. goods. I don't want to stop trade in food or medicines, but I don't want to reverse the ban on travel and other trade."

"The record shows you received a sizeable donation from Cameron and several from a Miami-based PAC. Did those donations cause you to flip-flop?"

"*Flip-flop!* Enough of your outrageous accusations. Get out of here. I don't need your vote. You're a goddam scumbag guide. A know-nothing and a do-nothing. Wasting your life fishing. You're a joke, Brooks. Don't give me any trouble, or you'll regret it."

"I think you may regret your position regarding Cuba when the Russians resume their domination in Cuba."

"You don't know what the hell you're talking about. How are the damn Russians going to restore their power and influence in Cuba?"

"They're trying to take back the Ukraine, and next it may be the Baltic states. Russia is determined to restore what they can of the Soviet Union. There's a rumor in Florida that Russia has offered oil to Cuba to replace the curtailment of oil from Venezuela. Cuba will send Russia medical personnel to work in rural areas. And the two countries will restore full trade.

"Russia plans to re-staff their embassy in Havana with the numbers they had in the 1980's, making it the largest embassy of any foreign nation that has diplomatic relations with Cuba. Plus, Russia will restore at least the 7,000 troops that were once in Cuba. Right now there are several thousand Russians living permanently in Cuba. Many because of marriage to a Cuban. Aeroflot still flies between Havana and Moscow.

"Remember that Russia loaned nearly $65 billion to Cuba over a thirty-year period. Apparently, the Russians are prepared to provide more loans in exchange for again controlling Cuba. What happens when Russia has missiles in Cuba, this time armed and pointed toward us?"

"You're paranoid, Brooks. Anyway, Montana's not a target. It's the East Coast that the Russians would target. Florida and D.C."

"If you *read* the papers, you wouldn't be surprised by all this. . . . I know you have a couple of brothers and sisters who live in D.C. with their families. You don't care about them?"

Longstreet got up from his chair, swearing and waving his arms uncontrollably. He came around the desk and stood face-to-face with me. Within five minutes a dozen people standing outside were watching their representative through the large window, pointing at him, and laughing.

I smiled, nodded, waved back at them, and left.

28

BACK AT THE MILL CREEK CABIN

WHEN I ARRIVED AT OUR CABIN after my summit meeting with Longstreet, Lucinda was watering some plants on the front porch. She watched me walk toward the cabin, put on her serious face, and asked, "What happened? You look awful. Did you meet with our beloved representative?"

"I did. I never should have gone. It didn't go well."

"Tell me," she asked quietly.

"He's of no use to us or to Elena. He's indebted to Cliff Cameron and in the pockets of a PAC in Florida. The only issue of importance to him is re-election. Let's forget about him."

"What did you two say to each other?" We sat on the steps in the shade of some pines, and I tried to relate our conversation.

"Macduff, isn't his role separate from our problems relating to Cuba. Longstreet has no real interest in Cuba or playing any part in developing U.S. policy toward Cuba. His only apparent concern is being re-elected. He's of no importance to whether we go to Cuba again."

"As usual, you're right. We won't affect his re-election plans. I don't plan to speak with him again. Nor with Cameron. The people we need to be concerned with are Senator García García, Minister Sandoval, and her son Francisco. Also Cubans in Havana who share Minister Sandoval's opinions, and some of the early exiles in Miami."

"Shouldn't we be worried mostly about the Miami exile group?" she asked. "They have political influence at both the state and federal levels. That doesn't include their extensive power within South Florida where their focus is so concentrated. We have more to worry about in Miami than in Havana."

"Agreed," I responded. "But what about our going to Cuba again?"

"It's mid-June. Elsbeth and Sue have to sign up by next week if they're still intending to go to Cuba. I'm sure they are. I'd like us to make *our* decision before they go. . . . I can't understand why you'd agree to have Elsbeth go. She's your *daughter*. Remember that there are *two* disappearances that increasingly appear to have been deaths and possibly murders."

"I want to talk to Elsbeth about her plans. She's a very mature young woman. Dial her on your phone, and we'll both listen. It's two hours later where she's working in the Keys, but it's early enough to call."

Elsbeth answered. She was in her room at the resort, reading a book recommended to entering UF students; Sue was working the evening shift on the front desk.

"Hi, guys, how are things in Montana? Still married?"

"Wait a minute," I said. "I'll ask Lucinda."

"I'll answer directly, Elsbeth. In ninety-seven days we'll celebrate our 'paper' anniversary. I'm giving him something paper. And it's not a divorce petition. He's stuck with me."

"What are you giving Lucinda, Dad?"

"It's a surprise."

"You're saying that because you've forgotten your first anniversary!"

"Something like that. . . . I have to put that behind me and move on. Don't get me in trouble." I felt the kick coming.

"We need to talk to you about your plans for Cuba. Still going?" Lucinda asked.

"Yes. We have to pay a deposit soon."

"Do you have a passport?" I inquired.

"I hadn't thought about that. But I have a passport because the Carsons took me to Canada twice."

"Then the name on the passport is Elsbeth Carson?"

"It is! Of course! I need to get a new one."

"Hold off. You are still Elsbeth *Carson* according to your passport."

"But I'm Elsbeth Hunt by birth. I'm the daughter of a married couple, Maxwell and Elsbeth Hunt."

"But you weren't born until after your mother died."

"That doesn't affect my being your daughter and being a 'Hunt.'"

"It doesn't. But we've never changed your driver's license, passport, or any other identification. Haven't you been checked, such as when you registered at UF?"

"No one asked for identification. They will when I get a new driver's license or passport or register to vote. Should we try to do that now?"

"No. If you go to Cuba, I want you to go as Elsbeth *Carson*. Whatever you do, don't use 'Brooks' in Cuba."

"I think I may keep the Carson name," she said. "It was a quiet, peaceful life."

29

ELSBETH AND SUE IN CUBA

E LSBETH AND SUE completed their summer jobs and stayed in Miami with a friend from UF the night before they flew to Cuba. Along with ten other UF students, they met at the Miami airport in the morning for a charter flight from Miami directly to Santa Clara's Abel Santamaría Airport.

Both airports processed the group without incident. Elsbeth entered as Elsbeth Carson. She hoped she had left anything bearing the name "Brooks" in her jeep at the Miami Airport.

The two inseparable friends spent much of their time at the Cuban university, formally the Universidad Central Marta Abreu de Las Villas, the third largest in the country and, along with Havana's university, the most highly respected. Many faculty and students spoke English. That hadn't been the case for long. Studying Russian had been *required* until the Soviet Union came apart and Russia lost its interest in supporting Cuba. English quickly became the foreign language of choice. That could change again if the rumors were true that Russia wanted to "reclaim" its position as Cuba's best friend.

Elsbeth and Sue found Santa Clara an ideal town for walking. Streets around the central Parque Vidal were reserved for pedestrians. A five-block pedestrian only shopping mall had shops and restaurants. But it served only tourists and those few locals with hard currency to spend. The two discovered a few restaurants when they felt a need to get away from the University's institutional food, which they ranked far below that both at UF and their year at the University of Maine. They had brought enough hard currency to have some meals at the Hostal Florida, where they ate their fill of seafood and chicken. Occasionally they invited a fellow student from the university to join them.

Neither Elsbeth nor Sue was inclined to spend much time in bars, but on a few nights they joined other students at the Bar La Marquesina, which often had local musicians playing Cuban music they both had come to love.

Only one incident caused them concern, and it was their own making—this time Sue's tendency to ask "why" questions about sensitive subjects. They had been taken on a tour of the town's main attraction, the Monumento Ernesto Che Guevara, where his huge statute overlooks the plaza. Sue didn't realize that the place was revered by many locals, including students at the university. Behind the mausoleum that held Guevara's remains were tombstones with the remains of thirty-seven of his comrades who died with him in Bolivia. Beyond that was a new cemetery that had more of Guevara's 8th column that fought with him in the Sierra Maestra Mountains. Gravestones were erected for all who fought, whether or not they had yet died. One's location in the cemetery was reserved.

When the group's guide asked if there were any questions, Sue raised her hand and asked, "We've seen T-shirts with Che's face all over the town. Isn't it strange that he fought to help the poor and oppressed in Bolivia and lost the fight, and now his face is being printed on thousands of T-shirts made by the poor and oppressed in Asia?"

"Sue, you shouldn't ask that," whispered Elsbeth, tugging on Sue's shirt to pull her away. "I can't believe you said that! We may see a firing squad in the morning."

That night at a party one of the Santa Clara students raised his Hatuey beer and said, "To Sue, who one tour guide in our fair city would like to see buried and not in the plaza with Ernesto." The student was wearing a gray T-shirt with "VIVA LA REVOLUCION!" in large, mostly black lettering, across the front. But the second through fifth letters of "**R**EVOLU-CION" were in red written as backward mirrored letters. They spelled "LOVE!"

The morning after their farewell party for the university part of the visit, the U.S. group piled onto a small bus and was off to visit some other places in Central Cuba. The students hadn't made it to bed until three and hoped they might someday again see their new friends. Maybe even share a beer in Gainesville.

As their bus pulled away from the dorm, Elsbeth and Sue saw that at least thirty students had come to wave them off. Each wore the same T-shirt as the one student had the night before."

"Sue turned to Elsbeth and asked. "I wonder if *those* T-shirts were made in Asia?"

"More likely in Miami," Elsbeth replied.

30

ELSBETH AND SUE RETURN TO FLORIDA FOR THE FALL

THE PHONE, WEDGED AMONG A PILE OF BOOKS
on the table next to our bed in Montana, woke me at 6:00
a.m. I didn't believe the clock, and I wasn't ready to get up, but
Wuff already was standing over me, breathing heavily and
prodding me with two paws to remind me she was ready for
prompt breakfast service. I wondered if she somehow had arranged for the phone call. With my phone in one hand and
Wuff's food bowl in the other, I padded around the kitchen.

"Buenas días, Padre," the voice on the phone said.

"Elsbeth," I mumbled, "you know I want to hear about
Cuba, but maybe not when I'm half asleep."

"Oh, Dad, I forgot there's a two-hour time difference."

"That's right; the sun has not yet arrived here in Montana.
It's pitch black on Mill Creek. Everything around here is
dormant—except me. Where are you?"

"On I-95 somewhere around West Palm Beach. Sue and I
got an early start from Miami. We crashed last night on the
floor of the Coconut Grove house of a UF friend because our
plane from Cuba landed after midnight."

"Plane trouble?"

"You got it! We had problems in Santa Clara. Our charter plane apparently was as bad mechanically as it was in appearance. Flaking paint, mismatched and torn seats, and two bathrooms that weren't functioning. The plane was an Aeroflot left behind by the Russians in the 1980's.

"Thank God the flight was only forty-five minutes, but it came after a six-hour delay on the ground. It's *not* pleasant to sit on a runway in summer heat and humidity in the middle of Cuba. We were soaked with sweat when we finally lifted off. But we're back in the Sunshine State, safe and sound."

"Now that I'm awake, give me a short version of your trip. Lucinda and I will hear the full tale when she's up and functioning, which may not be soon."

Elsbeth told me about the first six days they spent in Santa Clara, but not the last three. I thought she would be in Santa Clara the whole time and hoped the three final days were not in Havana. In any event, she was back in the U.S. and safe, to the extent that's possible driving on I-95 in South Florida.

Lucinda and I waited impatiently that evening for another call from Elsbeth to hear about the last three days in Cuba. She held off until we were getting ready for bed.

"Hi, you two. Sue and I are in Gainesville, settled in our Golf View house. Classes begin in three days. This is our first fall here. Football fever has hit the campus, but it's not our sport—it was never very significant for me growing up in Greenville, Maine. We're going to a UF women's soccer game tonight, season opener against Stetson. . . . What's up with you guys?"

"Your dad's guiding about every other day. He's set a record this summer—thirty-eight guide trips and no deaths on board *Osprey* or even nearby."

"Great, Dad! Sounds like a dull summer. Just what you need. . . . When will you two come east?"

"We'll stay here another six weeks, until early October. We like to fish together in late September. Toss hoppers along the banks of streams here and in Yellowstone Park's Firehole River. Plus, Lucinda's got some work to do."

"What are you photographing, Lucinda? Nude fly fishing guides for a calendar? Or are they all too old with wrinkled, sun-burnt skin and scars from fish hooks? If so, Dad should be on the cover."

"I'll talk to people at Trout Unlimited," she answered. "They do an annual calendar. They may like your idea."

"Come on, you two," I pleaded. "I want to hear about your last three days *in Cuba*."

"I'm not sure you do," interjected Sue.

"Did you two get into trouble?' I asked.

"Not that anyone knows about—we think," added Sue.

"Tell us," Lucinda said.

"OK. We had a real treat for the last three days," Elsbeth began. "It was a cultural and environmental tour. First, they drove us to Trinidad, a UNESCO World Heritage Site. What surprised us was the restoration being done in the city, thanks to funding that increased tourism has brought. We had lunch on the porch of an old hacienda at the nearby Valley of the Sugar Mills, where a group of old men—even older than you, Dad—were serenading us with Cuban love songs."

"And?" I asked.

"The next day we were driven along the coast to Cienfuegos. Both Cienfuegos and Trinidad seemed better restored than what you two told me about Havana. . . . By the time we finished in Cienfuegos, we were a little tired of seeing old forts and churches.

"The third and final day we stayed overnight where you won't believe—Playa Larga. We were there to see the Zapata Reserve, a huge preserved wetlands."

"I don't believe you," I said. "Tell me you're kidding."

"Will you believe me if I describe the Hotel Playa Larga, where we stayed, and the nice manager we met, Señora Busta-man. . . ?"

"OK, I believe you," I interrupted. "Did anyone know you're related to me?"

"Of course not, Dad. I'm not *that* stupid. . . . That doesn't sound right, but you know what I mean. Señora Bustamante came into the restaurant as we were starting lunch, introduced herself, welcomed us, and joined us for our meal. She sat between Sue and me! Remember I was Elsbeth *Carson*, not Brooks."

"I don't think I want to hear any more," I said, quietly.

"How long were you at Playa Larga?" Lucinda asked, worried I was on the verge of a stroke."

"Only one day. We got there, had lunch, and then were taken to the Zapata Reserve, about forty-five minutes to a little hamlet called Salinas."

I felt weak. If Cuban officials knew who she was, by now she could have been the third person to disappear.

"What did you talk about with Señora Bustamante at lunch?" Lucinda asked.

'She asked a lot of questions about our trip and how we liked Cuba. She asked me where I was from. I told her St. Augustine and that Sue and I were at UF. Oddly, she wanted to know whether I fly fished. I told her a little, but that my dad fished a lot, mostly in Montana and Wyoming. She was really interested in my name—she said Elsbeth was very unusual."

But not to Bustamante, I thought. I had told her when I was first in Playa Larga that my wife Lucinda would join me in two days, and that I had left a daughter in Florida. I'm sure I mentioned that her name was Elsbeth! Whatever Bustamante thought, she apparently didn't talk to government officials; Elsbeth left to come home with the group the following day.

"What else did you do at Playa Larga?" I asked, worried about her answer.

"Sue and I walked around the town . . . and visited the barracuda research center."

"You can't get onto the grounds. Weren't you stopped?"

"Yes, by one man, while we were walking down the entrance road."

"Didn't he throw you out."

"Two gorgeous college girls? Not a chance. He invited us in to see the barracudas! The pens were fascinating! Sue and I have agreed we may never go into the ocean again."

"Well . . . at least you made it home. Please don't tell me you're going to Guatemala for Christmas break."

"Nope. Sue and I are freeloading on you two at the cottage until Christmas day, when we fly to Jackson to stay with her parents through New Year's. . . . But there's more about Playa Larga."

"Do we really want to hear it?" asked Lucinda, turning her head toward me.

"You may be sorry you let us tell you," said Elsbeth. "The man at the barracuda center took us into the main building. It was very small, neat, and immaculate. He excused himself to make coffee and went down a hall and into a kitchen. . . . Sue had been looking into his office off the main room. She saw something that frightened her. You tell them about it, Sue."

"Hi, you two," exclaimed Sue. "If you're to blame anyone for all this, I'm at fault, not Elsbeth."

"Are you two good influences on each other?" Lucinda asked.

"Absolutely!" Sue replied. "Wait 'til you hear what happened next. I want you to open Lucinda's phone and look for pictures I just sent to you. . . . Mr. Brooks, do you remember telling us about the facial appearances of Juan Mendoza and Nacho Gomez?"

"Remind me."

"You said Mendoza had unusual teeth, gold crowns on almost all of them. Only the front four top and bottom were not capped, and the upper right was a porcelain cap resulting from a baseball breaking the tooth during college."

"I remember."

"You also said that a few years ago Gomez was in a terrible auto accident, suffered brain damage, and had a steel plate on the left side of his head."

"I remember that, too. What are you trying to tell us, Sue?"

"What bothered me when I looked into the barracuda center's office room were two things on the floor in a corner. I've sent you a photo of them. Do you have it?"

"I'm afraid I do," said Lucinda. Her face was ashen, and her hands holding the phone were trembling. She suddenly got up, dropped the phone, and ran to the bathroom.

I picked up the phone and looked at the pictures of two human skulls. One had a small steel plate in the skull on the left side; the other had gold crowns on all but four of the teeth, and one of the four front teeth was merely a stub.

"Unless I'm terribly mistaken," I said quietly to Lucinda, "they were the skulls of Juan Mendoza and Nacho Gomez."

31

THE FOLLOWING MONTH AT MILL CREEK

THE FACT THAT ELSBETH AND SUE found the skulls was traumatic for all of us. Less so but of concern were Playa Larga hotel manager Bustamante's questions to Elsbeth. It's not clear if her believing that Elsbeth *might* be my daughter affects our thoughts on traveling back to Cuba.

We didn't immediately call Elena and tell her we had seen a photo of what might be her brother's skull. And we didn't immediately call Dan and tell him about Elsbeth's and Sue's trip to Cuba and photographing the skulls.

We kept our doors bolted—which Lucinda commented was like living in her apartment in Manhattan—and went down to the music room and started a computer search for anything that might have happened recently in Playa Larga. It seemed to us that the employee at the barracuda center never knew that Elsbeth and Sue saw the skulls and, more importantly, never saw Sue take photos of them with her cell phone.

The next morning I guided a client on the Yellowstone River from Carter's Bridge to Livingston. The fish were taking small dry flies, but often my attention was elsewhere.

Several days later, when I was awakened at 6:00 a.m. by the wet nose of a hungry Sheltie, fed her, made a cup of coffee, and began to outline my day, my focus shifted from guiding to wondering how to tell Elena that her brother Juan was almost certainly a murder victim. I preferred not to tell her that his bleached-white skull was resting on the floor in the corner of an office of the barracuda research center in Playa Larga.

I also owed Dan a call. Lucinda and I used every reason possible to delay those conversations.

When I returned from a float that afternoon, I could hold off calling no longer. A few minutes before five, Lucinda poured a Gentleman Jack and put it in my left hand and dialed Dan on my cell phone and put it in my right. When he answered, I struggled to tell him word-by-word everything Elsbeth and Sue had told us.

"Have you been drinking, Mac? Bleached-white skulls on the floor of an office? What do I do with *that* information?"

"I haven't been drinking, but I'm starting now," I said, taking a sip. "The photos are at this very moment somewhere on their way to you."

"I have them in front of me. Damn! I was about to call it a day and go home. What the hell do I do with the photos? Have you sent them to the U.S. Interests Section in Havana?"

"I wouldn't do that. It's your decision."

"I appreciate that, but it doesn't often seem to happen that way. I'll take care of the Interests Section. We have some of our agents there, posing as various embassy staff."

"I'll call Elena when you and I are through, Dan. She has a right to know."

"Maybe you should tell her you know Juan was killed, but not how and not about the skull."

"I know she's going to press me about going back to find out about 'how' and 'by who' and 'why.' The moment she learns I'm labeling his disappearance a prelude to a murder, she'll insist that I at least find out how he died, if not who did it. . . . I'm *not* a private eye."

"Call her and see what she wants. Don't make any promises. Then get back to me."

I called Elena and wanted to hang up when she hadn't answered by the third ring, but I held on. Thankfully, she was not there and her "leave a message" speech came on. I hung up without saying a word, giving me time to think more about how I was going to answer some predictable questions. But I couldn't delay the discussion forever; Elena phoned an hour later.

"Thanks for trying to get me, Mac. Something new about Juan?"

"Juan is almost certainly dead."

"How do you know?" she gasped.

"Word from Cuba, specifically from Playa Larga."

"From who?"

"Don't know. Some evidence but nothing absolute. . . . The sources are not clear."

"What's been found? His body? Some remains? Any photographs? Or a letter or phone call?"

"Some remains. . . . The only thing we know is that the dead person had all but four teeth gold capped, and one of the front four was a stub where a cap had broken off. It sounds like Juan's dental work."

"Where are his remains? Has an autopsy been made?"

"I don't know. Elena, a photograph was taken in Cuba showing part of a skeleton. That's all we can say."

"All the more reason for you to go back."

"You know that Lucinda and I may be wanted in Cuba because we left without proper exiting; the fingerprint issue Francisco Sandoval raised can't have been resolved any way other than that they match."

"But they can't match?"

"Yes, they can. I won't say anything more about it."

"You have to go back, Mac. You *promised.*"

"I agreed to go to Cuba, Elena. I went. . . . I didn't agree to anything more and clearly not to solve a murder."

32

A MEETING AT A MIAMI HOTEL

HOW MANY CLANDESTINE MEETINGS of persons intending to do wrong are held in Miami hotel rooms each year will never be known, but it must be far more than even my vivid imagination might guess. It is a city of suspicion and imagination that gave us the movie *Scarface*, with Al Pacino efficiently adapting a chainsaw for use indoors in a shower.

One such meeting was beginning in an elegant suite at the Brickell Avenue Four Seasons.

The tension inside the cool suite—twenty stories high overlooking blue-green Biscayne Bay—was as stifling as the ninety-eight percent humidity outside.

Three people sat attentively in stuffed easy chairs covered with expensive fabrics in subdued colors unusual in exotic Miami. U.S. Senator from Florida, Jorge García García, wore a white linen Guayaberra and sipped on a mojito made from Havana Club rum. Not that produced by the U.S. Bacardi company in Puerto Rico and sold only in the U.S., but that made in Cuba and not sold in the U.S. García García also held a Cohiba cigar brought from Cuba that he prepared carefully by removing the label, slicing off the end with a double-bladed cutter without tearing the wrapper, lighting it with a special cigar lighter, and drawing the smoke in without inhaling while rotating the cigar for an even burn. García García enjoyed a good cigar as much as Winston Churchill or Red Auerbach did, and he didn't want his colleagues to think he was an amateur at the art of smoking arguably the finest cigar in the world.

The rum and cigars had been a gift of the second of the three present, Cuba's Minister of the Interior, Christina Sandoval, who this trip had entered the U.S. using her maiden name Christina Gutierrez and carrying no diplomatic passport. She sat on the left side of García García, wearing an exquisite silk dress she had bought last fall on a government-paid trip to Rome. She was drinking Dalmore 50 Year Old single malt.

Tall and aristocratic, the third person in the room was two decades younger than García García's seventy some years. He was Alfredo Luna, son of an immigrant named Alfredo de Luna from Zaragosa in Aragon, Spain, who, when he came to the U.S., had dropped the "de" preceding "Luna" to make the name sound less foreign. As the Hispanic population of the U.S. rapidly increased, his son Alfredo thought of resuming the use of "de Luna."

Luna wore a conservative Armani suit and held neither a drink nor a cigar, befitting the serious image he like to convey as the one who owned and presided over the largest sugar dynasty in the U.S. He made the poorer end of the Forbes 400 list of the richest Americans, his wealth estimated at only $2 billion and exceeded significantly by some forty other persons with at least $10 billion. But no one could claim that Luna did not live comfortably.

Luna sat close to the edge of his chair and began the conversation.

"Minister Sandoval, thank you for coming to Miami again. And for bringing up-to-date information from the highest levels of the Cuban government, to which the Senator and I obviously do not have access. . . . We are both hopeful you will be the next leader of Cuba."

"You are kind to suggest that, but there is no certainty of where Cuba is headed," Sandoval replied. "But I assure you that if it's within my power, there will be no abrupt changes in Cuba, either by holding free elections and fully opening foreign trade and investment or by terminating the limited trade we currently permit. Think of Cuba as a variation of China or Vietnam, with carefully controlled trade under socialism and a single party in power."

"It is the area of controlled trade that is troublesome in my view," said García García. "Commercial interests in the U.S. are very pleased with the foreign trade that now exists because they have a large share of that trade. I am pleased we all are in agreement that we must work to continue the status quo."

"Those who are pleased with trade as it exists include ranchers who have sold cattle to Cuba, such as the recent purchase from a Montana rancher," said Luna. "I think the Senator agrees with me that Montana is far more predictable than Florida with regard to its attitude towards Cuba. We depend on the actions of many other states to keep things as they are. Controlling the opinion about Cuba held by Floridians is critical to our interests. What is troubling is the increasing election of state and federal legislators who believe we should restore full trading relations with Cuba."

"Where do the greatest threats lie?" asked Sandoval, turning her head toward García García.

"The liberal members of Congress and younger Cuban-Americans who have been successful in business and wish to open doors to Cuba, but do not intend to press for restitution or compensation of property expropriated fifty years ago. Restitution is absolutely mandatory, in my opinion," García García ventured. "Nevertheless, it seems increasingly unrealistic to expect such payment from Cuba, which is why I believe keeping the status quo is the best we can hope for."

"My people are restless," said Sandoval. "On illegally watched programs they see what life is like in the U.S., hear about it from relatives, and want a share."

"Could there be an internal uprising," asked Luna, nodding at Sandoval.

"No," she responded. "The Cubans who remained in their country are largely indifferent. They prefer living in a poor Cuba to somewhere else. We have made the U.S., and particularly South Florida, appear to our citizens throughout Cuba as corrupt, racist, anti-Hispanic, lacking decent work opportunities for migrants, and rampant with serious crime. We control radio and TV in Cuba and broadcast many examples—true or false—of the bad side of Florida. It has worked. Cubans, of course, like the idea of having a better standard of living, but they feel threatened by what we let them hear about the U.S."

"Madame Minister," asked Luna, "reports of the disappearance of Representative Mendoza are disturbing and not helpful to our cause. The apparent death of the guide Gomez is of little concern. Are you satisfied that the Playa Larga deaths are history that will not be repeated?"

"I am," she replied. "Little if any evidence remains of either disappearance. The Zapata Reserve is now fully under my jurisdiction. Fishing there by foreigners has been increasingly lucrative to Cuba and to me. I am trying to think of a way to convince the U.S. government that recreational sports are not trade and should be opened—at the very least for fishing and bird hunting."

"Are you aware that there are churches called St. Peter the Fisherman in Playa Larga and somewhere in the Florida Keys, which have been successful in allowing some U.S. fishermen to travel to Zapata?" asked García García.

"The U.S. rules appear so foolish when false churches like St. Peter the Fisherman can be established and travel by church members follows easily," responded Sandoval. "I have met with Cuban guides in Playa Larga encouraging this fishing disguised as a religious exchange. There are a dozen such trips already planned for next month."

"I am not pleased with the church subterfuge," said García García, shaking his head. "But it is hard to stop any travel by church groups, who rant and rave about constitutional separation of church and state. I would personally like journalists kept out. They are a liberal group that advocates more travel and trade. Encouraging that group has been Elena Mendoza, Juan's sister. She has not been helpful to our goal. Her brother was worse, but he is no longer a problem."

"Do you know about a Florida fisherman named Macduff Brooks?" García García asked Sandoval.

"Yes. My son was assigned by the U.S. Interests Section to assist his wife in photographing Hemingway's favorite places in and around Havana. I think Brooks is harmless. But there is one concern."

Minister Sandoval told the other two about the fingerprint issue, that the prints left on entry this year matched those left at the Cuban embassy in Mexico City more than 20 years ago when Professor Maxwell Hunt applied for but was refused entry to Cuba.

"Are you certain the fingerprints matched?" Luna asked.

"Yes, but we don't know what that means. Professor Hunt, whose prints were taken in Mexico, died of a stroke a few years later. I suspect there was some mix up or confusion on our part; our record-keeping is not accurate.

"In any event, I don't believe Brooks represents a threat to our plans. However, there is another troubling matter. When my son confronted Macduff and Lucinda Brooks about the prints, the two Americans disappeared. They returned to the U.S. in the most outrageous and unlawful manner, on a stolen private plane flown from Cuba to Key West.

"Bringing Brooks into the church fishing exchanges and personally inviting him to participate is a thought. If we get him to Cuba again, we will interrogate him thoroughly. I will address that when I return to Havana tomorrow."

"I would watch him carefully," said Luna. "He lives in North Florida. I'll use my connections to watch him, and I suggest, Senator, that you use *your* office to also monitor his movements."

"What about Elena Mendoza?" asked Sandoval.

"Nothing to worry about; she is only a representative from a very small state that has few Cuban residents," Luna replied, with García García nodding."

"I'll start a file on Brooks—both him and his wife—tomorrow," said García García, rising, setting down his glass, and helping Minister Sandoval with her light jacket."

33

A FEW WEEKS LATER

FOR DAYS, LUCINDA AND I continued to discuss going back to Cuba. Or not.

"Elena is intimidating us to go," I said as we were driving to Emigrant for some groceries, watching an aroused sky that threatened snow. "I don't like being intimidated. . . . Dan approved the idea and just to be safe offered us diplomatic passports issued in different names."

"Elsbeth is enjoying the life of an undergraduate, Macduff, learning to balance time spent on academics and social life. She has a wonderful roommate in Sue. Have you given thought to how it would devastate her to lose her dad?"

"Or to lose you," I countered. "You two are inseparable when she's here with us."

"She's the daughter I could never have. . . . So much points to us not going to Cuba again," she exclaimed. "I don't trust the Minister. I don't think Dan is pushing us to go. It's dealing with Elena that we haven't done very well. I think we should tell her everything we know or believe and that we are *not* going. Not because we're afraid, but we don't see the likelihood of learning anything useful beyond what we already know. How best to tell Elena?"

"I'll do it," I said. "I don't look forward to the conversation but I was the one she called in the first place."

When I phoned Elena the next day and explained our position, she surprised me with her cordial response.

"Macduff. You've tried your best. I accept that Juan was killed by someone in Cuba. You decide. No pressure." After a few more minutes of pleasant conversation, she hung up.

"That she agreed with us wasn't what I expected," I said, nodding at Lucinda, who had heard our brief talk. "It didn't mesh with her previous insistence that Juan was alive. But people change, and it was welcome. Or, possibly she'd been threatened. In any event, the matter appears to be over."

Lucinda and I both had work to occupy us until we left shortly to enjoy the winter months in Florida. I was guiding a few late September and early October floats. Lucinda was beginning a two-year project—aerial photography of the Yellowstone and Snake rivers from their origins as nearly adjacent creeks in southeast Yellowstone Park, flowing their separate ways to the Pacific for the Snake and to the Gulf of Mexico and Atlantic for the Yellowstone. It would highlight dams and irrigation channels and note how the hand of man has altered the rivers.

"Ready for a winter in sunny Florida?" she asked one evening as we walked from the garage to the cabin shivering from our poor choice of clothing. The temperature had dropped to near thirty, and a light film of snow began to cover Paradise Valley.

"I'm ready. I have only three more floats scheduled. I'd like to wait until most of the aspen leaves have dropped and then we can scoot."

"Scoot?"

"That's right."

"Couldn't you use a more elegant word? Maybe 'hasten.'"

"Or maybe 'scram,'" I answered, while she looked at me and shook her head. "I'm a fishing guide; I don't have a Ph.D. like you, Doctor Brooks," I added.

"You promised never to call me 'doctor.' I'm not a professor. Call me an 'ace photographer.'"

"I did promise, but rules are made to be broken."

"Are they?" she asked.

"Only if they were coerced, like your allegations that I promised to marry you."

"But you *did* marry me and that nullifies any discussion of breaking promises and rules leading to the marriage. I think there's a statute of limitations on challenging a marriage."

"There's no statute of limitations on fraud." I answered, hiding some doubt. . . . "I'd like to change the subject."

"You always say that when you're losing a debate."

"It's time for me to run an errand—buy some groceries and wash the SUV."

"We bought groceries two hours ago. Wash the SUV in the snow? Bye. Enjoy the weather; it looks like about four inches have fallen, with no sign of stopping. You'll get stuck in Emigrant and spend the night freezing in the car wash."

"Let's quit and go to bed," I suggested.

"I thought you'd never ask. Let's scoot," she said.

I woke at midnight. The snow had stopped falling. I made a cup of tea and sat in the wooden rocking chair in the rear room by the windows, looking out at the moonlight reflections on the fresh snow. But my thoughts soon returned to what may have awakened me in the first place—what should we do about Cuba?

What we might accomplish in Cuba seemed to me to be quite limited. Mendoza and Gomez were almost certainly dead. The Cuban police, both national and local, apparently consider the cases closed. But the matter of the matching fingerprints bothered me. What if Juan Pablo Herzog in Guatemala got access to that information?

Lucinda was called every few weeks by a magazine encouraging her to photograph several of Cuba's parks and reserves. I would like to fish again, but had lost some interest in the Zapata Reserve because of the death of Nacho. But it made sense to go there because it was where Mendoza went missing. Not to mention it was also where there's some of the best fishing in the Americas.

The manager of the Playa Larga hotel, Celia Bustamante, was the most logical person to start with in further investigating the two deaths. Would Elena's conversation with her affect what she might now say? Maybe someone at the barracuda research center would help us. But if we arrived in Cuba using diplomatic passports with different names, might the government discover who we really were? This all led to our hesitation to put in motion *any* Cuban travel plans.

But that changed in the morning with a single communication we received.

34

THE EMAIL COMMUNICATION

WHEN I WOKE AT 6:00 a.m., prompted by increasingly vigorous nudges from Wuff, I made coffee quietly and took a cup downstairs to the music room to check email. From the shelf I removed a CD, placed it in the player, and turned the volume low. It was John Field's *First Piano Concerto*, played loudly enough to enjoy the variations but softly enough not to wake Lucinda.

The below ground music room was added when I first built the cabin. Entered by a staircase behind a bookcase across from the fireplace, it's where I store my weapons and work on an array of computer and electronic devices intended to keep me in touch with Dan Wilson in D.C. It's also where I *pretend* to be a world-class oboist, although I don't dare to play for anyone else, especially Lucinda.

There were two emails. The first was a "Dearest in the Lord, with Due Respect and Humanity" greeting from "Miss Bess in Christ" who apparently lives in fraud-produced comfort in Uganda. I'd heard from her before. Once again, she wanted me to invest with her and share in $4 million deposited in a

Kampala bank. To share in those riches—the source of which may have been U.S. foreign aid—I would only have to send a check for $1,000 and provide personal information that undoubtedly would lead to having all my financial accounts transferred to Miss Bess. I kept adding her name to my "send to spam without reading" folder, but she was so infatuated with me that she found another way to reach me the following week.

It was the second email that made me spill my coffee and change the CD to Wagner's *Siegfried's Funeral March:*

Dear Mr. Brooks

My name is Christina Sandoval, and I am the Minister of the Interior in Cuba. You and your wife know my son, Francisco, who escorted Lucinda around Havana and Cojímar on your recent trip to Cuba.

We know that the true purpose of your trip to Cuba was to fish although it was disguised as a religious-based exchange between members of the St. Peter the Fisherman churches in Playa Larga here in Cuba and at Islamorda in the Florida Keys.

Whether you were in Cuba in violation of U.S. law is not of interest to us—we encourage tourism. Thousands come from the U.S. as tourists under programs such as People-to-People. Many more Americans come by way of third nations, without disclosing where they have been when returning to the U.S. Adding the Cuban-Americans who move freely back and forth across the waters that separate us, the U.S. is a major source of visitors.

We are convinced that encouraging recreational fishing in Cuba by foreigners will provide many jobs for Cubans and has a good chance of being approved by the U.S., both because it is not a trade of tangible goods across our borders and it effectively fits into the People-to-People exchange concept.

Our records show that more than twenty years ago at our Mexican embassy a Professor Maxwell Hunt attempted to receive a visa to enter Cuba. He was fingerprinted by our embassy but was never given a visa because we knew he was working for the CIA.

Records in Washington, D.C., that we have checked suggest Hunt died of a stroke a decade later. The fingerprints match yours, taken when you entered Cuba last month.

After an investigation we have concluded that you were correct in suggesting that our records were in error. We lack needed modern equipment to maintain accurate records of the entry and departure of foreigners. Our records also do not show that you and your wife departed Cuba lawfully last month, but we know you returned to the U.S. That is all, as you Americans say, "water over the dam."

This email is to invite you and your wife to return to Cuba in the near future. If the U.S. government gives you a license, I can assure you a welcome reception. We know Lucinda was asked to do further photography in Cuba and assume that, as a fishing guide, you would like again to experience our outstanding fly fishing.

I personally hope to meet you both and look forward to your responding positively to this invitation.

Christina Sandoval
Minister of the Interior

I printed the email and rushed upstairs. Lucinda was standing on the rear porch with a steaming cup of coffee watching the tinted leaves of fall flutter to the frozen ground. She heard me coming.

"Macduff, what a beautiful sight!" she said turning toward me and handing me her French Vanilla coffee for a sip.

"Yes, it is. And you look just as good from the front."

She beamed and responded, "I meant the view."

"So did I."

"You're so sweet, sometimes. . . . What's the paper? An interesting email? . . . The snow is gone, and it seems to be warming up. Should we stay in Montana longer?"

"You may not feel that way when you read this email. . . . We've been invited back to Cuba by Francisco Sandoval's mother, the Minister of the Interior.

"What's in *your* coffee? Mostly Gentleman Jack?"

"Read it!" I said, handing it to her.

She did, and her composure changed with each paragraph.

"I don't believe this. What do you make of it?"

"I want to read it again, and this time read between the lines. I can't imagine the U.S. opening up recreational tourism to Cuba. Not either solely for fishing or more generally to visit the island with no control over where you go. But U.S. travel rules are an inconsistent mess. Because Cuba wants us doesn't mean we'll get a U.S. license to visit."

"Should we call Dan?"

"Not until I finish my coffee. I think I have indigestion. I didn't know one could get it from highland Guatemalan coffee."

"You can't, but you can from emails from Cuba."

"We have to forward this to Dan and also Elena. . . . I'm not sure I want to deal directly with her. I'd like to enjoy breakfast first. And maybe lunch and dinner. The trip Dan had proposed to us included using assumed names and diplomatic passports. Neither would be needed accepting this invitation, *if* Treasury says OK."

"Couldn't we do what Dan suggests and also accept the minister's invitation? Wouldn't that be safer? And let Dan deal with Elena?" Lucinda asked.

"Possibly safer—if we're not identified. And possibly disastrous—if we are. Do you suppose Minister Sandoval really believes we'll accept her invitation?"

"Why don't we forward the email and talk to Dan and maybe Elena and get their input?" she asked, less a question than a suggestion.

"OK. . . . What do *you* think is Minister Sandoval's motive?"

"I'm sure she has a motive. . . . I haven't the faintest idea what it is."

We revisited the invitation several times during the day, choosing not to make any conclusions until we had shared it with Dan and Elena. We did so after supper, hoping they wouldn't open their email until the morning.

They either didn't open their emails that evening or didn't read them or read them and wanted to give them some thought. Or figured Sandoval's communication was a joke.

The first call came from Dan about two minutes after 7:00 a.m. the next morning.

"Hi, you two. So, Cuba beckons again?" he asked. Lucinda and I sat together at the kitchen table, listening on my cell phone. Outside a cold wind was blowing. We turned the cell phone's volume to max and ignored the wind's howl.

"'Beckons!' Is that all you have to say?" asked Lucinda.

"I read the email late last night," Dan admitted. Then I couldn't sleep. I've called Celeste Jones at the Interests Section in Havana. She's soon to be transferred. She is the one to thank for getting you out of Cuba last time. About all she said was that Minister Sandoval is ambitious and likes the lifestyle being a minister provides."

"That doesn't help us. Macduff and I like *our* lifestyle. We like *staying* alive. . . . What's next?"

"Celeste is going to do some checking and get back to me."

"Is there any reason we should go to Cuba, Dan, other than for me to take more photos and Macduff to do more fishing? We can do those things here."

"The only reason to go is Elena. Your visiting Cuba doesn't do anything for us here at the Agency. Except possibly make my life more difficult. . . . Why *would* you go?"

"To keep a promise," I replied.

"To Elena? Would she want you to assume the risk? You did what you could."

"Not a promise to Elena. To ourselves," I said. "To finish something we started even at some risk. . . . But I'm not sure there is a risk. . . . So, it's just to finish what we started. To learn what happened to Juan Mendoza. We're reasonably sure he's dead. We don't know how or why. Elena deserves some closure."

"Maybe there's no risk now," Dan responded, "but you might *create* new problems while you're there. . . . If you go, will it be at Sandoval's invitation or under our giving you assumed names and diplomatic passports? Or maybe you're not going at all?"

"We'll decide that after we talk to Elena."

35

OCTOBER INTERLUDE IN MONTANA

WHEN DAN HUNG UP the phone, Lucinda and I took a walk along our drive out to East River Road and back along Mill Creek Road until we were across the creek from our cabin. The flow was so low we could ford the creek, something we couldn't do in the heavy turbulence of the spring and early summer, when it ran deep and swift and the round rocks were unforgiving.

"Macduff, shouldn't we be fishing rather than wading without a rod? Do you know how much fishing I've done since we went to Cuba? I never got to cast to a single bonefish, tarpon, or permit while we were in Cuba. Since we've gotten back from Cuba, I haven't fished much. You've guided, but you've been preoccupied in thought each time you left to meet a client. You haven't talked about one guide trip when you've come home other than with that rancher, Cameron. And that was because he had been to Cuba. . . . Today is the first day in a long time we've even walked."

"You're right about everything. Where would you like to hike and fish?"

"Anywhere."

"Name it."

"You don't have a guide trip for four days. Let's get our talk with Elena behind us and drive through the park to Jackson. Ask John to go with us on the Deadman's Bar to Moose section of the Snake."

John is John Kirby, long-time friend and Jackson Hole guide. We can't expect him to come to Mill Creek at the busiest time of the season. He loves fishing from *Osprey* and understands my emotions about Deadman's Bar to Moose. It's where I lost my wife El in a tragic boating accident nearly two decades ago and where Lucinda and I were shot by Park Salisbury. Although dead, his name causes my hair to curl; he sent the three of us—Wuff was along for the float—to the hospital. I came out reasonably unscathed, Wuff retained a slight limp, but Lucinda barely survived a coma and months of amnesia.

"Macduff, you OK?" Lucinda asked, wincing.

"Bad memories of nearly losing you on the Snake. That was not a good year."

"That was the year you proposed. Did that make it bad?"

"Not bad. Confusing. You tricked me acting as though you had amnesia," I said. She pushed me. It wouldn't have been enough of a push to have any effect if it hadn't been while I was taking the last step fording Mill Creek. Combined with a slippery rock I couldn't see, I pirouetted and lost without a trace of grace. The creek was shallow enough not to drown me, but deep enough to saturate me with cold water on a day the air temperature might reach sixty.

"Sorry, Macduff, I was trying to steady myself," she said, stepping out of the creek as dry as a bone and showing her trademark Cheshire cat grin that often accompanies some act of deception.

"You could have killed me."

"That's an idea I hadn't thought of," she answered. "You certainly made a big splash."

"And you want me to take you fishing and trust you not to make another attempt on my life?"

"Such temptation! I promise to be good, but only for the four days."

"Tomorrow we'll drive through the park, the following day fish with John, the next walk into Cascade Canyon, and the fourth day drive back. OK?"

"OK."

"I'm freezing. I need to dry off." Dripping water across the porch, I headed for a warm shower and then dressed as Lucinda dialed Elena.

"This is Elena Mendoza. I think I'm talking to one of the Brookses. It sounds like you're on a speaker phone."

"You're talking to both of us. We're in our living room in Montana. Macduff's drying out from falling in Mill Creek. He's getting old and unsteady."

"I assume you've read the email from Minister Sandoval," I added.

"I have and tried to contact you. What do you make of it; Lucinda knows the Sandovals."

"I only know Francisco," said Lucinda. "I never met his mother, Christina, the minister who wrote the invitation. . . . Francisco was wonderful to me for two days of taking photographs in Havana and Cojímar, but he changed his composure on the drive to Playa Larga after we finished. He was scary and threatening."

"I've learned nothing more," Elena admitted, "since you told me about Juan's probable death. I would like you to help and go again to Cuba."

"And do exactly what?"

"Go to Playa Larga and talk to the hotel manager," she suggested. "Talk to Nacho Gomez's wife. See what you can discover at the barracuda research center. Maybe talk to other guides who knew Gomez."

"And?"

"Nothing more."

"No work in Havana?"

"No. In fact, I suggest you fly directly to Cienfuegos from Miami. Flights go Saturday and return Tuesday. That gives you four to four and a half days in Playa Larga. Time to talk to people and time to fish as a cover for being there. Don't stay at the Playa Larga hotel; you might be recognized. Use the Hotel Playa Giron. It's about twenty miles further south along the coast from Playa Larga. You can rent a car at the airport in Cienfuegos in Lucinda's assumed name and pay for it with Canadian dollars."

"Elena, I'm recognizable in Playa Larga," I said. "I talked with the Playa Larga hotel manager and with several other guides. I never got into the research center. If I use an assumed name on a diplomatic passport to get into Cuba, how can I use that name in Playa Larga where I'm known as Brooks?"

"You'll use the assumed name for everything. That includes the flight, car rental, a hotel if you stay in Cienfuegos, and for lodging in Giron. You can use Brooks when you talk to anyone you might have met in Playa Larga."

"Is there any reason to risk taking Lucinda?"

"She's essential. She'll go as a professional photographer for a Canadian newspaper. You'll be nothing more than her spouse. If you go fishing, she'll book the trip, and you'll go along as her novice fisherman husband."

"I like that," added Lucinda. "I usually out-fish him anyway."

"Maybe I should let Lucinda go alone," I said.

"I've thought of that," replied Elena. "But couples tend to be the norm for visitors to Playa Giron. I want you to go as a quiet husband who is unlikely to make any impression on or be remembered by anyone."

"That's easy for Macduff. It's called typecasting," Lucinda said, nodding with a smile.

I didn't nod. Or smile.

36

THE FOLLOWING DAY IN JACKSON

I CAN LIVE WITH BEING UNIMPRESSIONABLE. Also quiet. Occasionally even innocuous. But being out-fished by a trophy wife? Not a chance. I would show her how to fish on our trip to Jackson.

When we began packing bags for Jackson, Wuff lay by the front door whimpering. She knew we were going somewhere, and she wanted an invitation. "What do we do with Wuff," I asked Lucinda. "She's not welcome at Dornan,s."

"We'll stay at Signal Mountain, and I won't have to cook," she declared. "Or sneak Wuff into Dornan's. She'll go with us in *Osprey* for the drift."

Wuff got up, walked to the bedroom where the closet door was open, pulled out her forest green L.L.Bean travel bag with "WUFF" embroidered on the top, dragged it to the living room, and fell asleep on top of it. She was ready.

"I have a proposition, Macduff. It deals with a four-letter word," Lucinda uttered quietly as I placed my rod bags in the SUV.

"The answer is 'yes.' Let's go back to bed?"

"You have a one track mind—the word I meant was 'Cuba.'"

"Darn! So, what's the proposition?" I said, showing disappointment.

"Promise me not to mention Cuba until we get back here. Then we'll sit down with *a* drink and decide what we'll do."

"I agree with everything except the singular reference to *a* drink. Can we change that to *a* bottle?"

"You want to make our decision in the condition and style Hemingway trademarked?" she inquired.

"You mean like: 'He watched her from across the table and liked the way her eyes moved and her chin wrinkled when he spoke about what they would do when they were old and the words did not come to him easily anymore and he poured another drink into the low glass in front of him and got up and brought another bottle from the cabinet and she took it back and looked at him.'"

"Why did I marry you?" she asked, her head in her hands and her elbows on the edge of the table.

"Looks. Charm. Money. Casting technique."

"None of the above. And I'm about to prove the untruth about the last one."

The first week of October in Yellowstone Park is unpredictable. Early snow can bring traffic to a halt, leaving park officials wondering if they should have closed most of the roads in September. But on days of sunshine and sixty degrees, they wonder if they should have scheduled the closing for the middle of November.

From our Mill Creek cabin to Mammoth meant an hour of gentle climb; there were no cars in line at the North Entrance at Gardiner—a mark of the late season. A sign a few miles further said the Mammoth to Norris road section had closed in early September for repairs. It would reopen in two days.

We had to detour and drive a section we rarely covered and even more rarely fished—Mammoth to Tower Junction. A friend had mentioned Blacktail Deer Creek as a good place for brookies and small cutthroats, not unlike Obsidian Creek on the closed portion..

Parking at the Blacktail Lake trailhead in the shade of some ponderosa, we let Wuff enjoy twenty minutes of play before we set her down in the back of the SUV, left the windows open an inch, and walked toward Blacktail Pond, also called Shaky Lake because of the surrounding soft bogs. We stopped at a section just before the creek enters the pond.

"Let me rig you," I offered Lucinda.

"Not a chance. This is serious competition. I don't want you rigging me with some dry fly certain to be rejected or putting the line through every *other* snake guide."

She turned her back, tied on a fly I couldn't see, and left to fish under the bank at a bend twenty yards upstream. I tied on a #18 Parachute Adams, walked downstream, and cast just above a good looking pool. Something hit it immediately, but either did not take it or I was too slow to react. The colors of what was probably an eight or nine incher suggested a brookie.

Out of the corner of my eye and above high grass along the bank, I saw Lucinda's rod bend and heard a "wow!"

Four more casts brought no movement around my Adams, and I bit it off and tied on a same size Elk Hair Caddis. Six casts with that didn't bring a single rise. I wanted that trout. Three more flies and a couple of dozen more casts didn't help. This was not good; plus I had heard a half-dozen more "wows" from Lucinda and knew she was keeping score.

Finally, I tied on a #12 hopper that seemed to be too large and too gaudy, but had been hanging from the small sheepskin patch on my vest that held past failures. I tossed the fly not to the pool but upstream along the opposite bank and watched it float along the edge beneath overhanging grass.

Just as it began to drag at the end of a float I should have stopped twenty feet sooner, the fly disappeared. I didn't see a splash. Not even a mild ruffle. Then a cutthroat broke the surface. I'm sure it looked at me before it dove underwater in search of shelter. Shelter was not to be had. A 12" cutty was soon in my net, and I let out a "wow" Tarzan would have envied.

I photographed the cutthroat not because I wanted another picture of another trout but because I knew Lucinda would demand evidence more reliable than my word. I don't lie about how many I catch, but I do have problems estimating lengths.

Lucinda soon returned around the bend, with a grin that forecast victory. She claimed seven fish, the exact number of "wows" I had heard.

"What did you use," I asked.

"I'm not talking. I'll tell you when were finished with this trip and are back at our cabin."

Then she dramatically broke off her fly—which I failed to identify from twenty-five feet away—and tossed it into *my* pool. It no sooner hit the water than a fish rose, slurped it in, and disappeared.

"That was a perfectly good fly," I pleaded.

"I have more of the same. I didn't want you poking through my fly box, searching for a fly that was still wet. So there!"

It was not a good start. I keep telling myself fly fishing is not a competitive sport.

Roosevelt and Tower Fall facilities had closed for the season as were most others further on at Canyon Village. The wrecker service remained open; apparently the management knew Lucinda was coming. Its service would be needed if I let her drive. On our detour we would not pass Old Faithful, where we planned to have lunch at the Inn. Instead, we ate potato chips and Ben & Jerry's ice cream sitting on a log in front of the Colter Bay convenience store.

"Is this the kind of dining you planned for me when we married," she asked.

"Nathan's hot dogs in New York. Ben & Jerry's in Grand Teton Park. Only the best!"

When we reached Dornan's at Moose, Lucinda disappeared while I checked in. She reappeared a few minutes later, gave me five minutes to get ready, and we beat the closing clock by two minutes at the Pizza Pasta Company. She ordered Buffalo Quesadillas and a Spinach Salad while I had Buffalo Bolognese and two scoops of Moose Tracks and Huckleberry ice cream. We slept soundly after the Dornan's cabin check-in desk closed, and we snuck Wuff in for the night.

John Kirby arrived in his pick-up at 8:00 a.m., overjoyed to see Lucinda, Wuff, *Osprey*, and me—in that order. We hooked *Osprey's* trailer to John's truck, which was loaded with food and drink. Not a drop of Gentleman Jack, but enough Wyoming spring water to bathe in.

Being an early October Tuesday, there was no line for launching at Deadman's Bar. For years John urged us to visit him at the close of summer *after* the early September One-Fly

Contest was over. During its twenty-some-year life, the annual one-weekend event had raised nearly $10 million to improve fish habitat. I wondered if I could get a grant from the contest sponsors to further alter Mill Creek in front of my cabin to "improve *my* trout habitat?"

John took to the oars to start the float with Lucinda in front, Wuff settling in for a long nap behind John. I was ignored in the rear. I've *never* sat in front when Lucinda and I have floated, deferring to John's opinion that when he's rowing she's a lot better to look at than I am.

It's easy to miss some good fishing along the moraine slope across from the Deadman's Bar put-in. John's strong rowing took us over there, and Lucinda and I responded with a double—both hooking a fish at the same time and about the best way to start a day on any river.

Lucinda's cutthroat measured at 17 inches. I thought mine was *much* larger—by at least a half inch. I didn't approve of the small notebook Lucinda used to keep count: Lucinda seven, Macduff two. By lunch time it was nine to two, but I pointed out that I had rowed for a half hour while John took the rear seat and landed three fish. I tried to get credit for his fish, but she just snickered.

Lunch on the east bank of the Snake has few peers. My collapsible table and three small folding stools were set facing the Grand Tetons. Early snow had started the winter's conversion of the high peaks' color from slate to white. John had stopped at Albertson's in Jackson and bought an Italian Specialty platter of assorted items I thought would be better as chum and some plain white-meat fried chicken for my culinary peculiarities.

Two hours into the afternoon brought little response to our casts and might have gone better had we slung hammocks between cottonwood trees and napped. Lucinda and I each caught three more fish. Two of hers were whitefish she insisted counted. The more I thought about her whitefish, the more I wondered what fly she was using. Whitefish hang out deep. When she next cast over me, I grabbed her line and looked at the fly.

"You're using a nymph!" I exclaimed.

"Only as a dropper under the dry fly John tied on. The dropper's a bead head Prince."

"What have you caught your fish on; the whitefish had to be on the Prince?"

"They were," she answered.

"And the trout, including the three in the morning?"

"I don't remember. Anyway, it's irrelevant. I caught the fish."

"John, did you tie on her nymphs?"

"I don't want to get involved in this. I'm sitting in the middle in the line of fire," he said, looking in the guide box for some tippet.

"Don't blame John," Lucinda said. "I tied on the nymphs when he was turned and talking to you. He never said anything about the nymph when he released the fish."

"John! Since when have you allowed nymphs on your boat?"

"It's your boat, Mac. You set the rules."

"Macduff, what fly are you using?" she asked.

"A streamer. I've been tossing it along the banks and stripping in."

"Does it float on the surface?"

"No, it's a *streamer*. It's supposed to be underwater."

"Like a nymph?"

"No, your nymph bounces along the bottom; my streamer is closer to the surface."

"You agree the streamer's not a dry fly?"

"Please don't call my streamer a nymph," I answered. "I'll concede it is not a dry fly. I'll even agree not to count fish I catch with it," I added at the instant something strong pulled at my streamer and turned downstream.

"Have fun handling your non-fish," she said, opening a bottle of water and laying her rod down while I struggled with what had to be a sizeable fish.

"Please, dear God, don't let it be a whitefish," I mumbled out of Lucinda's hearing.

A whitefish it was not. The colors of a rainbow flashed as it broke surface and for an instant was airborne. It looked big. I wanted to land it but obstacles remained. As always, I was using a barbless hook. John handed me the large boat net, telling me I was on my own. And Lucinda was cheering out-loud for the trout. But I was more determined.

The fish made four runs, two into my backing. But it stayed hooked. As it came close to the boat, tiring but with occasional short spurts of energy, I looked for an extra hand, but John and Lucinda were sitting stoically without offering. Only my determination not to allow the three a victory—man, woman, and fish—resulted in my netting the rainbow."

"John, hand me the ruler from the compartment next to you."

He opened the hatch, looked in, and said, "I don't see any ruler. I'd estimate the fish at about 18 inches. A decent rainbow."

"*There is a ruler there,*" I said, loudly enough to turn heads on the only other drift boat within sight on the river.

"Can't seem to find it. You want to come and look?"

"I can't. I've got to release it and you know it. *Please* look harder." Then I remembered a tiny tape measure hanging from my vest. I pulled it free. My rod was set beside me. I was holding the net with the fish in one hand and the tape measure with the other and pulling out the tape with my teeth. It was only a two foot tape! The fish was at least two feet long. I held it up for John and Lucinda to see.

"My best ever. At least 25 inches, maybe 27."

"Doesn't count," John said.

"What do you mean it doesn't count?"

"Inaccurate measure," added Lucinda.

I had to release the fish. If it could understand us, it was taking home a story about some strange humans. I watched it suck in some current and swim downstream.

"At least you know it was 24 inches. Let's say 26." I said, wanting verification.

"No way," said Lucinda.

"How about 25?"

"Doesn't count. The rules say the measurement must be *accurate.*"

"At least I measured 24 inches before the tape ran out. You saw it. Both of you."

"Did we see *anything*, John?" she asked. "I was watching Wuff; you were busy rowing."

"Did you have a strike, Macduff?" John asked, grinning.

"That was a great fish, and you both know it!"

"OK, Macduff," she said. "I saw you hook a fish and play it. Actually pretty competently. You had it in the net when I saw it was foul hooked through the tail."

"The streamer slipped out of its mouth and was caught in the tail while it was in the net."

"If you'll stop talking about it, John and I won't say a word about your catch being foul hooked. It's embarrassing to us to fish with someone who counts foul hooked fish."

"Drop me off. I want to fish alone."

"Drop you off? Do you know where you are?"

"In bad company."

"Macduff," Lucinda commented. "This is where you left a client to walk out. Remember Park Salisbury?"

"Don't remind me. OK. *New rules.* No flies other than dry flies. Any fish landed, foul hooked or not, counts. Fish don't have to be measured. Agreed?"

"Yes," said Lucinda, tying on a #14 Parachute Adams and catching seven fish before we reached Moose. I used the same fly and didn't have a rise.

John's wife Laura met us at Moose, and our foursome went to Dornan's Pizza Pasta Company and, swaddled in sweaters and scarfs, sat outside watching the sun set behind the Grand Teton range. When the sun's last flash of life was over, we went inside and ate. Laura never asked about who caught what, only whether we had a good day. Lucinda and John said "exquisite" and "spectacular." I mumbled something that was incomprehensible.

The next day Lucinda and I hiked up Cascade Canyon, an old favorite. We took our bambo 7' rods, a net, and a box of a dozen tiny dry flies. As I was leaning over alongside Cascade Creek to see if there were any fish, the fly box slipped out of my pocket, splashed, bobbed downstream, and was soon out of sight. Not another word about fishing was said.

When Lucinda asked me how the day had been as we stepped out of our SUV at the Jenny Lake parking area, I said "exquisite" and "spectacular." It was the truth because I had spent more time admiring Lucinda than the creek.

On the drive home to Mill Creek, we had lunch at Old Faithful, tossed some hopper patterns along the banks of the Firehole—with neither of us discussing success—and stopped at Obsidian Creek on the re-opened Norris to Mammoth road. The creek is a favorite Yellowstone stream to fish between the Moose Exhibit and Seven Mile Bridge. Large numbers of tiny brook trout hang in numerous pools and undercuts. We again used 7' bamboo rods and floated tiny dry flies, each catching a few brookies.

"Mac, I have a confession to make," she said as we walked on the trail alongside the creek.

"No need to confess," I answered.

"No, I want to tell you. When we were fishing in Blacktail Creek on the drive down, and I went downstream to fish, I caught all the fish on a red bead-head Copper John. I wanted to beat you so bad. I'm sorry."

"Any confessions about my big rainbow?"

"Nope, it was hilarious. John and I talked before we float-ed and decided to give you as much trouble as we could. He suggested the nymph. . . . Your rainbow *was* beautiful."

Impulsively, I turned, dropped my rod and net, and kissed her, lifting her and giving her my best grizzly imitation hug.

She yelled "uncle" and kissed and hugged back.

The voice from a ranger who had just parked and began to walk toward us called, "Do you have a license to do that?"

"I have a park fishing license."

"I don't mean that. I mean a marriage license," he said, smiling.

Two hours hour later, when the blinking light in Emigrant came into sight, I turned to Lucinda, and said quietly, "Cuba."

"I know," she answered. "I've been thinking about Cuba the past hour. Let's take the gear inside, pour a drink, sit on the porch, and decide what to do."

The drink part sounded like a good idea to me.

37

THAT EVENING ON THE CABIN PORCH

I T WAS AN UNCOMMON FALL SEASON. Two evenings ago Lucinda and I watched light snow fall that kept us inside at Dornan's in Moose. This evening, back at the cabin, we were able to sit out briefly in the last hour of sun. Half the leaves were dislodged from their bondage with the limbs, giving us a few more minutes of sun flickering behind bare tree limbs before it vanished beyond the edge of a slope of the Absaroka Range southeast of the cabin.

We were dressed for Montana's chilly fall. Lucinda wore jeans and an old L.L. Bean red and blue checkered flannel shirt under a heavy off-white Norwegian sweater she found in my drawer. A plaid scarf hung over her left shoulder, ready to be slipped around her neck to oblige the descending temperature.

I had on old Orvis heavy-weight khakis with the pockets trimmed with leather, a frayed burnt orange shirt ready for Goodwill or the trash, and my warmest Simms' guide jacket. We both wore wool caps and wouldn't last long on the porch. At least the air was still; evening breezes in October are usually intimidating.

"Time to choose," she said.

"Haven't we already?" I added.

"I think we've decided to go," she continued. "There are loose ends and you promised to try. The question is whether we go the way Dan offered or accept Minister Sandoval's invitation."

"If we accept the invitation, we'll be under the scrutiny of the minister," she added. "If we get into trouble, at best we may be on our own. If instead we accept Dan's help, using assumed names and diplomatic passports, if we get into trouble, we will have the 'protection' of our government, whatever that might mean. The most likely result would be expulsion."

"In theory, I *probably* agree," I responded. "But could we be charged with spying—with the Cubans ignoring our diplomatic status?"

"Not likely. What interest does Cuba have in the life of a U.S. House member? Or the life of a nonconformist Cuban fishing guide?"

"*Probably* none," I answered.

"If we can discover how and why Juan was killed without losing our cover and get back to the U.S., that's likely to end the matter for us. . . . What if we discover that some persons in the U.S. were involved in Juan's death?"

"*Probably* wouldn't even lead to an arrest. It's too difficult to pursue an investigation and trial where most of the evidence is in Cuba and kept under wraps."

"What if those persons in the U.S. were powerful public figures, such as another member of Congress or a high profile businessman? A Montana rancher or a Florida sugar grower?"

"*Probably* no difference. The evidence is even more likely to get buried."

"Too many 'probablies,' Macduff. But listening to you, I'm even more inclined to go to Cuba with Dan's help, and not even answer the minister's invitation until we get back. That means going soon."

Dan was surprised to hear from us when I called; he assumed we would accept the invitation from the minister the next morning.

"How soon can you go?" he asked. "I'll have it arranged in two days. You fly commercial to Miami from Bozeman. Lucinda goes on to Havana the next day; Mcduff follows two days later. You'll be given your diplomatic passports in Miami and travel as guests of the Interests Section. Each of you will have a driver from the Interests Section."

"Where are you putting us up," asked Lucinda.

"In the Interests Section building in temporary living accommodations for new employees and visitors. You'll have adjacent rooms with a door between them. We want our employees to believe you're unrelated."

"Is it safe? Staff people go home at night."

"Yes, there's a small marine detachment. Some are always on duty."

"What about our appearances?"

"Our folks in Miami will make you look so different you won't know each other. Macduff should remember how different he looked in Guatemala when he attempted to kill Abdul Khaliq Isfahani."

"I haven't heard that name mentioned since the Sudan last year," I recalled. "Let's not talk about him."

"Macduff, why am *I* going to Cuba this time? I don't have a contract for a photo assignment," she asked that evening, putting some warm weather clothes into her small pull-on suit-case. "It's clear you're staying in Playa Giron as a base to go to Playa Larga and talk to several people about the two disappearances. I'm going to Havana to do what?"

"You're bait in case I get into trouble. The U.S. could trade you to get me back if I'm detained by the authorities."

"I love you, but I don't believe you. You don't make sense. *Be serious*. Why am I going?"

"Because you're smarter and Dan is convinced that whenever I've been in trouble the past few years, it was your effort that saved us. He likes having you around me. So do I."

"How on earth could I help in this case?"

"You shoot better than I do. Remember Park Salisbury?"

"We can't take guns to Cuba!"

"The Interests Section has them."

"Mac, I don't want to be in a situation where guns are needed."

"I don't see how we could be. If I have any difficulty in Playa Larga, such as my disguise not working with the one person I already know and will speak with again—Celia Bustamante, the manager of the Hotel Playa Larga—I'll leave the country immediately. You'll follow as soon as possible."

"It sounds like you and Dan have been talking without me."

"I talked to him at noon today while you were running errands."

"After we have dinner in Havana somewhere we're not likely to be recognized, what happens?"

"I sneak into your room at the Interests Section and ravage you."

"Can we skip the dinner?"

38

LATE OCTOBER MEETING IN BOZEMAN

CLIFF CAMERON WANTED TO TALK with David Longstreet. They had met on the trade trip to Cuba. Cameron was unimpressed with Longstreet and worried about his ineptness and pandering to better experienced politicians and about the money of lobbyists. Cameron knew he could persuade Longstreet to agree to do anything that would help keep him in office.

Time was closing in on the end of October, which was fine with Longstreet because it was an off-year and there was no November election to fret about the following month. Longstreet could almost always be found in his Main Street office in Bozeman; he was terrified of Washington where he correctly felt out-of-place and overwhelmed. Sitting in his Montana office, with the large windows almost to the sidewalk, he leaned back in his chair, put his feet on the desk, and sipped from a cup of coffee as he looked out at his constituents passing by. He was troubled by the thought that each year fewer of them seemed to wave at him.

While he was trying to figure out why, his phone rang; the ring tone was the Marine Corps band playing Sousa's *Stars and Stripes Forever*. His phone played so many bars of the piece that callers often hung up. Today's first caller waited patiently for the last notes to fade.

"U.S. Representative David Longstreet speaking," he said.

"Representative, this is Cliff Cameron. I haven't had the privilege of talking with you since we were together in Cuba a few weeks ago. I'd like to talk to you about trade with Cuba. When can we meet?"

Longstreet had nothing scheduled for the day; his next obligation was three days away when he would attend something somewhere in the state to do something his secretary would remind him about.

"Mr. Cameron, I could have lunch today. I just had a cancellation; the rest of my week is booked solidly," he lied. "Ted's Montana Grill is just down the street from here at the old Baxter Hotel. Nice place. About noon?"

Cameron *never* ate there. He disliked Ted Turner and his pet herd of bison that grazed a few miles west of Bozeman. But playing politics required compromise and he agreed.

When they met—Cameron on time and Longstreet thirty minutes late—they both looked at the menu and Longstreet suggested, "The bison steak, Cameron; it's real good, much leaner that beef."

"I'll have a *beef* filet," Cameron said, loud enough to turn some heads.

"And I'll have the bison meatloaf," added Longstreet. After all, Ted Turner was a more important constituent than Cameron. At least so far.

Cameron noticed that Longstreet never looked him directly in the eyes and also had a habit of looking around the room
as though he might find a better lunch companion. Cameron
ignored him; he wasn't there for friendship, but to learn more
about Longstreet's position on Cuba.

"Representative, I did some research on your statements
and voting record with respect to Cuba. Until the time we went
to Cuba, you took a pretty strong position of permitting no
trade at all with the country, but since that trip you've been ar-
guing for retaining the status quo and allowing the current trade
to continue. . . . That's my view. I applaud you for having the
courage to change a position you realized was outdated."

"I keep up to date on our international relations, especially
when it affects Montana. I thought it appropriate to redefine
my position. I don't consider it a 'change.'"

Cameron was tempted to ask whether the "redefinement"
was based on his personal views about trading with Cuba or the
fact that the Florida-based PAC had promised a sizeable campaign donation if he changed his position. But Cameron held
his tongue. After all, he himself had written a check for $7,000
to Longstreet's campaign fund on the plane coming home from
Cuba. Longstreet remembered things like that.

"What I'd like to ask of you," Cameron said, putting down
his knife and fork for a moment, "is how are you going to be
influenced by the increasingly favored liberal movement to fully
restore trade with Cuba?"

"I'd have to know more about the movement. Is it strong
in Montana?" responded Longstreet.

"Probably in Bozeman or Missoula, left leaning university
towns. . . . But students don't vote," said Cameron.

"I don't plan to follow the socialists who want to restore all trade and travel with Cuba. But if my folks in Montana can benefit from some *specific trade*, I'm all for it."

"I'd like to think you'll keep that position," affirmed Cameron. "I see more trade opportunities for Montana ranchers and farmers."

Longstreet knew Cameron meant opportunities the rancher himself would benefit from.

"Of course I'll stay the course. And I appreciate your campaign contributions. . . . Let me change the subject for a minute while we're together. Do you know a Macduff Brooks? Or his wife Lucinda?

"I know him, assuming you mean the fishing guide. I floated with him last month. He's a good guide."

"You know he went to Cuba?" asked Longstreet.

"We talked about his trip. He said he went bonefishing. I tried to learn more, but he didn't want to talk about the details of the trip. He said he didn't remember the name of his guide, and he didn't recall if the place he went to was called Playa Larga. . . . Is Brooks any threat to our trade with Cuba?"

"Only if the pro free trade and travel group grows. He's in favor of ending the boycott. But as one individual he's not a problem. . . . I would like to see him kept out of Cuba. It doesn't help our maintaining the status quo by having him become a popular figure promoting change. . . . I'll do what I can to make sure he doesn't get a license to go."

39

HALLOWEEN AT THE FLORIDA COTTAGE

WE BID OUR FAREWELLS to the barren hills of Montana for the coming winter, driving faster than normal on the interstates. Swirling black clouds followed us, and the radio assured us that already six to twelve inches of snow had been deposited on the Western mountain states. When the gas gauge dropped between low and desperation, we refueled in little more time than a pit stop at the Daytona 500.

I didn't dare seek shelter at dusk because I knew we would wake to an unwelcome accumulation of snow. Usually we had left Montana and the other mountain states when the snow risk was moderate, but this year we dallied until the white flakes were falling too close.

When we judged we were far enough ahead of the storm, we began to work our way south and drove through the night nearly to Arkansas. The southern edge of the storm was a hundred miles north, and we found a dog-friendly motel and stopped at 3:00 p.m. The reception desk clerk had a Sheltie and waived the $10 fee for dogs. Within an hour the three of us were sound asleep.

We woke eleven hours later at 2:00 a.m., and left quickly since we couldn't fall asleep again. By evening, we rolled into our driveway at the cottage. Disconnected from real time, we went directly to bed. We were tired but had crossed the country in less than half our usual number of days, if not the same number of hours at the wheel.

Our internal clocks slowly became willing to function on Florida time. Jen, our local cleaning gal, had left the house immaculate and the refrigerator filled with a mix of necessaries and treats. The accumulated mail that she hadn't forwarded was mostly taxpayer postage-subsidized catalogs and brochures for such presumed unfulfilled needs as hearing aids, new cars, mattresses, sporting goods, prefabricated bookshelves, an array of performance enhancing medications, and credit cards offered with no limits to pay for it all. The onslaught of Christmas shopping catalogs was underway. Several advertised *only* clothing suitable for the below freezing temperatures Lucinda and I were content to have escaped.

"Here's something you need, Lucinda," I commented. "A windshield ice scraper that you keep warm by leaving it plugged into the cigarette socket. Ready for the next ice storm."

"And for you, Macduff, I've found a catalog of driveway and sidewalk snow removal devices. Would you like a snow blower for Christmas?"

"The first time we need it, we're moving further south."

"Where to? Cuba?" she said, only half in jest.

Halloween came and went without a trick or treat phone call from Dan. But on the afternoon of November 2nd, he reached us late, sounding as though he'd been fired.

"Are you both on the line?" he asked.

"Yes," Lucinda answered.

"I may be working my last day here."

"Early retirement? Health issues?" I asked.

"I wish. Yesterday our director Vance was called to the Oval Office at the White House. He told me to join him. I thought I was going because he wanted me along for moral support. . . . Nothing like that; it was the President who told him to bring me."

There was a long silence. Lucinda and I preferred to say nothing until we knew more. Dan needed a few moments to compose himself.

"When we were escorted in to see the President, he pointed to two chairs without saying a word. He came around from his chair and sat on the edge of his desk, giving him a position close to and above us. He was not pleased. It was obvious we had not been invited to see his collection of American art."

"You OK talking about this now, Dan?" asked Lucinda. "We can do it later."

"I'm alright. . . ."

After a long pause, Dan continued. "It was not a lengthy conversation. We were there only so the President could make a point about his opinion."

"This must have dealt with Cuba." Lucinda noted.

"Yes. We were ready to send you two back to Cuba. But someone got to the President's ear, undoubtedly about next year's election. He needs the electoral votes from Florida, or he's a one-term president. He didn't say much, but it came with an emphasis that suggested heads would roll if we didn't stop irritating the early exiles in South Florida. Senator García García was mentioned twice."

"What was García García upset about?"

"You two."

"Us? We've never met him."

"Somehow he learned we were planning to send you two to Cuba to learn more about Mendoza's death. The President doesn't want any more investigating by us. He told our director if we went to Cuba by any means his head would be the first to roll. Mine right behind his. . . . I don't have to tell you that your trip is canceled. . . .

"Another thing—the Treasury Department sent Minister Sandoval a request that she withdraw her invitation for you to visit. She denied extending any invitation for such a visit but agreed that Cuba would issue no further travel licenses to Lucinda or Macduff."

"Could we use our diplomatic passports for a different island—like Cancun?" Lucinda asked.

"Not in the Caribbean. But perhaps for a long stay on Elba," Dan replied with a twinge of the humor we often shared. He wasn't quite down for the count.

"How did García García know about the planned trip?" Lucinda questioned.

"He has too much power," I responded. "He hasn't served as long as he has without knowing how the system works and how to work the system."

"So, Macduff and I are not going. Could Elena go?"

"She's been once before and several times since her brother disappeared," Dan commented. "She hasn't told us. Something's fishy."

"Elena going to Cuba is news to us," called out Lucinda from across the room. "What was she doing in Cuba?"

"We don't know. But we're tracking her—like a hurricane."

40

THE NEXT DAY

AS LUCINDA WAS PREPARING LUNCH the next day, Elena called. She was cordial and acted as though nothing significant had happened.

"Macduff, I received word about the President's office overruling Treasury. I'm sorry."

"We're not," added Lucinda, sitting next to me. "I'd like to think it's over for us."

"What should I do?" Elena asked.

"Without much doubt, Juan is dead. What are you going to gain by pursuing the matter?"

"I want to know what happened," she pleaded.

"What do you think happened?" I asked.

"He was killed because he favored freer trade and travel."

"Killed by Cubans?"

"Of course."

"Maybe the trigger was pulled in Cuba, but the gun was loaded in the U.S.," I suggested.

"By?" she responded.

"People who want the boycott *strengthened*. That points to Miami and García García?" I said.

"I don't believe he was involved. He's a sheep in wolf's clothing."

"He could have been working with others. The PAC group, former Bay of Pigs invasion participants, or Cuban-Americans whose property was seized decades ago and never paid for. I could probably think of a dozen other suspects."

"Why would they kill Juan in Cuba? It could have been done here?" she asked.

"To shift the blame. Make it look like an exclusively Cuban action. Hide the evidence on that disorganized island."

"I buy that, Macduff. Do you?" Elena asked.

"No opinion."

"Are you through with being a part of my search?" she inquired, after a pause.

"Yes," Lucinda stated emphatically. "Macduff has put enough into it. He did it for you. I'm sorry we couldn't have helped more. There are much larger interests involved we aren't able to deal with. We're done."

"Well, I'm not through. I'm going to Cuba." Elena replied.

"Good luck," I extended.

"What do you make of that?" I asked Lucinda when we ended our phone discussion.

"She's frustrated. She realizes we're out of it. And still she doesn't know who killed Juan or why. Wouldn't you be frustrated?"

"I've been frustrated since we came back from Cuba. Maybe I should have pressed her about the trips she's made to Cuba, especially the one *before* Juan disappeared. . . . What should we do?" I asked, turning toward Lucinda.

"Get on with our lives!" Lucinda said, exasperated.

"Can we have lunch to start? . . . Maybe roasted chicken, beans and rice, tostados? A final Cuban meal."

"That's not a healthy meal. We're having chicken, but it's not roasted. It's called Chicken with Peppers, Fennel, Onions, and New Potatoes. Here's the recipe I took from a newspaper food section."

"What newspaper? The *Idaho Potato Farmer's Weekly*? The recipe has fifteen ingredients. The name of the dish has only five. The meal has three different bell peppers. It should be called Chicken, New Potatoes, and Pepper Medley. What's the rest?"

"Nothing you dislike. Like lemon wedges and brown sugar."

"It has *fennel*. Fennel is a food source of butterflies. You're depriving butterflies of their sustenance. People for the Ethical Treatment of Animals will be after you."

"I'll leave out the fennel."

"That's one down and fourteen ingredients to go. How about rosemary? It has medicinal properties. If there's a shortage of rosemary, you'll be in trouble with the Medicaid people."

"OK. The fennel and rosemary go. The garlic, olive oil, pepper onions, bell peppers, and bay leaf go. Are you satisfied?"

"Yes, I look forward to having Roasted Chicken with New Potatoes."

41

THREE DAYS LATER IN CUBA

CELESTE JONES HAD ONLY A FEW MORE WEEKS as head of public affairs at the U.S. Interests Section in Havana. She was then off to head public affairs at the U.S. Embassy in Paris, the City of Lights.

One of her last assignments in Havana was to provide assistance to Representative Elena Mendoza, who was coming for several days, purportedly to talk about the Cuban government's purchase of some medical devices from a Connecticut manufacturer, but Celeste had guessed Elena intended to make inquiries about her brother's disappearance and presumed murder.

At her apartment at Foggy Bottom on the day before she was due to fly from D.C. to Havana, Elena was packing light weight clothes that reflected the shift in weather 1,100 miles south, when Celeste Jones called.

"Representative Mendoza, this is Celeste Jones in Havana. I'm looking forward to meeting your plane tomorrow."

"That's kind of you. I can't wait to see Havana. When I was growing up in Miami, I heard hours and hours of stories about Cuba from my parents and grandparents."

"Have you ever been here?" Celeste asked, knowing the answer from a phone discussion with Dan the previous day.

"My father was twelve in 1960 when his family fled and took him to Miami. I was born ten years later and Juan four years after me. I haven't been to Cuba."

Celeste was surprised. Elena was lying. The Interests Section records that monitor Americans travel to Cuba showed that Elena had visited Cuba once before and three times since her brother went missing, each time traveling under a license routinely granted to family members. She had no record concerning where Elena went on her previous trips once she was in Havana.

"You're staying at the Meliá Habana in Miramar. Will you join me for dinner tomorrow evening?" Celeste asked.

"Yes, I'd like that. I'll call you when I reach the hotel."

Celeste met Elena at 7:00 p.m. and drove to the El Aljibe restaurant. Elena ordered a mojito. Celeste ordered a glass of white *Bordeaux* wine, which she considered preparation for her move to Paris. Both ordered the restaurant's famous roast chicken.

"What can I help you with while you're in Havana?" asked Celeste.

"I'm pretty well organized with names of persons to meet regarding trade. I would like to see my state—Connecticut— share in whatever sales to Cuba are allowed."

"Is there anywhere else you might want to visit while you're here? You're not bound to the usual closely monitored daily itinerary."

"My only interest is in developing trade contacts. I will remain in Havana."

"And your brother, Juan? He continues to be listed as missing."

"Juan is dead."

"Has that been confirmed?"

"No. But I need closure. I have to assume Juan's dead. That may not be true, but it's been months."

"Last question. Have you worked with Christina Sandoval or Jorge García García in arranging this trip?"

"I don't know what you mean. They are both very powerful people. I know who they are, but neither of them would be interested in me. I'm merely one of 435 members of our Lower Chamber."

"I meant have you talked to either about U.S. trade policy with Cuba?"

"No."

Celeste made a note to talk to Dan Wilson in D.C. and tell him that Mendoza was evasive, had been evasive about her past visits to Cuba, and may have lied about her involvement with Sandoval or García García.

As promised, Elena discussed Connecticut's trade with Cuba the following day, meeting with an assistant minister of foreign trade and investment. But by noon she was in a car arranged for her by the hotel. It took her to Playa Larga and left her at the hotel named after the town; it was the hotel where Juan had stayed. She walked around the town and learned the locations of the St. Peter the Fisherman church and the barracuda research center. She planned to visit both but wanted first to talk to Celia Bustamante at the hotel.

When she left the hotel after unpacking, she gave a note to Bustamante's secretary, asking if the manager would join her for dinner that evening. On her return a note placed in her room suggested they go to the Don Alexis Restaurant at 7:00 p.m.—that it was quite informal but the food was reputed to be good. Celia would drive them. Elena liked the choice because she was worried that dining in the Hotel Playa Larga would not be very private.

The restaurant certainly *was* informal. A group of five musicians—three on guitars that showed their age, one on bongo drums, and the fifth vigorously shaking a pair of maracas—was playing in front of faded green cement-block walls bearing the scribblings of many former diners. Around the corner, a man who must have been Alexis was preparing orders as the cook at one bench and turning around every few moments to mix drinks as the bartender at another.

A colorfully painted picnic table was reserved for the two women at the far corner along the outside wall. On it next to Celia were the words "We are *not* a nation in transition" and a small, poorly drawn U.S. flag with a black "X" across it. Cuba's limited permission to engage officially in private—but severely regulated—designated businesses was not to be considered a softening of Cuba's devotion to Karl Marx.

Both ordered mojitos, and both had the special of the day: freshly caught snapper grilled with onions and served with fried plantains, brought to the table with knives and forks wrapped in plain white paper napkins and sticking out of the pocket of the waiter's sweat-stained shirt. But the food was far better than what had been served to Elena the previous day at a "Cuban" restaurant in the Miami airport.

"I don't think I can help you," Celia began. "It really wasn't necessary for you to come to Cuba."

"Celia," asked Elena, ignoring Bustamante's initial comment, "you're university-educated, and you chose to work and live in this town of at most a few hundred. Isn't there something better for you? A hotel in Cienfuegos or even Havana?"

"*You* chose to live in Connecticut, Elena, a depressing state with a declining population. Isn't there something better for you? A larger and more sophisticated constituency by living in New York? . . . I chose to live here because I was born and raised here. I went to the University of Havana and came back after graduation. Playa Larga's a beautiful part of Cuba with none of the pollution and gridlock you face in Connecticut."

Elena knew she had a challenge ahead of her. Celia chose her words carefully and carried herself with dignity. And she wasn't through.

"Elena, I could have left Cuba a dozen times. I'm able to travel abroad. I've been to hotel management conferences in Mexico, Canada, and various places in Europe. Friends here often ask me why I don't leave Cuba. I have a very simple response: 'If you don't have a horse, you should cherish your donkey'. . . . Now, what is it you're interested in?"

"I would like to know what *you* believe happened to my brother Juan. I'm trying to put this to rest."

"I believe he was murdered," said Celia. "In Cuba it's not safe for a person like me to ask too many questions about a disappearance. People often disappear if they persistently question the system. . . . But since you're Representative Mendoza's sister, I'll tell you exactly what I believe.

"Juan was booked here for three nights. He was quiet, polite, and avoided contact other than being at my hotel and talking with his guide, Nacho Gomez. He ate in our restaurant or his room, wasn't demanding, and—to my knowledge—didn't talk with anyone other than Gomez. Then, one morning when we assumed he had left early for his last planned day of fishing, the police arrived and cleaned out his room. I didn't see them.

"A month or so later, Macduff Brooks, a guide who lives in Florida, came to fish. He also used Gomez as a guide. One evening they began to talk about your brother and Gomez suggested Brooks talk to me. We did, in the hall outside my office. I told him how the police had cleaned out Juan's room and that his guide had gone to the room early that morning with a staff member because your brother didn't show up on time to meet Gomez for a last day of fishing.

"Gomez told Brooks that in the room Juan's fishing gear for the day was in a bag by the door, clothes and a suitcase were on the bed, and the last inch of rum in a bottle was on the nightstand next to a couple of cigar butts."

"Did you go to the police?" Elena asked.

"No. I never asked the local police to explain why they cleaned out the room quickly and left. One doesn't challenge police actions in a town in Cuba. I tried to put it out of my mind. I did until Nacho Gomez went missing."

"What did you do about Gomez?"

"I didn't go to the police for the same reasons, but I began asking questions to people in this area I know and trust."

"Who were they?"

"I won't disclose their names. It's for their safety."

"I understand. Can you tell me what you were asking?"

"Little more than whether they had seen or heard anything about the disappearance of the two."

"Did any of them tell you anything of value in learning why and how the two men went missing?"

"Yes, but most of their responses involved rumors or that someone else said so and so."

"Are you satisfied with what you now know?"

"I still have questions, but, for the most part, I'm satisfied."

"Have you reached any conclusions in your mind about the disappearances?"

"Yes."

"And?"

"I won't say much, but I believe the two were abducted and taken to the barracuda research center. That was the last anyone saw of them. My guess is that your brother was fed to the barracudas. . . . Elena, I'm really not comfortable with talking about this anymore."

Elena had remained calm as she listened to Celia's opinion. "That's fine, Celia. You've been helpful. I think it confirms that they were murdered. Why and how aren't clear. But I accept that Juan's dead."

"I'm glad you agree," said Celia. . . . They had finished their meal. Celia got up from her chair and, after an affectionate and understanding hug, added, "I need to be getting home. Let me drop you off at your hotel."

"It's not far," Elena responded. "I'd like to walk and breathe in this wonderfully clean salt-flavored air. I understand why you live here. . . . I wish I could."

Elena walked leisurely toward the hotel, using the light of dusk and the moon to guide her. Her walk took her past the barracuda research center where she hoped there might be someone to talk to. The short driveway into the center was rough with deep pockets filled from an afternoon shower. A sweeping curve avoided an attractive group of palms and passed a depression that appeared to be a man-made retention pond. The research lab building was dark, showing only a single bare bulb hanging askew alongside the front door.

She went to the windows of the first floor, looked in, and saw no sign of anyone. Before she tried to enter the building, she was drawn by some emotion to the barracuda pens. She had little trouble finding her way with the moonlight and a small flashlight she carried in her bag. The pens were noiseless as she walked out the suspended ramp that hovered above them, holding onto the sides as the ramp undulated under her steps. There was no sound of any movement below, and when she used her flashlight, she learned it was quiet because the pens were empty. She couldn't imagine why.

Retracing her steps to the office, she tried the front and rear doors without success, but discovered a rear window where the lock had rusted. With some effort the window opened, allowing her barely enough room to slip inside. Her flashlight told her she was likely in a storeroom, but the room was empty. Carefully she opened the door to the hall, which led to the main office. Opening the door to the office, she took a chance and turned on the lights. The office was mostly bare, but there were a half-dozen packed boxes marked simply "Camagüey," the name of a Cuban city 250 miles to the east.

There was another storeroom to the rear, the door partly opened. She opened it further, reached in, turned on the lights, and froze. On a table on the far wall next to a carton lay two white sculls. One had a number of gold crowns other than on the front four teeth, one of which was a stub and apparently had been capped. The other skull showed that teeth were missing and those remaining had received little attention over the years. There was a small metal plate on the left side of the skull.

Elena knew that one skull was almost certainly her brother Juan; she knew he had gold crowns and a porcelain cap on one front tooth. The other skull could be that of Nacho Gomez. When her composure returned, she noticed that the empty carton had a label, and the bottom was filled with recent issues of *Granma*, suggesting that it served as packing insulation for something. That something had to be the skulls.

One flap of the carton was bent down in back. Elena pulled it up and gasped as she read the mailing label. The box was to be sent to Senator Jorge García García at an address in Miami, Florida. There was no sign of an accompanying letter.

Elena panicked. She took the box, placed Juan's skull in her large shoulder bag, set the second skull in the carton, left the office—leaving it as she had found it—and quickly headed out the drive toward the main road.

She felt Juan's skull bouncing against her hip as she walked rapidly back toward her hotel room. What should she do with the skull? If she got it back to the U.S., she could bury it. She thought the skull should be decently buried. . . . Her Catholic education never addressed such questions.

On the edge of the hotel property, a trash pile burned several weeks' accumulation of trash. It was unattended but located where it posed no threat of spreading. Without thinking clearly, Elena tossed the carton with Gomez's skull on top of what appeared the hottest place. She knew cremation was done at extremely high temperatures and the skull might survive the fire. She hoped it would be charred, mixed with the remains of the trash, and quickly disappears into some landfill.

Elena hurried to her room and sat in a chair by the bed, Juan's skull stowed in her locked bag in the closet. Sleep did not come easily that night, when it came at all. She never left the chair, at best nodding off several times before the dawn began to creep into the cabin.

In the morning, Elena struggled with exhaustion from lack of sleep and emotional trauma. She wanted to get out of Playa Larga and out of Cuba. She shouldn't fly on a commercial plane without risking the discovery of the skull, but she might have to take her chances.

Before she left Playa Larga, she had two visits on her list to complete. The first was to St. Peter the Fisherman. She thought that Macduff Brooks had something to do with its establishment in Playa Larga. . . . Her second stop would be the home Nacho Gomez to talk to his widow.

She walked the slight rise behind the local school to an unimposing building of cement block painted grayish silver that was certainly an attempt to match the color of the tarpon, known as the "silver king." On the front lawn a simple sign—written in Spanish—said:

St. Peter the Fisherman
Playa Larga, Matanzas, Cuba
Non-denominational
Pastor Alonzo Figueres

The front door was open and Elena walked in, was nearly knocked over by a man leaving the church with a fishing rod in one hand and studying a box of fishing flies in the other.

"Excuse *me*," she said. "I'm looking for Pastor Figueres."

"He's in the back room, lady," the man answered in English without the trace an accent. He was wearing a Columbia fishing shirt and a baseball cap embroidered with "Jackson Hole One Fly Contest 2009." He looked to be American.

Elena went beyond the altar and stopped at an open door. A man was sitting at a desk tying a fishing fly. He heard Elena, turned and asked, "Can I help you?"

"I'm looking for Pastor Figueres."

"I'm the pastor," he responded.

"My name is Elena Menendez. My brother Juan dissapeared from Playa Larga several months ago. He had been fishing with Nacho Gomez."

"I remember that."

"Can you tell me anything about Juan's disappearance?"

"Nothing, other than that everyone here in town believes he was murdered."

"Why do you say that?"

"The manager at the barracuda research center was drunk a couple of weeks ago and talked about a U.S. politician who was taken to the research center one night and not seen again."

"Who is the manager of the research center and where might I find him?"

"His name is—or was—Ricardo Arias."

"Was?"

"He was drunk, as he often was after dusk, and killed in an auto accident on the way home that evening. Head on into an old truck without headlights that was carrying sugar bagasse."

"I have one other person I'd like to talk to in Playa Larga. It's Nacho Gomez's wife."

"That would be Lydia. But she can't help."

"She isn't willing to talk?"

"She can't. The week after Nacho went missing, she had a stroke. She's paralyzed and unable to speak. Or comprehend anyone else."

"Pastor Figueres, is there anything else you know that would help me find out who killed my brother? Is there any talk in the town about who might have done it?"

"Not really. There's talk about a group of three who meet in the U.S. who were unhappy with your brother's trying to open trade and tourism with Cuba."

"Who are the three?"

I don't know their names, but one is a powerful political figure in Miami, another a wealthy sugar producer in Florida, and the third is a Cuban."

"Who is the Cuban?"

"I won't say anything more. It wouldn't be prudent."

"Is that person a minister in the Castro government?"

"I can't say anything more. Please leave, I've told you more than I should."

"One last question. Did any of these three actually do the killing of my brother and Nacho Gomez."

"Of course not. They had someone from Cuba do it for them. I'll say nothing more. Goodbye."

With that he got up and took Elena by the arm and escorted her out of the church and went back in and closed the door. Elena heard the lock click.

Elena left Playa Larga on a public bus for Havana the following morning. She stayed at the Melia hotel, took a flight the next afternoon to Nassau, then another to New York City, and lastly a train to Hartford.

Juan's skull accompanied her the whole way; not a single search of her bag was made.

42

TWO DAYS LATER

THANKSGIVING AT THE COTTAGE began for us when Elsbeth arrived Wednesday afternoon, twenty-four hours before turkey time. Sue came with her. I was down at the dock replacing the depth finder on my flats boat when I heard the Jeep drive in and walked up and met them at the stairs to the cottage.

"Were you invited to stay here?" I asked them, blocking the stairs and looking from one to the other. Sue looked embarrassed. Elsbeth looked combative.

"I live here," Elsbeth said. "Sue's my guest. She's staying in my room with me."

"Where're you going to eat?" I asked.

"Right here. Lucinda's in charge of the kitchen. That means *what* she serves and *who* she serves."

"And I suppose you both want laundry done?"

"No. You forget we're living in your old house in Gainesville. It has a laundry."

"Now what? I don't seem to be doing too well."

"Our bags are in the rear. Please carry them to our room."

"Anything else, miss?"

"We'll let you know."

Lucinda's been training Elsbeth how to deal with me.

Laughing, they edged by me and went upstairs to a warm welcoming hug from Lucinda, who was on the porch applauding another defeat for me.

I was standing at the bottom looking forlorn. I might have cried if I were not so tough. Then Elsbeth ran back downstairs and jumped on me with her arms around my neck and kissed me on my cheek. A tear ran down and dripped from my chin. It wasn't from Elsbeth. I guess I'm not so tough.

When we walked up the stairs and went into the cottage, Sue gave me a hug and kiss on the other cheek. I was beginning to enjoy the holiday.

"Lucinda," Elsbeth asked, "we having turkey tomorrow?"

"Of course, it's wild turkey with wild mushroom gravy."

"Why wild?" I asked. "Why not a fat Publix butterball?"

"Supermarkets sell turkeys with an added sodium solution," she answered. "Ours is organic. I'm trying to keep our sodium down."

"What kind of mushrooms? Shitake?" Sue asked, nodding to Lucinda.

"Probably psychedelic. From Mexico," I interjected.

"Not yours, Macduff," said Lucinda. "You get Inky Caps."

"They're poisonous!" I exclaimed. "They cause a rapid heartbeat, lightheadedness, and nausea—you trying to kill me?"

"Don't give me ideas. At least you'll go out happy . . . I'm cooking the turkey in white wine."

The meal was delicious, and I didn't feel lightheaded or nauseous. I did feel the wine.

Thanksgiving evening we all kayaked down Pellicer Creek, past the old Princess Estate, and to the Whitney research center on the Intracoastal Waterway where we'd left a vehicle and trailer.

Back at the cottage I opened a bottle of Freixenet Cordon Negro *Cava* from Spain. Elsbeth sat with Lucinda on the porch swing; Sue and I were in rocking chairs. We watched an osprey drift high above the pines and glide down and land on the highest piling on our boat pier. It stared into the water for a moment, dropped talons-first into the water, and lifted off, struggling with an 8" sea trout.

Sue turned to me and asked, "Are you two going back to Cuba?"

Before either Lucinda or I could answer, Elsbeth looked at me and added, "You *should go*. It's beautiful and. . . ."

Lucinda interrupted, "We can't go back. We were turned down."

"Why?" asked Sue.

"We don't know, but it has to do with Juan Mendoza."

"His death hasn't been solved?" asked Elsbeth, turning her head toward me.

"Ask Lucinda," I suggested to Elsbeth. "She's the family Hercule Poirot. I get us in trouble; she gets us out."

"I like that," Lucinda nodded and smiled, then turning to Elsbeth next to her, added, "The only evidence is the photos you brought back of the skull," her hand affectionately tapping on Elsbeth's knee. "Dan Wilson had the photos examined from every possible angle. He's satisfied Mendoza's dead. The Agency's lab in D.C. did find an indication of some tooth marks on the skull. Dan said they could be from a barracuda, a very big one."

"Sue and I didn't know about that. Do you agree, Dad?"

"I don't dare to disagree."

"Were you this wimpy before you went to law school?"

"No, it happened when I met Lucinda."

Lucinda smiled again.

"Tell the girls your feelings about Mendoza," she suggested, looking at me.

"One, Mendoza's dead, and you two brought back the evidence. Circumstantial, but the best produced thus far. Enough to proceed on the assumption that Mendoza died in Playa Larga and that it wasn't from natural causes. I believe he was thrown into the barracuda pens. If he fell in, they would have pulled out his remains and reported it as an accident."

"And not saved his skull and bleached it," Sue added.

"Good point," I agreed. "So we move to the who and the why."

"But if we know who did it, shouldn't we know why?" Elsbeth asked.

"Of course, especially if there's to be any conviction for murder. It's hard to talk about one without the other."

"So *why* was he killed?" Sue wondered out loud.

"He might have walked into the research center uninvited and witnessed a crime," I surmised without support. "He paid the price of losing his life. That means he was most likely killed by locals. But not necessarily. Mendoza might have had enemies who traced him to Playa Larga and killed him."

"Then the research center is out of it?"

"Not necessarily. We don't know if the marks on the skull *are* from a barracuda. His body could have been taken into the center and fed to the barracuda to get rid of the evidence."

"This is getting grim," noted Elsbeth.

"Murder is grim," I said, and continued. "In addition to someone in Cuba wanting to kill Mendoza for any of several reasons, it could have been someone from outside Cuba, most likely someone from the U.S. The why issue could be jealousy of his status or success. He was considered a likely next senator from New Mexico. That might have meant he stood to gain power in D.C. at the expense of someone else. Someone jealous. It could have been retribution. Maybe the one Mendoza beat in the last election. Or possibly some woman scorned. Too much 'maybe this' and 'maybe that.'"

"*Who* did it is no less clear; too many possibilities," said Lucinda. "Macduff, aren't you saying there is simply too little to go on to proceed?"

"Exactly. Far too much speculation. And you and I aren't going to be the ones who try to sort it out. We're through. We need to move forward with our lives."

"I have one question, Mr. Brooks," stated Sue. "Are Lucinda and you under any danger because you were involved with trying to help Elena Mendoza find out about her brother's disappearance?"

"Possibly. But we're not the only ones in this room who may be in danger. You and Elsbeth found and photographed the skulls. If the killer knew you photographed the skulls, your lives might be in danger. And, if there were a trial, you'd have to testify about photographing the skulls."

Elsbeth and Sue looked at each other as though they had been caught doing something wrong. Lucinda looked at me as though I was responsible for bringing the two into this mess.

I guessed she was right.

43

THREE DAYS LATER IN MIAMI

MIAMI WAS UNDER A CLOUD OF STORMS drifting slowly northward from the Caribbean. Slanting rain pelted the twenty-fourth floor windows of the headquarters of the American Sugar Company. Two multi-deck cruise ships on their way home from a week of holiday for the masses could be seen through the rain blurred windows entering Government Cut.

Two men and a woman sat in deep, soft lounge chairs in a U-shape facing the windows; a small table in the center held three full coffee mugs bearing the logo of the sugar company.

After a few moments of quietly sipping their coffee, each head turned from the gloomy outside, and the three began their conversation.

"My staff has informed me that six days ago Elena Mendoza returned to the U.S. after a brief two-night trip to Cuba," said Cuban Minister of the Interior Christina Sandoval. "She had spent the first night and following morning in Havana, where she met with some of our trade people."

"She didn't go to Cuba with *our* endorsement," interrupted Senator Jorge García García. "Why did she go?"

"In Havana Mendoza had dinner with a Celeste Jones," said Sandoval. "Jones is the public affairs officer at the U.S. embassy . . . rather, the U.S. *Interests Section.* We have no idea what they talked about, but my contacts at the restaurant say they were very cordial to each another.

"The next afternoon Mendoza was driven to Playa Larga. She had dinner with the manager of the Playa Larga hotel, Celia Bustamante. The hotel, as you both know, is where Juan Mendoza stayed three nights before he disappeared.

"Our reports indicate Bustamante and Mendoza ate at a small restaurant on the edge of the town, after which Mendoza returned to her hotel room. Early the following morning Mendoza visited the St. Peter the Fisherman church and talked to the pastor, then left on a bus to Havana where she boarded a flight to the Bahamas. She next flew to New York City and went to Hartford by train.

"That's all we know. I assume she was seeking information about her brother's disappearance that Macduff Brooks had failed to learn or had not told her about. He is the fishing guide who both the Mendozas had previously fished with in Montana. He has an unusual past which is not fully clear but involves several murders on his fishing boats in Florida and Montana. I wouldn't be surprised if Brooks doesn't know Elena went to Cuba."

"Is Brooks a threat to our plans?" asked the third person, Alfredo Luna, CEO of the sugar company, looking attentively at Sandoval.

"Don't worry about him, Alfredo. We would like to talk to him about how he and his wife Lucinda departed Cuba recently, but especially about a trip he may have attempted two decades earlier under a different name while consulting for the CIA. If he ever revisits Cuba, we will detain him for questioning about that unsuccessful earlier attempt to visit Cuba."

"Didn't you invite Mr. & Mrs. Brooks to visit Cuba recently?" asked Luna.

"Yes, but for some reason the U.S. Treasury Department rejected that trip," she replied. "And we withdrew our invitation."

Luna rose from his chair and walked slowly to the window, looking out and saying nothing, lost in thought. Neither Sandoval nor García García interrupted him.

Turning to face the others, Luna said, "If the U.S. completely opens trade with Cuba, my sugar interests will be in chaos. Any re-opening the debate about the continuation of the lucrative sugar supports we receive from Congress is troublesome for me. Has Elena Mendoza made any public comments about trade with Cuba? I thought we had talked to her about that."

García García thought for a moment before he answered. "She has spoken in favor of ending the boycott, but not as forcefully as had her brother Juan. Also, she cast several votes in the House against bills her brother sponsored that would have completely opened trade and tourism. Juan paid the price for his position.

"Elena's plans for being elected to the Senate are no longer threatened. She backed off supporting another trade expansion bill when the PAC group here in Miami donated generously to her campaign fund. She is a popular Connecticut figure, but she faces a much admired former mayor of Hartford in her next primary. He's advocated either no change or tightening the noose the boycott created. That's probably why Elena has shifted from supporting open trade to keeping the status quo."

"Which is exactly what we want," said Luna quietly. He nodded and returned to his seat, then added, "It's what we instructed her to do."

Luna sipped his coffee, looked at García García, and said, "Senator, you know what goes on in Congress. Can we be assured of Elena's support."

"If we continue to pay for it, yes."

"Do we trust her?"

"As much as you trust me."

Luna thought to himself that no politician was trustworthy when the issue was re-election. He also thought that Elena had served her purpose to the group.

"I don't know the Brookses—husband or wife," said Luna, changing the subject. "Are you telling me, Senator and Madame Minister, that the Brookses are absolutely no threat and we can drop any thoughts of having to deal with them?"

"I agree," said García García, "but I don't know them personally. Minister, you know them, don't you?"

"Not well. My son assisted Brooks' wife for several days. She was photographing in Havana for a Canadian travel magazine. After they returned to the U.S. on an unauthorized flight which was embarrassing to my government and to me personally, I invited them to return to Havana. I planned to have them detained until we received a full explanation for the fingerprints. It could be treason, if Brooks were Hunt. When Hunt was with the CIA in Mexico, they were planning to assassinate Fidel Castro. However, the U.S. government—apparently because of the President's intervention—rejected that invitation. I never spoke to the Brookses about whether they would accept my invitation. I have no trouble were we to decide to get rid of the Brookses. Including Macduff Brooks' daughter."

"That leaves us with only one problem—what to do with Elena Mendoza," Luna noted. "Should we merely reduce that threat, or eliminate it? We can't have her acting on her own."

"Before we deal further with to Elena, perhaps we can talk about two new faces in the picture," said García García.

Luna looked at him questioningly, but nodded.

"There are two new players. One is the sole House Representative from Montana, David Longstreet. The other is an influential and successful Montana cattle rancher named Cliff Cameron."

"Do they affect our control of the U.S.'s Cuban policy?" asked Luna, appearing agitated by any such possibility. Turning to Sandoval, he asked, "Do you know either of them?"

"I do not," she responded.

Luna turned back to García García. "Go on."

"Longstreet is a multi-term unpredictable clown," said García García. "For years he openly favored more trade, thinking he could gather new trade for Montana. Now he favors no change because of pressure from Cameron and receiving PAC money from here in Miami. But tomorrow he will change his mind if the wind shifts overnight."

Luna wrinkled his brow, stared at the floor, rested his chin on his hands, and rocked on the edge of his chair. "Longstreet sounds weak; it's a matter of how we use him. Cameron sounds different; it's a matter of how we *satisfy* him. . . . Tell me about Cameron. I may have met him. I would suspect he shares my concern about change in Cuba."

"But for a different reason," Sandoval suggested. "He sells to Cuba. You do not. He wants to maintain the status quo to protect his near monopoly in marketing cattle to Cuba. You want to maintain the status quo to assure that Cuba does not export sugar to the U.S."

"Are you supporting a position that hurts your country?" challenged Luna, staring at the Minister. "If Cuba restores relations with the U.S., it will only be able to pay claims for confiscated property if it is able to once again be America's source of sugar. Cuba again becomes dependent on the U.S."

"You forget that I wish to be president of Cuba, but not to have a free democratic election. The status quo with the U.S. works best for me."

"And you *will* be president, just as I will continue to be a powerful senior senator," added García García.

"We may have to meet again; I am unclear about the intentions of Elena Mendoza and what she has already done," noted Luna. "And I am not convinced that we should forget about the Brookses."

"We may have to do more than talk about Elena," added Sandoval.

44

THE FLORIDA WINTER SEASON

THE ONLY REMINDER OF CUBA after Thanksgiving was a Christmas card we received from Celeste Jones in Havana. But it did not depict Cuba. It showed the Place Dauphine on the Île de la Cité in Paris under freshly fallen snow at dusk, the only lights flowing from streetlamps and the windows of Le Caveau du Palais restaurant.

Celeste was anticipating Paris; working there in public affairs after Havana would be like changing planets, if not professions. But the card noted that her transfer was delayed until spring. Lucinda and I knew that the card would likely be the last correspondence between us; Celeste came into our lives because of an unhappy event in Cuba, and she would likely spend the next decade or more in various capital cities around the globe, with Cuba a fading memory.

The Christmas and New Year's holidays passed uneventfully for us, beginning with Elsbeth arriving from Gainesville at the completion of her first year at UF. The grades she transferred from Maine gave her one full semester of credit; in January she thus began what would be the second semester of her sophomore year. She would soon have to declare a major and hadn't given us a hint about the direction she was headed.

January proved balmy. On more than one occasion Lucinda and I dined on the wrought iron railed porch at the A1A restaurant in St. Augustine, under a galaxy of seasonal white lights that attracted thousands to the city each year. We didn't hear a single word from Dan or Elena about Cuba.

February saw many trees leaf out and azaleas blossom. For most of the month we added only light cotton sweaters to reduce a few evening chills. But occasional modest thrusts of cold northwest winds had their impact; Lucinda and I escaped a few of these "cold" spells by spending three weeks on No Name Key in the Lower Keys of Florida. Again, we didn't hear a word about Cuba, which continued our joy of the winter season.

March found us frequently together on the water in our flats boat, fishing the salt marsh flats near the cottage for sea trout and blues. And with less enthusiasm, occasionally fishing deeper for redfish and flounder. We still didn't hear a word from Dan or Elena about Cuba, nor do I recall that the word "Cuba" was spoken even once by either of us.

Could it last? Was the Cuban experience becoming as distant in our memories as the gill net, wicker man, shuttle gals, and earlier murders? It seemed too good to be true. And so it proved with April—*too good to be true*.

"It's time to think about heading West," Lucinda announced abruptly in mid-April as we sat on our dock, looking thirty feet away at four roseate spoonbills searching for food on a mud flat. Half the flat was jammed with oysters being uncovered by the ebbing tide at the rate of an inch every ten minutes. The oysters looked like a scattered arrangement of tiny fountains as they sent squirts spraying upwards from their seemingly closed shells.

"Never eat an oyster that hasn't recently squirted," I observed.

"Is that scientifically supported?" she asked, sitting on the arm of the one-person Adirondack chair I occupied and had bolted to the dock after she left me for Manhattan over a year ago, when I vowed I would never again share my dock-seating with a woman.

"It's the result of years of research I have done, eating oysters from many sources: hotel buffets, fish markets that had lost their refrigeration for unstated hours, conference dinners in the middle of the country far from salt water, and these oysters off our dock that assure me they are alive by squirting. I discovered a relationship between how long the oyster has been dead and the frequency of my trips to the bathroom."

"You make oysters sound so appetizing!"

"They can be, taking them from our flats and cooking them. . . . I love raw oysters; but from experience I'm not as convinced that they love me."

"I like them, but they're so hard to pull open," she observed.

"A man may as well open an oyster without a knife as open a lawyer's mouth without a fee."

"Enough philosophy. . . . When *are* we going West?"

"It's still April, an 'iffy' month on Montana rivers."

"Could we put off the 'iffy' and go a southern route, maybe to New Mexico and then north?"

"And check out the San Juan River starting at the Texas Hole below the Navaho Dam?"

"Sounds good," she said. "Have another raw oyster."

45

MID-APRIL TO MONTANA

DRIVING ACROSS THE COUNTRY by a southern route, we swiftly tired of traffic on I-10 and angled northwest to cross the Mississippi River at Natchez, passed through Louisiana, and then confronted North Texas on U.S. 82. Thankfully, we missed Lubbock by shifting to U.S. 70. We headed straight to Albuquerque and altogether avoided facing the Great Plains states. But I may never again complain about boredom entrapped in the "amber waves of grain" of Kansas after enduring North Texas.

The one Texas motel we stopped at, only because of exhaustion, was built in the 1950's and since then the owners had done little more than change the sheets. The rug was stained in multiple colors, the sink rusted and the faucet dripped, and the 11" black and white TV brought us a single snowy station.

"Macduff," Lucinda asked the next day as we passed a "Welcome to New Mexico" sign, "did you do that on purpose?"

"What?"

"Take the scenic route across Texas. Wuff's had her head under her blanket ever since we crossed the Mississippi."

"It *was* pretty grim. Maybe Mexico would take Texas back."

"They're too smart," she said. "We'd have to throw in something more, like Minnesota or Connecticut."

"Mentioning Connecticut makes me think of Elena Mendoza," I noted. "That's her state. What do you suppose she's up to with the search for her brother's killer?"

"I don't want to think about Elena at all or the Sandovals or Cameron or Longstreet or especially García García. I want to enjoy a Montana summer."

"How did we get so involved? I just want to fish and play with Wuff and look across and see and think about you."

"In that order?"

"I must have dyslexia. I get things backwards."

"I dream that someday you'll love me as much as you do Wuff."

"Not until you've learned to fetch."

The silence that followed was finally shattered by my phone. Lucinda reached over and took it from my shirt pocket, opened it, tapped "speaker," and said, "This is Macduff Brooks."

"Your voice has changed. This is Dan Wilson. Remember me?"

"Every midnight when the nightmares set in."

"Remember *Cuba*?"

"We think about it daily," interjected Lucinda. "But we are *not* going back. Have a nice weekend. Goodbye." She hit "off" on the phone.

Thirty seconds later it rang again. This time I answered.

"Hello again," Dan said. "You can't get rid of me that easily."

"Do you have any good news, Dan, like you have a new grandson or your cholesterol is under control or you've solved the homeless problem in D.C.?"

"I want you to go back to Cuba—tomorrow."

"Great! You finally got us fishing licenses for Cuba from Treasury. How did you do that?" I asked.

"No. I got you new Glocks from our weapons supply. They're on their way to the Interests Section in a diplomatic pouch."

"That does not sound good, Dan," said Lucinda, setting the phone down on the console between the seats because her hands were shaking.

"It isn't good. Two nights ago Celia Bustamante was shot in her office at the Playa Larga hotel."

"Dead?"

"No, but we quickly had it announced as a murder to suit our interests. Celia's recovering at our Interests Section in Havana. We have a small medical clinic there for minor problems for our staff."

"Being shot isn't minor. What happened?"

"We learned about it only through Celeste Jones' replacement to be, Will Kenny. Because of a mix-up about Celeste's delayed departure, he arrived in Havana early and was being introduced to Cuba, including a trip to the Bay of Pigs area that had a stop at Playa Larga. Kenny was unknown there and was instructed to check on a group of fishermen from the Florida Keys who use the two St. Peter the Fisherman churches as a way of getting to Cuba to fish. You of all persons know that's not permitted."

"Did Kenny see the shooting?"

"No, he was in the bar having a drink with a fishing guide from Key West named Brian Hawes. Know him?"

"I hate to say it, but yes, I know Brian well. I use him as my guide when I'm in the Keys. I don't want to get him in trouble if he came to Cuba without a U.S. license. But I believe he has dual citizenship and carries a Canadian passport along with one from the U.S. Was Brian involved?"

"He was the first to reach Bustamante. He and Kenny weren't far from her office and heard a door slam shut and what Brian thought was a voice calling. Brian ran to her office with Will close behind. They found Celia on the floor in a widening pool of blood. They stopped the bleeding. She was conscious and asked them to get her away from the hotel. They carried her out the back door; put her in the back of Kenny's car, and drove to the Interests Section in Havana. She's there now. . . . One other thing, we never heard shots."

"Why has it been called a murder?"

"We didn't want the shooter coming back to finish what he, or she, started. Celia's going to survive, and we want to talk to her. She's weak, but stable. I'm going to Cuba tomorrow. I want you both with me, using assumed names and carrying forged Canadian diplomatic passports.

"Lucinda will pose as the owner of a large tour agency in Toronto that wants to shift tours from Mexico and Central America to Cuba. Macduff, you're with the Canadian Tourism Commission. I'll be Quentin Ross with the U.S. Interior Department. We'll be met by Kenny, talk to Celeste—and to Celia if she's up to it—and then go to Playa Larga."

"Is Brian Hawes still in Cuba?"

"As far as we know, yes."

"Dan, are Macduff and I related in your new drama?" asked Lucinda.

"Husband and wife. You'll be Hugh and Gabrielle Brown. . . . Pack lightly. My plane will be at the St. Augustine airport at nine in the morning."

"We won't be there."

"Backing out already?"

"We're in our SUV driving west. We just passed a sign that said 'Albuquerque – 50 miles.'"

"Damn! Then be at the Air Force base adjacent to the Albuquerque airport at the same time—9:00 a.m. mountain time. I'll leave here two hours earlier than I planned. We're not due in Cuba at any specific time, and we have landing permission for the José Martí airport in Havana. . . . Gotta lot to do. See you in the morning. Bye." With that he hung up.

"What just happened?" I asked Lucinda.

"I think we're going to Cuba in the morning!"

46

CUBA REVISITED

WE REACHED THE AIRPORT AT 8:50 a.m., drove around for fifteen frustrating minutes before finding the Air Force base entry, and left our SUV locked in a hanger after loading two small bags into Dan's agency's jet. Most of what had been packed carefully in those bags four days earlier destined for Montana was now scattered in the back of the SUV. Lucinda and I each took one casual outfit from the SUV pile—Lucinda by careful selection and me by random grabbing—and added some lightweight clothes we bought at an Albuquerque Banana Republic ten minutes before the doors were locked for the night.

Wuff was dropped off to stay with a Sheltie breeding couple who our vet from Florida once mentioned ran a reliable Sheltie boarding house in the foothills of the Sangre de Cristo Mountains. Wuff didn't want to leave the SUV until she saw a dozen other Shelties, jumped from the vehicle into their midst, and immediately forgot about us.

Dan was waiting on the plane with coffee and pastry.

"Does the plane look familiar, Macduff?"

"It's a Gulf Stream. Nothing but the best when taxpayer dollars are used. By any chance, has it ever flown to a private ranch in Guatemala?"

"You remember! This is the plane that flew you to take out Abdul Khaliq Isfahani nearly a decade ago."

"Don't remind me. The plane looks better than I do. . . . Remember that I didn't kill Isfahani."

"But you got him two years ago in the Sudan. Anyway, he's out of our lives."

"Are you going to try to coerce me into an assassination attempt in Cuba? It won't work."

"If I thought we could knock off Raul and get out safely, I would say 'yes.' But no, we want you two to help us with the Mendoza case. It's gotten complicated."

"How so?" asked Lucinda.

"We bugged the CEO's office at American Sugar in Miami a month ago. Two weeks ago we hit gold."

"Why the American Sugar Company?"

"Its CEO and biggest shareholder is Alfredo Luna. We learned—and you don't need to know how—that Luna has been meeting with Senator Jorge García García about Cuba and the Mendoza death."

"Why Luna?"

"He's paranoid. If the U.S. opens relations with Cuba, it will also agree to open the U.S. to buying Cuban sugar. Possibly even restoring the sugar quota of the 1950's. That would be the end of Luna's forty years of having nearly all the U.S. sugar market. He's a billionaire. He wants more; his greed has made him unpredictable."

"What does their meeting have to do with our going to Cuba?"

"Let me finish?" asked Dan. "A third person was at the meeting—Cuban Interior Minister Christina Sandoval."

"What did they talk about?"

"First about Elena Mendoza's most recent trip to Cuba. The group of three that meet in Miami didn't know she was planning to go. . . . Elena had dinner with Celeste Jones, then went to Playa Larga the next day and had dinner with Celia Bustamante. *We* don't know what they said, nor do we suppose the three meeting in Miami know.

"One last thing, Mac. The three talked about whether you two are a threat to their plans, whatever those plans are."

"Do they believe we're a threat?"

"No, but Sandoval said Cuban officials would like to talk to you if you ever go back."

"What else did they discuss?" I insisted on knowing since we were going back.

"The heart of their conversation was the need to preserve the status quo in trading with Cuba. Luna fears competition from Cuban sugar, especially combined with a reduction of U.S. sugar subsidies. García García fears loss of his power in Florida if the Cuban dialogue goes away. And Sandoval doesn't want her chances to be the next president of Cuba harmed by any dramatic changes like those in parts of Eastern Europe."

"How does this involve who killed Juan Mendoza?"

"It involves his sister, Elena. The group in Miami started to discuss her and even raised the possibility of eliminating her, but got diverted to discussing Cameron and Longstreet. They concluded that those two were not a problem. We assume Sandoval would know more about what happened in Cuba, but she didn't offer any information. We don't know about Elena Mendoza. With Celia Bustamante shot two days ago, we have to think about Elena as the possible shooter."

"But Elena's reliable. You said so yourself recently."

"We have some reason to rethink that," explained Dan.

"You're not saying she might have been responsible for her brother's death? Or Gomez? Or shooting Bustamante?"

"I'm only saying I want to rethink her role. . . . I'm going to tell you something about her that we dug up. . . . Elena is four years older than Juan. She was sexually active at sixteen and seduced her brother Juan as part of an initiation to a high school sorority in Miami. She forced herself on him several more times before she went off to college"

"Was any of that made public?"

"No. The family was prominent and apparently paid off or threatened the few who knew."

"What does this have to do with Juan's death?"

"We did some investigating in New Mexico. Juan's wife died of breast cancer a year before Juan went to Cuba. She had told a friend the story of Elena's seductions and that Juan was receiving demands from Elena to stay in the House and not run for Senate. And of course not to pursue any presidential aspirations. Juan rejected her, embarrassed that he had never been able to do so years before when she humiliated and abused him."

"That's a motive, but it doesn't make Elena a murderer," Lucinda observed. "Unless she was *working* for the three who were meeting in Miami."

"We don't know," Dan continued. "But, they aren't happy with her acting on her own and going to Cuba without their knowledge."

"You two hopefully are going to talk to Celia in Havana. She knows and trusts you. If she is able to talk, find out what she knows. Then go to Playa Larga and check around some more. Lucinda's going partly to keep you from splitting to go fishing like you did last time."

"That's unfair! I was in Playa Larga because of a fishing exchange with the churches, and I had to make it look serious by fishing."

"Whatever. This time leave your rods with me if they're in your bags."

"Damn! I've bought a new four-piece Winston rod I want to try fishing for bones."

"See what I mean," Dan said wincing and shaking his head.

Lucinda smiled and nodded a "What do I do with him?" silent response.

The flight to Havana took us across a calm and cloudless Gulf of Mexico. Freighters going and coming to places like Tampa and Veracruz left long contrail-like wakes in the Gulf waters. Soon after the Keys appeared to the left and Cuba ahead, we landed in Havana and passed through security using our assumed names on diplomatic passports. Not a question was asked.

Will Kenny was waiting with an Interests Section car, and we melded with the usual assortment of Havana's methods of transportation—a few cars and trucks, double busses, tractors, and occasionally a horse-drawn cart. It was gridlock in slow motion. At the Interests Section building, we were taken immediately by a Marine guard to a room where Celia Bustamante was sitting up in bed reading *Granma*.

She looked up at us, smiled and said, holding up *Granma*, "This is Cuba's answer to England's *Punch*. . . . I guess I'll be emigrating to North Cuba, which you folks call Florida. Or to Spain, where my grandparents were from and fled to Cuba during the late 1930's. Ironically, Elena Mendoza pressed me about why I hadn't defected.

"I still don't want to leave, but I agree my life here is of uncertain duration. I have a cousin in Tampa. He visited here last year and said he'd take me in anytime. I didn't realize how soon 'anytime' was going to occur. . . . Thanks for coming to see me."

"I'm Dan Wilson, Ms. Bustamante. I work for the U.S. government. Lucinda and Macduff and I go back a number of years. We're going to take you to the U.S. in a few days. We have the go-ahead from the Cuban government. Do you feel well enough to talk?"

"I'd like to. It gets boring lying here and having my blood pressure, temperature, pulse, and who knows what else checked every hour. I guess you'd like to hear my version of the shooting?"

"Anytime you feel you can," Dan answered.

Celia repeated what Dan had learned from Celeste. The shooting happened so quickly Celia had little to tell: Sitting at her desk, engaged in preparing boring reports for the government, she had looked up as a person with a long coat and mask came into her office with a gun pointing at her. She hadn't gotten a word out when she was hit by a bullet. It knocked her off her chair. Maybe that saved her life because two more shots went into the back of the chair and desk.

She could add nothing more about the incident, except for one thing. She thought the person to be slim and perhaps little more than five-and-a-half-feet tall. The most telling mark was that the person's hands were not covered and the fingernails were painted red. Celia assumed her shooter was a woman.

As Celia finished her brief comments, another Marine escorted two men into the room and left. She held out her arms as best she could and hugged each of them. I knew one was Brian Hawes, my guide friend from the Keys. The other was Will Kenny. He smiled at Dan, and they shook hands warmly, which I took to confirm Kenny was joining the CIA mission staff in Havana.

"Brian, I'm Dan Wilson. You know Macduff. This is his wife, Lucinda. We're here with diplomatic passports, mine as Quentin Ross of the Interior Department and the Brookses as Gabrielle and Hugh Brown from Canada. Use those names outside this room. I'd like to hear what you and Will have to say. Unless Ms. Bustamante feels too weak to continue."

"I'm fine," Celia stated.

"Brian and I were at the bar at the hotel in Playa Larga," Kenny began. "We'd been talking about our planned meeting with Celia, and as we got up from the table, listened to a door slammed in the hall toward her office. We entered the hall in time to see someone running out a door in the hall that led outside. We never heard shots; the shooter must have used a silencer.

"Celia's door was closed and we made out a whimpering sound and something fall. We opened the door and saw her on the floor by her desk. She was struggling and had pulled on the cord to a desk lamp, knocking it over and causing the noise we heard. She tried to move but passed out. Brian and I stopped her bleeding; she had been shot in the left shoulder, close to her neck and not far from her carotid artery. The bullet came out her back and shattered a picture frame on the wall behind her desk. The damage seemed to be to her muscles and soft tissue around the shoulder."

"Why did you move her?" Dan asked. "Wouldn't it have been better to keep her still and call in a local doctor?"

"We didn't know whether the shooter was interrupted and got off only the one shot and might return," said Hawes. "And we didn't know how to find a local doctor who wouldn't call the police."

"Also," interrupted Kenny, "Brian was a medic in the Army in Iraq. He took charge and agreed that Celia could travel. We carried her to the Interest Section's car I was driving and came here. I phoned and said to have a doctor present when we arrived and that the matter had to be kept quiet."

"Did anyone at the hotel see or hear anything and come to help?" asked Dan.

"We left too quickly to know," responded Kenny.

"What happened to the bullet? Was it lodged in the wall behind the shattered picture?" Dan asked.

"I went back to Playa Larga the next day and nosed around, mainly listening," said Brian. "The word at the hotel was that the police arrived an hour after the shooting. Like Juan Mendoza's case, the room was cleared and cleaned. The police apparently discovered and removed the bullet. Why that happened again is a mystery, and no one's talking."

"Macduff is going to Playa Larga tomorrow. If you have anything that might help him, let him know now," suggested Kenny.

"Mac," Brian said, turning toward me, "talk to Pepe Cañas. He's a guide and can be found through the St. Peter the Fisherman church. He has a good knowledge of Playa Larga and the Zapata Reserve area, including who knows what and who knows who."

I turned to Dan and asked, "Is Lucinda going with me?"

"No. She's staying here. She's meeting with some Cuban interior ministry officials who deal with tourism. They work for Christina Sandoval. Lucinda might pick up something useful."

"Dan, I'm known in Playa Larga as Macduff Brooks, not Hugh Brown."

"You won't look like you do now when you go tomorrow. We'll work on you in the morning. Anyway, you didn't know anyone there except Nacho Gomez, who's dead, and Celia. Remember that you're a lower level Canadian Tourist Commission official trying to increase recreational tourism by Canadians, including fishing. *You* don't fish. Don't even think of going fishing. Understand?"

"But this is a great time for fishing the Hatiguanico River. The tarpo. . . ."

"*No fishing!* Period!" Dan responded, turning his head away from me.

We'll see about that, I thought.

47

LATER THE SAME DAY

WHEN CELIA SHOWED SIGNS SHE NEEDED TO REST, Lucinda, Dan, and I went directly to the office of Celeste Jones. She was expecting us.

"Let's go where we can talk. Hungry?" she asked.

"Sure," Lucinda quickly answered, "our last meal was in New Mexico."

Kenny joined us, and Celeste's driver dropped the five of us next to the cathedral in Old Havana.

"Aren't we near La Bodeguita?" asked Lucinda. "Are we going there?" she added.

"It's around the corner. Too crowded and not very good food," replied Celeste. "We're going to a new paladar named after and run by a woman who used to work at a state-owned restaurant and always thought she'd open her own place when the rules changed and private enterprise was restored. The rules were changed a few years ago, and her paladar is the best in Havana for traditional *ropa vieja*—shredded beef. OK?"

"Right now shredded anything sounds fine," I said.

Our first mojitos were downed and refills brought to the table as we talked about Celeste's next assignment in Paris and Will's acclimation to Havana after transferring from Belgrade. Then we turned to Celia's shooting.

"Who do you suspect shot Celia?" asked Lucinda looking at Celeste.

"I have my suspicions based on what I've learned in my brief time here," Will answered, after Celeste nodded toward him to answer the question and perhaps provide a new perspective. "But not enough to make any accusations. It's kind of off the top of my head."

"Tell us."

"Celeste filled me in on three people who meet to discuss what can be done to keep U.S.-Cuban relations the way they are. Each member stands to gain by no change."

"Benefit enough to murder two persons and attempt to kill a third?" Lucinda asked.

"You decide," Celeste directed.

"Is your information coming from conclusions reached here or with others in D.C.?" I asked.

"Both," said Will. "Dan knows some of this. It's his agency that's involved here. I'm just a foreign service guy."

"I know little," Dan responded, looking embarrassed, knowing that Lucinda and I would have expected him to share his information.

"Can you tell us the *names* of the group?" Lucinda asked, wondering if she had heard of them before.

"I will," said Celeste, with Will and Dan nodding their approval. "One is a Florida senator from Miami—Jorge García García."

"What Lucinda and I know about him," I interjected, "—only because he's our senior senator in Florida—is that he's powerful, ambitious, and short on brain matter. That's not a good combination."

"He's been in office too long," Celeste suggested, nodding. "He's always interfering with U.S. relations with Cuba. He thinks decisions about Cuba are to be made in Miami by himself as the leader of the exiles. As long as enough Floridians think he's important to keep in office, he stays. His views are always consistent with a Miami-based PAC that spreads money around at election time proportional to the PAC's motives."

"What are the motives?" Lucinda asked.

"At first they were to overthrow Castro and put Cuba back in the hands of the likes of those who fled in 1959. That view is changing, and not to García García's liking. But he has to go along, or he'll be gone from office at the next election."

"What's he conceded?"

"He's willing to accept Cuba as it is, but he doesn't want any more movement that might create a Cuba that is like China or Vietnam—a mixture of a communist government and a tightly controlled amount of capitalism."

"Do the early exiles accept the status quo?"

"Not with any enthusiasm. But the younger generation Cuban-Americans are changing. They seem untroubled by the slow movement toward a Cuba that trades with the U.S."

"Does García García worry about any *direct* threats to his next re-election campaign?"

"Yes, or rather he did," expressed Dan. "He was worried that Juan Mendoza would become a senator from New Mexico and increasingly dilute García García's standing as the godfather of Hispanics in Congress. Remember that Mendoza grew up in Miami."

"Doesn't this suggest that García García ordered Mendoza's death?" I asked.

"Not García García alone," Dan responded. "He's too scared to get his hands dirty."

"Then who?" I continued.

"The group also includes one Cuban—Interior Minister Christina Sandoval."

"How do the three meet?" asked Will. "García García isn't welcome in Cuba. And he doesn't *want* to go there. Does Sandoval travel to Florida?"

"Yes," said Dan, interrupting. "Recently, she has flown commercial to D.C., where she allegedly does some work at the Cuban Interests Section, Cuba's de facto diplomatic mission in Washington. At some point, she flies to Miami in a private jet and lands at a private airport west of Miami."

"Which airport?"

"*Very* private. It's the airport on the property of the American Sugar Company."

"What's that company's interest in all this?"

"It's the interest of the company's owner, Alfredo Luna," Dan said.

"Luna is the third member of the group," interjected Celeste.

"Why is he interested? American Sugar doesn't trade with Cuba?" Lucinda asked.

"He's the head of the PAC that funds campaigns. His interest in keeping the status quo is the fear that, if the U.S. restores full trade with Cuba, any deal involving even a modest payment for Cuba's expropriations of U.S. property will have to restore Cuba as the main supplier of sugar to the U.S. That will be Cuba's only way to earn hard currency."

"Could Luna have been involved in Juan Mendoza's death?" I asked Dan.

Will quickly responded, confirming in my mind who pays his salary. "We've investigated Luna. He stands to lose hundreds of millions of dollars if he loses dominance of the U.S. market. Remember that U.S. sugar production is highly subsidized. That could come to an end if we reach a deal with Cuba. Politics will rule, not economic sense."

I was puzzled by all that had been laid out before us.

"Dan, Luna isn't any more likely to travel to Cuba than is García García. And we know Sandoval goes to Miami. Do you think the group meeting in Miami gave the go-ahead to kill Juan Mendoza?"

"This is where I have to speculate more than I'd like," responded Dan. "I suspect Juan Mendoza was identified as a danger to the group's interests. I believe they would like to have *learned* of Mendoza's death. But I doubt that they ordered anything more than encouragement."

"Did the three ever meet with Juan Mendoza?"

"Not to our knowledge. But they could have before Juan went to Cuba. We know they met with someone who was very close to Mendoza."

"Close enough to be his sister?" asked Lucinda, certain of the answer.

"Exactly," answered Will, who repeated what he knew from the Interests Section's files about Elena Mendoza's abuse problems with her brother and her frequent trips to Cuba.

"Is it possible that Elena killed her brother?" Lucinda asked.

"Possible? Yes. Provable? Not so easy."

"Will or Celeste, did Celia say anything to you about Elena before we arrived?" I asked.

"Yes," answered Celeste. "Enough to convince me that Elena . . . she had dinner with Celia, who said Elena acted strangely. Less like one who was trying to collect information than one who was trying to be assured that information available was not incriminating."

"To Elena?"

"Yes. . . . Celia also mentioned that the pastor of St. Peter the Fisherman in Playa Larga, Alonzo Figures, came to her office the day Elena and Celia had dinner and asked about Juan."

"Did the pastor have anything to add?"

"Yes, that the head of the research center was drunk a few nights before he died in the auto accident and he talked about Juan Mendozo being brought to the research center and placed in the barracuda pens the night he disappeared from the hotel."

"Didn't anyone at the research center see Juan?"

"The head of the research center is dead. If one or more others were there that night, they were the ones who were paid to abduct Mendoza and toss him into the pens."

"Where is Elena now?" asked Dan.

"I assume she went back to Connecticut," Celeste said.

"She's either there or in D.C. The House is in session," Dan replied, and, nodding at Celeste, asked, "By the way, where is Minister Sandoval?"

"She was in the U.S last week to meet with García García and Luna. Presumably, she's back here in Havana now."

"Would it be worth talking to Sandoval?' asked Dan. "Just Celeste and me. She might recognize Lucinda or Macduff. And Will can stay here and see if Celia is able to think of anything more about her shooting."

"Lucinda and I could go to Playa Larga one last time. We might find out something. OK with you, Dan?"

"Don't you dare go to Playa Larga. What you might find are some tarpon and bonefish and maybe even a permit."

48

THE NEXT DAY IN HAVANA

MINISTER SANDOVAL DID NOT WANT TO MEET AT HER OFFICE. Nor did she want to be seen going to the U.S. Interests Section. She chose to meet on the grounds at Morro Castle—the "Pearl of the Antilles" to pirates in colonial days—at the entrance to Havana harbor.

Fifteen minutes before their planned meeting time, Celeste and Dan entered the main gate and walked along a wall where anyone watching would assume them to be simply two admirers of the immense centuries-old stonework. Promptly at 10:30, Sandoval entered and walked past them with only a flick of her eyes and slight nod, leading them further into the fort near one of the former powder storage rooms. There they found a quiet corner with a low wall that served as seating. Behind them were views of the sea swells rolling in to self-destruction on the rocks seventy feet below.

Neither Celeste nor Dan had ever met Minister Sandoval. Her English was excellent and her demeanor professional. She opened the conversation.

"Miss Jones, my staff told me you are about to leave our island for Paris. I assume you believe that to be a step up in the world."

"Yes and no," Celeste answered, not surprised at Sandoval's knowledge. "I am leaving, but my time here has been the most challenging of the twenty-four years I've served at various embassies. Paris will be different, but my heart remains among the Cuban people on this beautiful island." There was the slightest smile on Sandoval's face.

"And you're Dan Wilson from the CIA?" she stated firmly, turning to Dan.

"My name is *Quentin Ross*," Dan responded, amazed at the minister's knowledge. "I'm here from the Interior Department in D.C. You must be mistaken."

"Whatever game you want to play is no concern of mine," Sandoval added. . . . "So what is it you have to tell me?"

"As I mentioned on the phone yesterday," Celeste said, "we have yet to close the Juan Mendoza disappearance. We were hoping you might be able to help us."

"I doubt that I can. He was never found. He may have returned to the U.S. The matter is closed."

"Do you know Alfredo Luna and Jorge García García?" Shock was immediately expressed on Sandoval's face.

"Whoever they are, what do they have to do with Juan Mendoza?"

"We believe they, along with one other person, planned Mendoza's death. That person is you, Minister Sandoval."

Dan outlined the dates of the several meetings Sandoval attended with the other two. She decided it wasn't worth trying to deny they met.

"We never planned Mendoza's death," she stated.

"What did you plan?" asked Celeste.

"We merely wanted to convince Mendoza that he should moderate his view about the U.S. ending the trade boycott."

"By what means?"

"García García promised PAC money. Luna promised further financial incentives if Mendoza would publically downplay his position and back a continuation of the status quo in our two nations' dealings."

"How did Mendoza react?"

"He had no chance to react. He was giving thought to his response while he was here in Havana with the trade group. I met with him and urged him to go slowly."

"But he didn't agree?"

"He neither agreed nor rejected my suggestion. He disappeared."

"Are you saying that you had no role in his disappearance?"

"None. Nor did Luna. Nor García García."

"Then who was behind Mendoza's death?"

She paused, struggling with what she had already said and what she was being asked.

"It was his sister Elena. She acted alone."

"But she met with you and Luna and García García."

"She received her instructions from us by phone," Sandoval lied.

"What were those instructions?"

"Only to persuade her brother to change. Not to hurt him and certainly not to kill him."

"Juan wasn't the only one to disappear or be shot," said Dan. "Nacho Gomez disappeared, and we have evidence of his death in Playa Larga. Also, three days ago Celia Bustamante, manager of the Playa Larga hotel where Mendoza stayed, was shot in her office."

"Bustamante was reported as missing two days ago," said Sandoval, embarrassed by her government's lack of knowledge of Bustamante's present location.

"Celia Bustamante is safely in the United States. She will surely be allowed to stay," Celeste added, knowing that Celia had not yet been taken to the U.S.

Sandoval's face reflected her anger, but she said nothing for a few minutes, staring out over the fort's wall high above the water. Finally, she turned and spoke.

"I hope these incidents will be settled without further involvement of my office. We are not interested when a U.S. House member kills another U.S. House member, and neither is the average Cuban citizen. If Elena Mendoza comes here again, she will be returned immediately to U.S. authorities.

"We have investigated the Nacho Gomez disappearance and believe it had nothing to do with Juan Mendoza's murder. Gomez owed money to some bad people in Playa Larga. One was Ricardo Arias, the manager of the barracuda center. Arias copied the method used to murder Mendoza. Nacho Gomez is dead, thrown into the barracuda pens. His wife later was paralyzed from a stroke and is unable to function, and we believe Arias himself died in a car accident. There's no reason to do anything more about Gomez."

"And what of Celia Bustamante's shooting?" Dan asked. "That likely involved an American citizen attempting to kill a Cuban national. Certainly you're interested in that?"

"If Celia has defected, our government will drop the matter. They will have no more interest in her than in any of the other *gusanos* who have left."

"And you, Minister Sandoval? You are a party to the conspiracy," stated Celeste.

"There was no criminal conspiracy; we never ordered or approved of any action by Elena that would result in her brother's death. I am convinced Elena shot Bustamante to prevent her from pursuing any further investigation of her brother's death."

"Where do we go from here?" asked Dan. "We still have a murder, possibly two, and a shooting."

"You deal with Elena. She's one of yours, and she's no longer in Cuba."

"But it is effectively impossible for us to try her for crimes committed in Cuba," said Dan. "She might be charged with conspiracy, but with the tenuous relations between our countries, any trial is doubtful because Cuba would have to provide evidence. If Cuba wanted, it would be possible to try Elena here *in* Cuba, *if* we would be willing to extradite her. I doubt that will happen."

"I agree," Sandoval responded. "But we are simply not interested in Elena. An American murdering another American *in* Cuba obviously violates our law. But it is better dealt with by you."

"Elena didn't commit the murder of her brother alone. She had to have hired Cubans to do that. Aren't you interested in that?" asked Celeste.

"Of course, but there are problems of proof. Our system is not as developed as yours. We don't have the forensic services present in the United States. There is *no* body. For all we know Juan Mendoza is alive."

"Do you believe that?"

"No, but I don't make decisions regarding ordinary crimes committed in Cuba. That is a matter for our prosecutors. . . . I would be in trouble if what we've discussed were known by our internal security people. Or for not asking 'Mr. Wilson,' or as you say 'Mr. Ross,' for proper identification, which I will not do. . . . I want to see our countries remain as we are. And I hope to serve in higher office. . . . As far as I'm concerned, the matter is closed. . . . I must leave."

She rose and walked away, not turning back, and was soon through the entry gate and gone.

49

THAT AFTERNOON

C ELESTE CALLED LUCINDA AND ME and suggested we meet with Dan and Will at the Interests Section at 3:00 p.m. Lucinda and I had been tense and irritable all morning. We could think of no reason we should remain in Cuba. There was no need for me to go to Playa Larga. Dan had brought us on a wild goose chase in a land without geese.

Lucinda and I went for what we hoped would be a last meal in Cuba at El Aljibe

"I hate to leave here," I said as I tasted the first bite of our roast chicken.

"We talked this morning about how we couldn't wait to leave Cuba. Sometimes I wonder about you."

"I didn't mean leaving Cuba; I meant leaving El Aljibe. Can you duplicate this meal at home?"

"I've already sweet-talked the cook into giving me his recipe. He said it was as much a secret as the formula for Coke in the U.S. . . . But because of my exceptional charm, he gave it to me anyway."

"Maybe you could open a restaurant in St. Augustine. Or Livingston or Bozeman. Or all three. Specialties would be roast chicken and roast bison."

"I cook *only* for you. If I ran a restaurant and were up late, I'd sleep in and miss checking on what you ate for breakfast."

"Ever vigilant."

"You bet."

At 3:00 p.m. the two of us, with contented stomachs, walked into Celeste's office at the Interests Section. Dan was already there.

"I can't wait to wrap this up," said Celeste. There were a half-dozen cartons along one wall addressed to her at the U.S. Embassy in Paris.

"Macduff and I agree. We want to get back to the U.S. and finish our drive to Montana."

"There's one matter we can't just leave," said Dan. "Elena apparently is in the U.S., presumably headed back to D.C. and her work. We seem to agree that she at the least arranged for her brother's murder and shot Celia Bustamante. I have to contact our Department of Justice in D.C."

"I agree," I responded. "You do it, Dan; leave us out of it. We had no part in the murder or shooting."

"Leave me out," Lucinda added, "I was in Cuba taking photographs of Hemingway's favorite places."

"But you both will be a part of Justice's investigation. You're part of the case however you look at it. Especially you, Macduff," he said looking at me.

"I guess," I whispered. "But Minister Sandoval was right this morning. This case is going nowhere. Justice will do an investigation and drop it because Cuba won't cooperate. Of course, if the investigation is made public, it will impact Elena's continuation as a House member and affect any attempt on her part to run for the House again, much less the Senate. But because Justice will know they're going nowhere and Elena is popular, they may keep it out of the news."

"What do you suggest, Dan? We left Wuff and our SUV in Albuquerque. I planned to be at Mill Creek today and begin some floats."

"And I have a deadline for some photos on the Snake River I haven't finished for the *Jackson Hole Magazine*," added Lucinda. "They're my first photos for that magazine, and I want to start off by meeting my deadline."

"OK. I'll fly you to Albuquerque directly from here early tomorrow morning. You'll have breakfast in New Mexico and be in Montana in two days, sooner if you drive through the night. . . . I'll fly on to D.C. and prepare a report for Justice. Today is Thursday. I'll send the report first thing Monday morning. You'll be contacted pretty quickly."

"Is Elena a flight risk?"

"No. She doesn't know we're in Cuba," Dan said. "She should be back in D.C. by Monday—I assume because the House is in session."

"I'm leaving Saturday on a direct flight from Havana to Paris," Celeste affirmed. "I check in at the embassy Monday. If Justice wants me, they know how and where to reach me.

We were finished by 4:30 p.m. and convinced Dan to fly us that evening. Lucinda made a lodging reservation at a place near the Albuquerque airport and, having picked up a happy Sheltie, we were on the road to Montana by 9:00 a.m. the next morning. By 7:00 p.m. we were so far along that we kept on driving and pulled in to the cabin on Mill Creek before midnight.

The Havana we left two days before was in the high nineties, humid, and sunny. At breakfast time Mill Creek was in the mid-forties, drizzling, and overcast. We wouldn't have traded places. We were thrilled to be home. And have the matter of Juan's death resolved.

At least we thought that was so.

50

A WEEKEND IN MONTANA

I WOKE UP at 6:02 A.M. hearing Wuff express her impatience with the slow meal service by barking at Lucinda. After prodding her and telling her to feed *her* dog, I fell asleep again and didn't move until 10:00 a.m.

Shuffling to the kitchen expecting that coffee would be brewing, I found the pot empty. Lucinda's favorite mug was missing. I called out to her, but the cabin was silent. I assumed she had gone to Emigrant to pick up some food, so I made my own coffee, doubled the sugar, and stepped out onto the porch overlooking Mill Creek.

The creek hadn't suffered from the force of the spring snowmelt coming down from the Absaroka heights above us. I looked upstream and watched the creek tumble over large familiar boulders. Then I turned toward downstream where we had reorganized the creek to make a calm area along one bank.

Someone was standing in the creek fishing, facing away from me, wearing drooping waders and a baggy jacket with the hood up to deflect the chilly wind. A perfect back cast told me the person knew how to fly fish, reinforced three-fold when the fly set down gently at the upper edge of the calm area, and was immediately engulfed by a cutthroat. Not large, perhaps nine inches.

"Wow!" a voice called out, "I wish Macduff were here to see my first trout of the Montana fall."

It wasn't a poacher; it was Lucinda wearing my fishing clothes.

I watched her slip the hook out and return the fish to the creek, waited a couple of minutes, and called, "Hey! Want a sip of my coffee?"

"Yes!" she said turning and showing her Cheshire cat grin. "My cup's on the bank and the coffee's cold. You saw my fish?"

"Fish? Are you claiming you caught something?"

"You *saw* it!"

"I just got here. And I don't believe you anyway."

"If I knew you'd be like this, I wouldn't have thrown it back. I would have taken it into the cabin and put it on your breakfast plate. Eyes and tail included."

"That's not catch and release."

She laughed, picked up her empty cup, and tossed it to me. I caught it only after dropping my nearly full mug of my favorite Guatemalan coffee.

"And to think I could be in Playa Larga by myself bone-fishing," I exclaimed.

"I'll take you to the Keys for a couple of weeks, and you can fish for bones," she promised. "We'll be safe. No need for licenses from Treasury. No barracuda pens. Now, I'd like a re-fill of my coffee, please."

And it's only our first day back in Montana!

51

A WEEK LATER IN MONTANA

"MACDUFF, WE'VE ONLY BEEN HERE a week, and it's like paradise, sitting in our living room with its warm log walls and a roaring fire as the sun goes down. Who ever said that fires roar? This one has a soothing crackle."

I moved closer to her so our shoulders touched and leaned my head against her hair. "It *is* paradise. So close to Mill Creek and so far from Playa Larga," I responded.

"Agreed! Should we get new unlisted cell phone numbers?"

"Or no phones at all. And quietly spend winters in Hopetown on Abaco?"

"And summers fishing for trout in the Picos de Europa in Spain? No one would ever find us, Macduff."

"Let's just change the cell phone numbers. I love Mill Creek and St. Augustine."

"I hope we've heard the last from Dan about Cuba," she commented. "We can cross it off our bucket list of places to visit. Been there. Done that."

"Before we put Cuba and the Mendozas and Sandovals and others out of sight and out of mind, let's have one last discussion on Cuba. I never solved the deaths of Juan Mendoza or Nacho Gomez, much less the attempted killing of Celia Bustamante," I suggested to her. "I'm lost trying to reach any conclusions, but it's on my mind."

"You're asking *who* did it," she stated. "We know who was on the receiving end and how it was done."

"OK, crime solver. Solve it!" I responded.

She put down her drink, turned and looked at me, and gently put one hand on my knee. "First, I'd eliminate the Nacho Gomez death as in any way related to Juan Mendoza and Celia Bustamante. There was no motive to kill Nacho Gomez on the part of anyone who had a motive to kill Juan and shoot Celia."

"Agreed, but out of curiosity, who do you think killed Nacho?" I asked.

"Maybe someone we don't know about," she said. "Someone with a grudge. Nacho may have been hitting on someone's wife. Or he stole from someone. Remember, Cubans don't have much, and the theft of even a kid's bicycle could lead to retaliation. There's no one *outside* Cuba who had anything against Gomez. Do you agree we can eliminate him?"

"Yes, for the sake of your analysis, he's gone," I replied. "One down, how many to go?"

"Seven!"

"Seven?"

"Maybe ten."

"Ten! Who?"

"David Longstreet, Cliff Cameron, Juan Mendoza, Elena Mendoza, Minister Christina Sandoval, Senator Jorge García

García, and Alfredo Luna. And another trio—maybe you, maybe me, maybe Wuff."

"Wuff! Drop her or I call in the SPCA. And PETA."

"OK. Wuff's eliminated."

"Drop me. I don't murder people; I just watch others being murdered from my drift boat."

"Wimp! OK. You're eliminated."

"Also, Wuff and I agree it was not you. If you wanted to get rid of someone, you'd poison them with one of your meals. You're eliminated. Were back to the seven. Who first?" I asked.

"I'd eliminate both our Montana House member David Longstreet and rancher Cliff Cameron," she said. "No motives."

"But they didn't agree with the position Juan took on extending trade and tourism with Cuba."

"True. But Longstreet had no *consistent* view on trade with Cuba. He was interested in keeping himself in office. Juan didn't pose a threat to Longstreet's re-election. Once re-elected, he would first check which way the wind was blowing and ride with it."

"Cliff Cameron?"

"Somewhat the same, but his interest was making money selling cattle to Cuba. Juan didn't pose a threat to Cameron. Maybe if Juan were running for the Senate from Montana rather than New Mexico, Cameron would have been concerned. But he has both Montana senators as well as Longstreet in his pocket."

"Five left. Who's next?" I asked.

"Juan Mendoza?"

"Come on, be serious," I said. "Juan didn't abduct himself and jump into the barracuda pens. And I don't believe it was an accident. Did he fall in, and then someone found his remains and saved his skull? Not likely."

"OK," she stated. "Four left. What about his sister, Elena?"

"What about her? She adored her brother!"

"Did she? One of several reasons to have her brother killed was to prevent him from disclosing the sexual abuse he suffered from her as a teen. If it got out, Elena would have been dead in the water. Remember that she was going to run for the Senate—and most likely win—and had visions of being the first woman and first Hispanic president. Juan was the only serious roadblock. With Juan gone, there was no threat from disclosure of her abuse and no roadblock on the path to the White House."

"If she had Juan killed, Lucinda, why did she ask me to go to Cuba and investigate? I might have found out that *she* did it."

"She wanted to know what the Cuban authorities thought. You did her a real service by reporting that the police didn't want to spend much time or money investigating the death of a foreigner. Especially a Cuban-American."

"Why would Elena have asked me to go to Cuba and then kept in contact with me when all along *she* was traveling to Cuba herself? She even went once before her brother made his trip!"

"Macduff, I don't know. It is suspicious. She was always protective of Juan, in a strange sort of way. She abused him, but she always stood up for him. She told us she didn't want him to go to Cuba in the first place. She may have gone to judge for herself whether Juan would be at risk."

"I think that's farfetched," I said. "How do you explain her later trip? Dan told us she went three times after Juan disappeared."

"Maybe she thought we weren't doing anything of value to help. She might have decided to do her own investigation, but not embarrass us."

"You have a vivid imagination. When you combine it with your—well, I hate to admit it because I'll never hear the end of it—your intelligence and logic and good judgment and. . . ."

"Go on. I like this, Macduff."

"What I was trying to say is despite all those assets, your decision can be overwhelmed by your unbridled imagination."

"So I'm imagining everything about Elena?"

"I didn't say that."

"Macduff, . . . we'll never know. No investigation is going to be made. Elena isn't likely to tell her reasons for going to Cuba on her own after asking you to go. I thought we were not going to get into this mess deeper, but try to outline what we know logically and then, when we finish, put it aside—permanently."

"If you say so. We know Elena made a trip to talk to Celeste in Havana and Celia in Playa Larga. Does what we know about that trip allow you to conclude that Elena didn't kill Juan and wasn't involved in his death?"

"I haven't decided anything yet," she said. "First, from what little we know about her meeting with Celeste in Havana, Elena lied about why she was in Cuba. She told Celeste it was only to talk about trade, but she went to Playa Larga. Her conversation in Playa Larga with Celia confirmed Juan was dead."

"And that Celia and the police didn't have *any* evidence that *Elena* might have been involved. Why would Elena go back and try to kill Celia?"

"Celia was the only person in Playa Larga who could make trouble for Elena. She may not have been thinking rationally."

"OK. Let's place her on hold," I suggested. "Neither of us wants to eliminate her . . . yet."

"Three left, Macduff: the group that met in Miami several times—Sandoval, García García, and Luna."

"What about a conspiracy to murder by all three?" I asked.

"I don't think so. All three had far more concern with their careers than getting one New Mexico House member out of the way. Juan had little if any impact in Congress about widespread acceptance of his views on trade and tourism with Cuba."

"They didn't pull the trigger, but could they have paid someone to kill Juan?"

"Yes. So could Elena, which is troubling to me. And her motivation was greater. Without question, all of the three believed the world was theirs. Luna to keep and increase his enormous wealth. García García to hold his Senate seat. Sandoval to become President of Cuba."

"That's it," I concluded. "There's no one left."

"No one we know about. I'd like to keep it that way. I don't want Dan calling with some new idea about who killed Juan and how we had to go to Cuba again."

"He's not going to send us back, Lucinda."

"He tried once, and the President stopped him."

"But we went!"

"Yes. If it's known, Dan may lose his job. Director Vance is not what one would call an admirer of the President."

"Are we through?" I asked.

"Enough. Want a straw vote?"

"Why not. I say it was Elena."

"I hate to admit it, but I have to agree," she said.

"Beyond a reasonable doubt?"

"Without question. Over. Decided. Ended. Closed. Wrapped up. *Finis.*

"All over but the shooting?" I added.

"Don't say that!"

"I know Dan and Celeste believe Elena was the killer. . . . That's four to zero. Add Will Kenny, Brian Hawes, and Celia Bustamante, and we have a unanimous seven-person jury."

"Macduff, it's time to live a normal life again. Spend time with Elsbeth. Enjoy Montana and St. Augustine. Go fishing. Take photographs. Feed Wuff on time."

"You've solved another murder and shooting," I exclaimed. "This was easier than the Park Salisbury case, the shuttle gal murders, the wicker man and mistletoe explosions, and even the gill net deaths."

Lucinda got up and came over and grabbed my hand, pulled me out of my comfortable chair, and led me to our bedroom.

"I have some recollection about being seduced in Manhattan years ago by a beautiful woman who pulled me up off the couch and took me to her bedroom," I reminisced. "I don't remember much more."

"Let me refresh your memory," she said, showing her best grin as we stumbled in the dark and fell onto the bed.

52

THREE MONTHS LATER AT MILL CREEK

KNOWING "WHO DID IT" and apprehending the guilty party or parties do not always bring closure to those who remain aggrieved about their losses. For three months the death of well-liked U.S. House member Juan Mendoza of New Mexico had been subjected to unending, repetitious, "breaking news" TV coverage, without regard to the mourning of Mendoza's family and friends.

Secluded in our Mill Creek Montana cabin, Lucinda and I were unaware of—and uninterested in—what the lead characters of Juan Mendoza's saga might be conspiring about. We could assume that Cuban Minister of the Interior Christina Sandoval was back in Cuba plotting her ascent to be president, U.S. Senator from Florida Jorge García García likely was focused on recent opinion polls about his chances for re-election, and sugar czar Alfredo Luna was working to elevate his *Barron's* ranking among U.S. billionaires.

Closer to our Montana home, we had heard that Representative David Longstreet was enmeshed in a scandal involving a student intern from Montana State, which he doubted would affect his re-election. A neighbor told us that rancher Cliff Cameron had just signed an agreement to sell another 20,000 cattle to Cuba.

Lucinda and I talked little about Cuba and extensively about our dreams for a quiet, uneventful future. We had tried breakfast in Bozeman early this windless, cloudless, and moistureless morning, at a new coffee shop that proved not to justify the hour drive each way. The coffee was adequate, but the hardening, stale pastry was ready to be sent for sale at a Merita bakery outlet. But we had found a copy of *The New York Times*.

As we dropped down the unassuming Bozeman Pass to the more reserved eastern side of the Gallatin Mountains on our drive home, Livingston appeared around bends in a progressively more defined panorama. A long freight train passed slowly through town, loaded with coal likely destined for China.

Lucinda used her cell phone to call longtime friends whom we hadn't seen since the previous year. Their place is where I often stayed when I was building my cabin.

"How are our favorite B&B hosts?" Lucinda asked when Joan answered.

"Tired and retired. We closed the B&B part of our house, took it over for ourselves, and, along with our Jack Russell terrier, are enjoying some privacy. We've kept our rental on Mill Creek near your cabin. . . . Where are you? Is Paradise Valley's most notorious guide still with you?"

"Can't seem to get rid of him. He's dozing in the seat next to me—practicing for retirement. This very moment we're turning off I-90 on the sweeping curve into Livingston."

"Stop and have coffee."

"Give us ten minutes."

The thought of Joan's freshly ground coffee caused us to make it in five. After hellos we all settled in the comfortable living room, with grand windows looking at the foothills of the Gallatin Mountains. A single bull elk was moving across the slopes in the distance, bugling for another cow to add to his harem.

Joan's coffee achieved its usual perfection. After a few sips, Johnnie turned to me and asked, "Any chance you two have been in Cuba recently?"

"What prompted *that* question?" I asked.

"Have you read the *Times* today?"

"I haven't read a paper in a week. Lucinda and I picked up today's edition in Bozeman; we're saving it for lunch on our porch. Why?"

"There's an article reminiscent of the kind of trouble you two get into around here. And that you faced in Florida with the gill net murders."

"What do you mean?" asked Lucinda, squeezing my knee with a hand that quivered in worried anticipation.

"Read this," he said as he handed it to me. "Read it out loud; Joan hasn't seen it yet."

I took the folded paper, sat back in a soft chair, and began to read, not knowing where it would lead:

House of Representatives member Elena Mendoza from Connect-icut was found dead at her Hartford home yesterday. Death was pre-sumably caused by an overdose of drugs.

Mendoza's death comes only months after the disappearance and assumed death of her younger brother Juan, also a House member but from New Mexico. Both were favored to win Senate seats in next year's election, and both regularly had been mentioned as possible presidential candidates within the next decade.

Juan Mendoza participated in trade negotiations in Havana, Cuba, a few days before he went missing at a popular recreational fishing town named Playa Larga near the site of the infamous Bay of Pigs on the south coast a couple of hours' drive from Havana. An avid fly fisherman, he had remained in Cuba after the trade meetings for a few days of fishing the flats off the Zapata Reserve. His disappearance has not been solved.

Elena Mendoza left a letter on her word processor. The letter was addressed and mailed to three prominent people: Senator Jorge García García of Miami; Alfredo Luna, controlling shareholder and CEO of American Sugar Company, the largest grower in the United States; and Christina Sandoval, the Cuban Minister of the Interior. Sandoval was known to be close to Raul Castro and was rumored to be a possible successor to the Cuban presidency. Minister Sandoval could not be reached; she was in Paris attending a meeting of interior ministers from developing nations. García García and Luna have refused to discuss the matter.

Elena made three copies of her letter and addressed them to the recipients, leaving them on her desk where they were discovered and mailed by her secretary. A copy of the letter—printed below—has been obtained by this newspaper:

I have buried the few remains of my brother Juan that I recovered. I took his skull from the barracuda research center, brought it back to the U.S., and had it examined. The dental work is what assured me that the skull was Juan's. A forensic professional told me that there were marks on the skull that were consistent with marks made by barracuda teeth.

As you know, I agreed to go to Playa Larga at your urgings as soon as we learned that Juan was planning to go to Havana for the trade meetings. I went first in July, the week before Juan. I was not aware that Minister Sandoval traveled from Havana to Playa Larga the day I returned to the U.S.

It was the intention of you three to embarrass Juan in two ways. One was if he appeared too friendly with or approving of the Castro administration, your hope was that he would lose his attempt to gain a seat in the Senate. The other was that if he deviated from his trade work to fish for several days after the trade mission, he would be violating his Treasury Department license that was restricted to the trade meetings. Juan should have returned to the U.S. at the meeting's conclusion, as did all the other participants. Fishing in Cuba was clearly not lawful under U.S. law.

In return for my assistance, you promised me substantial funding for my own race in Connecticut for the Senate and for my agreement to change my preference for freer trade and tourism to favoring maintaining the current rules.

It was never your intention, nor mine, to harm Juan. I was devastated when I learned in August that he was missing and immediately went to Cuba for a second brief time. I spoke with several people. First was to Juan's fishing guide Nacho Gomez. He knew nothing but said I should talk to Ricardo Arias, manager of the barracuda research center. Gomez said I should be careful as Arias was known to be dishonest and possibly re-

sponsible for the death of a Playa Larga resident two years earlier. According to Arias, that resident fell into the barracuda pens and was savagely killed. I talked to Arias, but he was evasive and refused to continue after I mentioned Juan.

I also talked to Alonzo Figures, the pastor at the St. Peter the Fisherman Church. He said he met Juan briefly. He also said I should be careful of Arias.

I wanted to speak with Celia Bustamante at the hotel, but she was in Santiago visiting her family. Her assistant, whose name I did not obtain, was evasive when I asked about the investigation of Juan's disappearance.

Two months after I returned to the U.S.—as I recall, in October—I called Macduff Brooks, a fishing guide in Montana who Juan and I had retained a few years earlier to guide us on the Yellowstone River. I had learned that he wanted to fish in Cuba and was involved with the establishment of the two St. Peter the Fisherman churches, in Playa Larga in Cuba and in Islamorada in the U.S. I begged Brooks to go to Cuba to learn out what had happened to Juan. I arranged Treasury Department licenses for him and his wife, Lucinda.

In mid-January they went to Cuba and Brooks fished with Gomez for two or three days. Then, suddenly, Brooks and his wife disappeared. I learned soon thereafter that the Cuban government apparently confused some fingerprints of a different person with those taken from Brooks on his arrival. The U.S. Interests Section helped the Brookses flee the country illegally in a small plane, much to the anger of Minister Sandoval and the embarrassment of the Cuban government.

311

I returned to Cuba and Playa Larga for the third time a couple of weeks later to carry on Brooks' search. I did not tell any of you three that I was going. I went to the barracuda research center. Before I got out of my hired car, I watched as Minister Sandoval and Ricardo Arias came out of the office, laughing about something I could not hear. I hid and returned the next day to speak to Arias. He was very upset I was in Playa Larga.

In May, I talked on the phone with Brooks about the disappearance of Nacho Gomez. I wanted Brooks to go to Cuba again. He arranged such a trip with the State Department, but it was canceled under pressure from the President.

It was August or September when I learned from Brooks about his daughter's trip to Cuba and her discovering and photographing two skulls.

I made a fourth visit to Cuba in November and found and took the skulls of Juan and, I assumed, Nacho Gomez. I disposed of Gomez's skull and brought Juan's back to the U.S., where—although it involved the only discovered part of him—I carried out his wishes regarding cremation and dispersal of the ashes.

In my last meeting with the three of you in Miami, Minister Sandoval told me I was no longer needed but that I would receive the promised support for my future campaigns. Unlike the earlier meetings she appeared to be in charge—García García and Luna hardly spoke. When Minister Sandoval left, the re-

maining two profusely apologized for their being unable to control her and for Juan's apparent murder.

Not much later, a U.S. government official called me and told me about Celia Bustamante being shot. I am convinced that Celia Bustamante was shot by Minister Sandoval. Just weeks before the shooting, the two had a meal together, and people who overheard their conversation said Sandoval drank extensively and threatened Bustamante.

While I cannot provide proof to support my view of Juan's death, I am convinced that it was the act of Minister Sandoval, possibly working with several Cubans in her ministry who would personally gain by her assumption of the presidency. In the past few weeks, it became increasingly clear that Sandoval and others in the government planned a coup to remove Raul Castro. That proved to be true. The coup failed and Cuba is seeking to have Sandoval returned from Paris.

After Celia Bustamante was shot, Celeste Jones from the Interests Section and another U.S. official using an alias met with Minister Sandoval, aborted a planned trip to Playa Larga, and returned to the U.S.

I believe that Minister Sandoval arranged with the manager of the barracuda research center, Ricardo Arias, to have him carry out the murder of Juan. Sandoval intended to mail the skull to García García to scare him and convince him to adopt her views on Cuba. I suspect she also may have been responsible for the car accident that later took Arias' life.

The disappearance and similar murder of Nacho Gomez was unrelated to Juan's death. Inquiries during my trips to Playa Larga determined only that Gomez and Arias were enemies and that after Arias had disposed of Juan, and shortly before the car accident, he used the barracuda pens in the same way to kill Gomez.

It is my intention to end my own life. I have lived with secrets about my relationship with Juan years ago that I could not bear to see become public. If the truth were known, it would show that Juan raped me repeatedly when we were teens. But I was the older sibling and the one blamed. There is neither proof to know exactly what happened nor any interest on my part to cast blame on a brother I dearly loved despite his treatment of me.

I leave a wonderful and devoted husband, Robert Macintosh, and two beautiful children, whom I have embarrassed by my conduct, as I have also embarrassed so many of my constituents.

Elena Mendoza

The Times has learned that Minister Sandoval has fled Paris but presumably remains somewhere in Europe, possibly Spain. The U.S. has been surprisingly quiet about the events, stating that any discussion would jeopardize sensitive ongoing discussions with Cuba to further open trade and tourism.

Fearing further attempts on his life, Raul Castro has allegedly made overtures to the U.S. about Cuba agreeing to meet the strict conditions in the Helms-Burton law for renewal of full relations. No comment has been forthcoming from Havana.

53

A WEEK LATER IN MONTANA

IT TOOK A WEEK FOR LUCINDA AND ME to be able to discuss the Mendoza letter rationally. We had both been smug in our conclusion that Elena Mendoza had been responsible for her brother Juan's ghastly murder and the shooting of Celia Bustamante, who is in D.C. and fully recovered physically but is not yet able to accept the fact that she cannot safely return to her homeland Cuba.

Lucinda and I have been wrong before in guessing on guilt, but with less conviction than we had about Elena Mendoza as the killer. We never thought about Minister Sandoval acting alone outside her role as part of the three who met several times and who—we concluded correctly—as a *group* did not order Juan Mendoza's death or killing Celia Bustamante.

Perhaps some good may come from our terrible mistake. Elena Mendoza's final letter and Minister Sandoval's apparent defection in Paris have convinced us we shouldn't play "Nick and Nora Charles," Dashiell Hammett's fictional duo, unraveled murder mysteries far more complex than our Cuban drama.

"Mac," Lucinda asked, putting down a book of Ansel Adams' photographs of the American West and turning to me in our bed while we read far into the night, unable to sleep the way we wanted and needed, "are we to blame for Elena's death? If we had figured out that Minister Sandoval was the guilty party and acted, perhaps Elena would be alive."

"Don't play the 'if only' game. We did what we could. Remember that our past embroilments have not always been clearly resolved in a just way."

"We've lost Elena and that's tragic," Lucinda observed. "I'm satisfied that her letter is the truth."

"It's hard to believe that had the coup attempt by Minister Sandoval had been successful, she might be serving as the President of Cuba," I added.

"Are we being fair to ourselves?" she asked. "We were never part of a crime in any of our past cases. Not part of a conspiracy. Not accused of having a wrongful thought. When we acted, it was to protect ourselves and people we viewed as friends. . . . Let's put Cuba and the other cases to bed."

"There's one case I can't put to bed. Indirectly, it led to all the others we've survived. . . . Juan Pablo Herzog in Guatemala wants me dead. And you. And maybe Elsbeth if and when he learns about who we are and where we live."

"Every time you mention him, Mac, my stomach begins to churn. But I know he's busy running for president."

"Maybe not too busy to avenge the deaths of his niece and nephew. I did kill his niece, as she was about to shoot both the UF president and the law dean. Herzog incorrectly also blames me for the shooting of his nephew."

"Herzog doesn't know that you are former Professor Maxwell Hunt," stated Lucinda.

"But he knows that Professor Hunt did not die of a stroke in D.C. He knows that his friend Abdul Khaliq Isfahani is dead and likely assumes that I killed him in Khartoum. We hope he doesn't know that it's Macduff Brooks who he's after."

"But there's something added now."

"What?" I asked, anticipating an answer that would terrify me.

"You believe that Herzog knows a lot about the life of Professor Hunt before he purportedly died of a stroke."

"Yes. Herzog was my student and a friend. He was helpful in my getting over the death of El."

"He knows she died in an accident on the Snake," she stated, "and that her name was El, short for Elsbeth."

"True, but I told him several times that El was lost along with an expected daughter."

"Who you were planning to name Elsbeth, not the more common Elizabeth?"

"Correct."

"There is an Elsbeth enrolled at UF."

"There is."

"As Elsbeth Brooks."

"Yes."

"What if Herzog learns about Elsbeth? Plus that she was Elsbeth Carson of Greenville, Maine, the adopted daughter of two people who found her and your wife El floating on the Snake River, saved the daughter, and raised her?"

"Not likely, but possible. You scare me, Lucinda. If the matching prints of Hunt and me in Cuban customs records are ever discovered by Herzog, we're in trouble. . . . Thankfully, Elena's letter doesn't mention the name Hunt."

317

"It doesn't," she said, "but something seems to come out of every episode of our lives that comes closer to providing Herzog with what he wants to know. . . . I'm terrified of the danger we pose to Elsbeth."

"I don't like to think about that."

"Have you given *any* thought to all this and what could happen when Herzog decides to renew his attempt to find you?"

"Not much."

"Maybe it's time you thought more about it. At this very moment Juan Pablo Herzog could be sitting in his Guatemala City condo planning your end."

At this very moment Juan Pablo Herzog was *not* in his Guatemala City condo. He was in Antigua, where years earlier he had been responsible for the savage murder of his Catholic priest cousin known as Padre Bueno. Herzog sat sullenly in the corner of a bar, consuming the sweet flavor of the country's Ron Zacapa *Centenario* rum, aged in barrels stored on the slopes of nearby Guatemalan volcanoes. Six empty glasses lay on the table; Herzog held a seventh with unsteady hands.

Rum made him think he could achieve when drunk what he had not been able to achieve when sober. It made his focus shift from gaining the mantle of the presidency of Guatemala to seeing the death of the person who once was known as Professor Maxwell Hunt.

"Where is Hunt?" he thought out loud, turning the heads of the other patrons, who, recognizing Herzog, quickly left the bar. "I will find him and when I do I will ..." he mumbled, and slumped on the table, knocking the glasses aside to shatter on the cement floor.

EPILOGUE

Elsbeth's Diary

It wasn't long after my Dad and Lucinda married that they once again found themselves in the middle of murder—this time two grisly deaths and an attempted third. After the killings, the players in that drama mostly went on with their lives.

Florida Senator Jorge García García was re-elected three more times, outliving Fidel and Raul Castro and nearly all the early exiles in Miami. He collapsed and died while smoking a cigar in his D.C. office, expecting that a bronze statute would be raised in Miami acknowledging his service. The most acknowledgment came in the form of a book award given once at the University of Miami and forgotten. Mentioning his name now brings a 'who's he' response.

Alfredo Luna's fears were fulfilled. The U.S. re-established both relations with Cuba and a special generous quota for renewed sugar imports to the U.S. from Cuba. The world sugar price dropped in half when Luna died at his retirement party years ago.

Elena took her own life, leaving her letter that identified Minister Sandoval as the killer of her brother Juan and the shooter of Celia Bustamante. Elena's ashes, like those from Juan's skull, were scattered off Playa Larga; she wanted to be near where her brother Juan died.

The apparent murderer of Juan and shooter of Celia, Minister Christina Sandoval, successfully fought extradition to Cuba. After a quiet decade, she became a prominent activist and promoter of Hispanic interests in France. A decade ago, she was shot and killed at a rally in Carcassonne in Southwestern France. Some placed the blame on members of the Mendoza family, especially Elena Mendoza's two children, but nothing was ever proved.

David Longstreet lost the next primary election in Montana. I don't know much about what happened to him, but his Main Street Bozeman *office is now a controversial store selling sex toys and adult movies. The windows have been covered with blinds.*

Cliff Cameron continued to sell cattle to Cuba and now owns the largest cattle ranch on that beautiful island. He sold his Montana interests when bison became more popular than beef and lives comfortably on his ranch in Western Cuba.

I've been back to Cuba several times, always with or to visit my dear friend Sue who loves Cuba so much that she now owns an old restored house in the center of Trinidad. But I will spend the remainder of my life in my house here in Captiva. It is the house that was once the St. Augustine cottage owned by Dad and Lucinda.

This is a house of memories.

AUTHOR'S NOTE

I enjoy hearing from readers. You may reach me at:
macbrooks.mwgordon@gmail.com
Please visit my website: www.mwgordonnovels.com
I am also on facebook at www.facebook.com

I will answer emails within the week received, unless I am on a book signing tour or towing *Osprey* to fish somewhere. Because of viruses, I do not download attachments sent with your emails. And please do not add my email address to any lists suggesting for whom I should vote, to whom I should give money, what I should buy, what I should read, or especially what I should write next about Macduff Brooks.

My website lists past and future appearances for readings, talk programs, and signings.

72277787R00202

Made in the USA
San Bernardino, CA
23 March 2018